Tainted Times 2

In Valerie Brooks' scintillating new suspense novel *Tainted Times 2*, Angeline Porter, the tough but vulnerable Oregon attorney who first appeared in the author's remarkable debut *Revenge In 3 Parts*, continues to unravel the sinister narrative threads woven around her sister's tragic death. And once again Brooks keeps the pages turning by constructing an intricate and engaging story. From the first paragraph to the last, *Tainted Times 2* unfolds at a breakneck pace, each startling new revelation about Angeline's troubled family adding to the book's genuine emotional depth. A muscular, laser-focused, compelling new entry in this one-of-a-kind trilogy.

–Tim Applegate, *Flamingo Lane* and *Fever Tree*

With *Tainted Times 2*, Valerie J. Brooks has delivered an intriguing thriller that crackles with tension. Amid the cast of fascinating characters Brooks has created, disbarred attorney, Angeline "Ang" Porter emerges as a gutsy, likable heroine. You'll find yourself caring about her and rooting for her. Filled with clever plot twists, *Tainted Times 2* is a real nail-biter from the first page to the last.

—Kevin O'Brien, *New York Times* Bestselling Author

Revenge in 3 Parts

has been said, 'well-behaved women seldom make history'—or good novels."

—Wendy Kendall, "Kendall and Cooper Talk Mysteries" podcast

"Revenge is a dish best served hot, at least in Valerie Brooks' *Revenge in 3 Parts,* a sexy fast-paced tale of family, love, and murder. Brooks' settings are characters too: two-faced lovers who charm as they kill. Can't wait for Brooks' next noir!"

—Cindy Brown, Agatha-nominated author of the Ivy Meadows mystery series

"Jan Myrdal famously said, 'Traveling is like falling in love; the world is made new.' In *Revenge in 3 Parts,* Valerie J. Brooks offers up a darker, if no less enthralling view of globetrotting. With *Revenge,* we follow jaded criminal lawyer Angela Porter as she seeks to avenge her sister's tragic death. With a whip-crack voice and delicious twists, *Revenge* is a thoroughly engrossing page-turner."

—Bill Cameron, author of the award-winning Skin Kadash mysteries

"Button up your trench coat! Valerie J Brooks' *Revenge in 3 Parts* puts an original twist on the classic elements of noir. *Revenge* successfully and poignantly balances travel destinations with the darkest compulsions of the human heart. Brooks' future travel destinations promise more creatively chilling mysteries!"

—Chris Scofield, author of *The Shark Curtain*

"*Revenge in 3 Parts* in twist after twist keeps our senses reeling as Angeline, an ex-attorney who believes in ultimate justice, comes closer and closer to the truth of why her sister committed suicide. Follow Angeline to the edge. Does she ever find what she seeks? Is she willing to go for the ultimate revenge, one that might tear her own life apart or even take her life? Find out in this tense noir mystery set in Paris, Portland, Oregon, and Kauai."

—Patsy Hand, *Lost Dogs of Rome*

TAINTED TIMES 2

2ND IN THE ANGELINE PORTER TRILOGY

VALERIE J. BROOKS

This is a work of fiction. All characters, organizations and events
in this book are either products of the author's imagination or are
used fictitiously. Any similarity to real persons, living or dead, is
coincidental and not intended by the author.

BLACK LEATHER JACKET PRESS

ISBN 978-1-7323732-2-8 (paperback)
ISBN 978-1-7323732-3-5 (e-book)
Library of Congress Control Number: 2020914494

To Jason Holden
Always

Secrets have a way of making themselves felt, even before you know there's a secret. - Jean Ferris

PART I

1

I t was noon. I'd just sat down in the tiny kitchen with my second mug of coffee and the local newspaper. My gun rested near my elbow on the counter, and my dog slept at my feet.

As cozy as that could be at times, I missed Oregon, my home. This morning, I woke with an ache, the kind you feel when you realize a loved one is dead, isn't coming back, never, nada. This time, instead of it being my sister's suicide or my husband's death, I ached for the loss of me. For the loss of being a lawyer and fighting for justice. That was the woman I once was and wanted to be again, not this person who was "on the lam," almost useless.

Not that I was running from the cops or FBI. I wasn't running. I was hiding on Kauai under the name of River Atwood. In self defense, I'd killed two leaders of a Boston extortionist mob. They wanted the money my sister had stolen and me dead. The gun at my elbow served as my only protection, except for Tempest my dog. The FBI had done nothing.

I lit a cigarette. Outside the storm flung anything not

nailed down. Maybe I was fooling myself. I didn't have a home to go to, but I did have a hometown. But everyone probably thought I was dead by now. How could I ever start over? I wanted to be back in the game. I missed being a lawyer, missed the fire from getting justice for a client. Being in my mid-forties and I couldn't envision a future? That was pathetic. I rubbed my chest, sighed, and went back to my paper.

Paris headlined in the news again, more protests, more violence, more outrage against the government. Oh, how I remembered Paris. More than a year ago I'd gone there under an alias to kill Gerard, the undercover FBI agent who was the cause of my sister Sophie's suicide.

But I'd failed. With him being FBI and undercover, he was hip to the tricks of someone like me. Even with everything I knew from being a former criminal defense attorney, I'd failed. Failed at protecting my sister. Failed at killing her lover, a man so blinded by her beauty, so infatuated with her that he hadn't understood her deep sense of insecurity. A man married to his job and unable to put that ahead of Sophie.

I, however, understood why she'd fallen so hard for him. I'd almost caved to his charms too. I wondered where Gerard was now. But I'd never know, not after refusing his personal invitation to meet him in Paris. He'd messed with my life enough. Messed it up so much that I was now hiding out under an assumed name from the same criminals he was undercover with. I wished I'd protected my sister better. Perhaps none of this would have happened.

I sipped my coffee, the paper mangled beneath my arm. Tempest rested her head on my foot. "It's just you and me, girl." She'd refused to go out that morning to do her business, and who could blame her? It was nasty out there. Rain had cut deep arteries of water into the gravel path leading to my porch and left a mud moat around the house, cutting me off even more from the world.

A deep growl vibrated through my foot. Tempest's head and shoulders slowly rose, her growl now loud enough to hear over the storm. I grabbed my gun. My eyes followed hers riveted on the cottage's front door. I patted her head.

"What's up, girl?"

Tempest rose, fur bristled. I stood and waited.

At the door, I snapped off the gun's safety and turned on the outside light. Nothing. When I unlocked and opened the door, the dog bolted into the storm.

"Tempest!" I screamed.

I waited, but she didn't come back. I called for her again. And again. After an hour when she didn't return, I put on my rain gear, tucked my gun in a large pocket with a protective overlap. In the storm, I scoured the road and hillside, yelling Tempest's name until I was hoarse. After my fourth attempt, I was close to tears and giving up.

Soaked, I stepped inside the porch, locked the doors, slid off my mud-covered boots and rain gear, pulled the gun from my pocket, and towel-dried my shoulder-length dyed-red hair, no longer short and spiky as when I'd first arrived on Kauai.

It would be dark in a few hours. When my burner phone vibrated, I knew the caller. I'd given my number to only one person.

"Aloha, River," Iolana said. "I'm leaving the library and have something for you. I'll be there in twenty minutes."

"What is it?"

"A sealed envelope with your name on it. Right after your name in parentheses is the name *Angeline*. It's handwritten and—"

"Who gave it to you?"

"One of the school kids. Someone paid them to give it to me. Should I throw it away?"

"No, it's fine," I lied. "See you in a few minutes."

After pouring two fingers of scotch and drinking half of it, I looked out the window again for Tempest and checked the locks.

Someone knew I was on the island. I finished my drink and poured another, then put water on for tea. Iolana doesn't drink alcohol, and I keep her favorite blend on hand. She's my closest friend here, actually my only friend, but even she didn't know my story and that I was hiding.

When the wind came up, the shutters banged and the lights flickered. I opened the door again and yelled for Tempest, trying not to think the worst and hoping Tempest had taken shelter someplace. She'd once survived as a stray on this island and could again. But I didn't like how she'd taken off like that. The thought made my heart bang so hard my chest hurt. The only reason she'd do that is if she sensed a threat. I yelled for her again and waited. Nothing.

I closed the door. I didn't like this. First Tempest taking off and now this envelope. Someone had found me. It had to be someone from the extortion ring. I slugged down more scotch. Gerard, Mister FBI Undercover Man, was probably still embedded in the extortionist ring, trying to find the identity of the mastermind, possibly a rogue FBI agent. While undercover, Gerard had had quite the plum job. In Sophie's case, he'd forced her to steal millions from my husband's business. But while doing so, they'd fallen in love.

Gerard's mob boss smelled not only the lust, but a double-cross. So he turned both against each other, told Sophie that Gerard had used her and just wanted the money. She'd already stolen the money, but when she thought Gerard had used her, she stashed the money in a Maryland bank under her and my name, then hung herself.

Gerard thought she'd trust him, but he didn't know how insecure she was. Hey, when a woman looks like Marilyn Monroe, she gets used—a lot.

Talk about star-crossed lovers. I picked up my scotch, slugged it back, then set out a mug, spoon, and honey for Iolana. At the front door, I yelled for Tempest again, over and over until my throat hurt. The scotch wasn't doing its job. I was still agitated.

Plus, I had my suspicions about Gerard. He was no where around when Link tried to kill me, he'd showed up too late to save poor Gus, the FBI agent assigned to protect me, and if I hadn't outwitted Betty, I would have gone over the cliff instead of her. So where was Mr. FBI Man when I'd needed him? Conveniently *in absensia*.

It had been a rough year.

I checked my phone. Iolana would be here any moment. I loved that woman. As the head Waimea librarian, she maintained a quiet and self-contained exterior but had a backbone of steel, a fighter. I could trust her. At least I thought so. I really didn't trust anyone anymore.

Iolana's headlights broke through the rain and darkness, and swept across my cottage. Then I remembered the gun in my hand and stashed it under my raincoat. Iolana hated guns.

She bounded down the lit path bracing against the wind. I opened the door, and she stepped inside. Water dripped off her face and long, dark braid. I handed her a towel and looked beyond her.

She glanced back too. "What's going on?"

"Tempest hasn't come home."

As she took off her rain gear, Iolana said, "She'll be OK, River. She's no *haole* when it comes to the island."

I hung up her poncho. "True. But I think she bolted after something. You know how she hates storms like this." The scent of frangipani wafted from Iolana.

"Did you hear anything outside?"

"With this storm? Not bloody likely."

In the kitchen, I made Iolana tea and handed her the mug, honey, and spoon while waiting for her to give me the envelope. She climbed onto a barstool at the counter and, in the unhurried manner of the island, fixed her tea. She started to take a sip when her cell rang with Bobby McFer-rin's "Don't Worry, Be Happy." I smiled. She dug in her fanny pack for the phone and answered, "Aloha."

When she stood, she almost knocked over the stool. "What?" "Oh, no." "Not good." "Yes, keep me updated."

Iolana hung up. Her chin trembled. "It's bad news."

I set down my drink. "How bad?"

"The Grim Reaper is dead."

"What?" I leaned back against the counter.

"They found him beside the road to Hanapepe."

The Grim Reaper protested transnational companies that had taken over the island. He stood at various main road and town intersections in his grim reaper costume and jumped in front of cars, waving one of his signs: "Dow & DuPont Kill" or "Dow & DuPont=Corpses." The locals complained about it being bad for tourism because he scared drivers, but tourists loved taking photos of him.

"Was he hit by a car?"

"It'll be on the news." She hovered on the edge of the barstool.

"TV?"

Iolana nodded then met my eyes. "He was killed."

We remained silent, letting the news sink in.

I didn't like the way this day was going. "Any idea as to who would do that?"

Iolana shook her head. "He was harmless."

Not seeing the Grim Reaper out there anymore seemed unfathomable. Nobody knew his real identity or where he lived, but people from our group, the Kāne Crew, took care of him. Our environmental group fights four transnational companies that poisoned the island. The fight for the island's health is complicated. Emotions run high. I believe in their cause and want justice for the islanders. I do legal research in secret for the group's lawyer.

She slipped her cell into her fanny pack. "I suppose now we'll find out his identity, where and how he lived. How tragic for his life to end this way."

Before I knew that Betty headed the Boston crime group, and before she tried to kill me, she told me about her brother who had lived with other hippies at the far end of the island. That piece of paradise is now a state park, but isolated places still exist where someone can live undetected —like The Reaper.

My legal mind couldn't resist. "Did you find out anything else? What happened to him? Do they have a suspect? Are the cops taking this seriously?"

"Aisake will call with the rest of the info. He went to the scene."

Aisake, the original founder of The Kāne Crew, routinely dropped off food, rain gear, toiletries, and medical supplies for The Reaper.

"When did it happen?"

"He doesn't know."

One of the local police had to be a member of the Crew because we often received info like this as soon as it became available. No one acknowledged it, though. No one wanted to blow that inside contact.

My mind spun, thinking that whoever did this had to have a motive. One of my law school mentors told me that, if it wasn't a crime of passion, to follow the money.

"What if it's a desperate move by the multinationals? They were after the police to crack down on the protests. Plus, they were bringing in big guns to stop the lawsuits."

"Murder seems extreme."

"Why not? They could get away with it." I paused. I was no stranger to homicide. How he died would tell us a great deal. I'd killed two people in self-defense, and that had never come to light. It didn't matter that they were extortionists and killers. Having those deaths on my conscience would follow me my whole life even though it had been them or me. I would forever see Betty falling backwards off that cliff.

I noticed the envelope sticking out of Iolana's fanny pack. "How was he killed?" I poured more scotch.

"With a fishing spear made of a hardwood like *kauila*." She put down her mug. "Driven up under his ribcage into his heart." Tears filled her eyes. I went over, gave her a hug, then returned to my drink.

"Damn." I took a deep breath. "Someone had to know what they were doing and be strong enough ... and brutal."

"Maybe somebody good at spearfishing."

I laughed then realized she was serious. "Why do you say that?"

She tapped the counter. "It would have been easier to kill him with a gun or knife. But with a spear, the killer could have been making a statement. What that would be, I don't know."

A shudder passed through my body. Time to find out

who had blown my cover and how much trouble I was in. "Can I have the envelope?"

"Oh, yes. I'm so sorry." She handed it to me. "With all that's happening, I forgot."

River Atwood (Angeline) was handwritten on the front. Sweat pooled under my arms and formed on my upper lip.

"Who gave it to the boy?"

"Billy didn't know the guy, but he said he liked him."

Yeah, I bet. The guy paid him five dollars. I stared at the envelope. My arm hair rose. Reluctant to open it, I finished my scotch.

Iolana reached out for my hand. "Are you OK? You've gone pale."

I ripped open the envelope and pulled out a folded piece of white paper with four words written on it.

"WHERE IS THE MONEY?"

I stared. My stomach heaved. Then I ran to the door.

2

Iolana ran after me and grabbed the paper. "What? What is it?" She examined the paper as if there should be more. "Does this have to do with you hiding here on the island?"

I pulled on my rubber boots. "I have to find Tempest. I'll tell you about it after I find her."

"I'll help."

We pushed out into the storm with flashlights, but the beams couldn't cut through the downpour, and we were forced to turn back.

On the porch, we slid out of our rain gear and hung it up, both of us quiet. The people who were after me could take Tempest and would think nothing of killing her if I didn't give them the money.

I handed Iolana a towel to dry off. Had she given someone info on me to someone? No, not purposefully or for money. I truly believed that she was one of the good people. And for some reason, she had trusted me from the beginning—without knowing my history. I glanced over at her as I slipped on my Crocs. She was watching me like a poker player looking for a tell. I could smell my sweat.

"Do you know how Tempest was injured?" I didn't wait for an answer. "A woman named Betty purposely cut the dog's leg so she could pretend to save her then meet me. That's why Tempest limps."

"Who was this woman?"

I made a decision I swore I never would. But now, all bets were off. "Someone is hunting me, Iolana. I could be killed."

She sat down on the stool and pulled a leg up under her. "It would be good to tell me your story. In case something happens to you."

Her coolness calmed me. "Like I've said before, you should be a lawyer."

She huffed as if she found this distasteful.

"I was once a lawyer," I said. "But I was disbarred."

Iolana's mouth dropped open. I'd never seen that before.

"I bet you thought I'd been a legal aide, right?" I didn't wait for an answer and told her my long, sad story.

When I finished, I picked up the note. "Those sons of bitches."

Iolana sipped her tea, not reacting, looking every bit the wise woman. "Let me see if I have this straight."

She leaned on the counter and recited everything I'd just told her about my sister and Gerard. "Do you have the money she transferred to the Maryland bank?"

I nodded. "It's still there."

She sipped her tea and shifted on the stool. "What a sad story. What a stupid Frenchman."

"He had his reasons," I said. "I'm not making excuses for him, but later I found out that he was told they would kill Sophie if he went back to her."

Iolana looked into the mug as if reading tea leaves. When she looked at me, sorrow clouded her face. "But you didn't know that at first. You thought the Frenchman, this Gerard, had used your sister, so you went to Paris to kill him." She sat up and swallowed hard. "You now had the money, right? After your husband died, you left town in disguise, trying to escape the gang. But one of the leaders of the gang tracked you down in Portland, and before he killed you, you poisoned him."

I shrugged. Iolana kept shaking her head as if she couldn't believe the story. Or my actions.

"That's how you came to be here on Kauai under a new name. You were at the Waimea Plantation when the other partner in this criminal enterprise—Betty? Right?—tracked you down. You didn't know her. She befriended you. Finally, she demanded the money. When you said no, she tried to push you off a cliff. But she went over instead." Iolana searched my face. "Good so far?"

I gave her a thumbs up.

"After Betty died, you went back to the car. The Frenchman was there. You thought you'd killed him in Paris. How surreal." She searched my face. "Did you faint?" Again I shrugged. "He drove you back to your cottage. That's when he told you the whole story about him and Sophie and the extortionist gang." She drew in a long breath and let it out. "No wonder you passed out."

I waited to see what she'd say next.

"That's when I found you at the hospital where he'd dropped you off then disappeared."

"I'm glad I had one friend on the island," I said as I marveled at this woman who had listened to this story and not bolted from my life forever. "That's an excellent summation." I paused, then said, "Iolana, if you want to leave now, I won't blame you. I don't want you to be a party to any criminal charges that could be brought against me."

I hoped she'd stay. The week after I left the hospital, Iolana stopped by my cottage every other day after work and brought me food from the market and her garden. She was kind and generous that way. She didn't even know why I'd been in the hospital, only that I'd gone through a trauma of some kind and needed help because I had no one.

I watched Iolana's face as she processed all I'd told her.

Finally, she said, "River's not your real name."

"No."

"The note means someone took over the extortion racket."

"Obviously."

Iolana finished her tea and let out a laugh. "You are one kickass *haole*," she said. "I thought you were running from an abusive ex. I had no idea."

I glanced out the window, wishing my past was dead, and my dog would come home safe and in one piece. I didn't feel like laughing.

"Let's go look for Tempest again," she said.

I nodded. It looked like Iolana would stick by me. At least for a bit.

After no sign of Tempest, we made it back to the house just before the storm worsened. Wind whipped the palms and Poinciana trees so loudly I couldn't hear the rain. The last few lychee nuts ricocheted off the roof. I left the porch light on for Tempest.

I pulled the gun from my pocket, trying to hide it from Iolana.

"River! Is that a gun?"

I sighed. "Look, I need it. Pretend you didn't see that." I figured I'd better change the subject. "Do we have a cop in the crew?"

Iolana's expression didn't change. Her words were clipped, disapproving, when she said, "That would be convenient."

I took that as a *yes*.

"Is he or she trustworthy?"

She didn't answer.

"Can I make you something to eat?" I asked, not trying to hide the gun anymore.

"No, I'd better go."

"Please don't judge me, Iolana."

"I don't, River. I'm just afraid for you. Guns draw bad energy."

Thankfully, I didn't have to say anything. Iolana's phone rang. After she hung up, her eyes turned downward, tired, and her lips seemed pinched.

"Are you OK?"

She shook her head. "Will you be all right? Should you come home with me?"

"Thank you, but I need to stay here for Tempest." My gut said she'd been taken so I'd give up the money. I set down the gun.

Iolana hugged me. "She'll come home."

After Iolana drove away, I grabbed my blanket, my gun, a butcher knife, and pulled a chair up next to the front door so I could hear if Tempest scratched to come in. I'd made a big mistake—I'd become too attached to that dog. And that dog had become too attached to me. That wasn't safe for any human or animal.

At sunrise, I woke up stiff from sleeping in the chair. I stood, stretched, and rubbed my sore back. The storm had stopped, and the air was thick and stunk like jungle rot. The feral rooster strutted and crowed incessantly. Water dripped from the trees. Frogs croaked. Something moved through the bushes, not big enough to be Tempest. After coffee, I'd go looking for her again.

Like an old man in slippers, I shuffled to the kitchen. My stomach knotted in pain. Last night, I'd been wrong telling Iolana my story. Now I had to worry about that, never mind Tempest and the note. I filled and turned on the electric kettle, then set up the Melitta. Images of Tempest dead somewhere, her throat cut or. ... I rubbed my temples.

"Get a grip!"

I said it so loudly, I made myself jump. I needed food.

After eating leftover mango rice to calm my stomach, I made coffee, dumped in cream, and inhaled it. The rush of caffeine hit.

"Enough is fucking enough."

No more hiding from the world. Dead people—Sam, Betty, Gus—have been gaslighting me. I wasn't crazy. I haven't been driven mad, only underground, and abandoned. But it seemed like the same thing sometimes. Even my poor dead sister, who instigated the whole thing, left me to clean up the mess.

No, not a mess. She'd put me in danger, and now I was hunted. How impossibly cruel of her.

But the dead were dead. I was still alive, and I needed to act like it. I had to quit sleepwalking through each day. Waiting for something to happen. Reacting. Ever since Betty nearly killed me, I'd been scared someone would try again. Now someone knew where I lived and knew I still had the money.

"Screw you. You're not getting the money." I took a swig of coffee, and it went up my nose. With a paper towel, I wiped my face. This was a matter of principle. If they've touched a single hair on my dog, they'd be sorry. I lifted my coffee mug in mock salute to the dead—the two I'd killed. "Just try it, motherfuckers."

I was going to get my dog back and go home. But first I needed to find my way out of this mess.

I'd been suppressing and running away from the pain and trauma, thinking I could stay safe.

Not anymore. No more victim. Ironically, I once helped victims seek justice, and now I was victimized. But you never know what it's like to experience violence until you do.

I didn't need to hide. The principal players were dead. I had no arrest warrants under my legal name of Angeline Porter. No one had evidence that I'd killed Sam. And if some scuzzbag had taken my dog as a way to get info from me, I'd hear from them soon. *If* Tempest's disappearance connected with the note.

As I drank my coffee and ate more mango rice, my mojo maxed, my brain caught fire. So did my gut, that uncanny messenger that sometimes did what the rational mind couldn't. What if the timing on all this wasn't a coincidence? The Reaper was killed, my dog disappeared, and I got this threatening note, delivered to me via the library. I knew none of that made sense right now. Still, I'd won some diffi-cult cases by not ignoring my gut and the connections that at first seemed flimsy and that others had ignored.

Action would help me get back into the fight. Iolana would call me when she found out more about The Reaper. Still, for now, I needed a strategy to find out how I could get home and stop the Boston gang because I'm sure that's where the note came from.

They knew where I lived if they'd followed Iolana to my house after she received the envelope.

That made me an easy target. Maybe that made my job easier, so I could flush out the assholes.

I took my coffee to the porch and checked for Tempest again. The feral rooster continued with his piercing, insanely repetitive noise while his brood scratched up the path to my house.

I opened the door and yelled, "Give me back my dog!"

The rooster and his harem skittered into the underbrush.

Back in the kitchen, I poured another cup of coffee, grabbed a new sheet of paper to make another list. This one would force me to face these criminals who kept me bottled up in fear and hiding under a new identity in a place that wasn't my home. They'd be sorry if anything happened to my dog.

But I jumped ahead. Now that someone knew where I lived, why hide anymore? I could get back online. No more trips to the library every time I had to do research. That meant buying a new laptop. Plus, I needed a new burner. I knew nothing right now. I needed info. I wrote:

- Research the Boston gang.
- Contact Snoop, my old hacker pal. If reachable.
- Contact the Frenchman. (if possible, if I want to open up that old wound) As FBI, he had connections.
- Ask both for info on the Boston crime group. Did it still operate? If so, who's running it?
- Figure out how to go home to Oregon.
- Find out who sent the note. How?
- Buy a new laptop and burner; get back online.

The rooster started in again. I added to the list: Kill that fucking rooster.

5

Again, I walked the road in an attempt to find Tempest, but I was losing hope. I headed back to the house. Iolana waited in the driveway, and when she saw me, she lowered the window.

"Tempest not home yet?"

"No, but can I come by the library to use your computer?"

Iolana looked me over. I know I looked a mess. "I'm worried about you, River. I'm not worried about Tempest. She can take care of herself. But with you, an FBI agent was murdered. *They* won't stop investigating. And now you've received that note. You're in danger."

"I know, Iolana." I leaned on her open window. "But you know what? Screw them. I'm tired of living in secrecy, under an assumed name, on the run. If the FBI wants to find me, they can, they will. If Betty and Sam's gang is still active, screw 'em."

"I understand. You're angry and—"

"I'm way beyond angry."

Iolana said nothing.

I needed to tone it down. I wasn't mad at Iolana. "Sorry, but I'm in action mode and a little ramped up."

"No worries. I just want you to take care of yourself."

"I will. I've made it this far. But if they've done anything to Tempest. ..." I stopped and took a good look at Iolana. Something bothered her, and it wasn't just me. "So what's up with The Reaper's case?"

"I didn't want to tell you on the phone, but I'm worried about Aisake." She sucked back tears. I laid my hand over hers. "Remember last week's meeting?"

I did. Just the three of us met, and Aisake jumped all over me for making a joke, calling the transnational companies "The Po Foe." I thought I'd cleverly named them after *Po,* the god of endless dark chaos in Hawaiian mythology. He'd jumped up and shouted, "There's nothing funny about those murderers." Iolana tried to calm him, but he grabbed his coat and left.

"Is he all right?" I asked.

Iolana looked like a mother who feared for a son. "I don't know. I'm afraid he'll do something ... rash ... about The Reaper's murder."

Now I felt bad for adding to her worries with divulging my history. "Look, don't worry about me. Take care of Aisake, OK? I'll be just fine."

She didn't look convinced. I squeezed her hand.

"See you at the library," she said, then left.

Inside, I poured more coffee and lit a cigarette, the first in a long time. The first drag made me dizzy, but after that, I practically swooned with the sensation. In my predicament, lung cancer took a back seat.

The cigarette wasn't the only thing giving me a buzz. The island never felt like mine, my land, my home. Maybe

I'd felt the first surge of freedom or escape now that my cover was blown.

An urge came on heavy. I wanted to go home to Eugene. I guess it's true that you don't really know what you've missed until you lose it. I loved that small city and its eccentricities. I could see me walking Tempest as I took on some cause, something normal. Whether some criminals wanted my money or the FBI wanted me to help them catch these thugs, I'd either say bring it on or get the hell out of my life. The idea of taking back my name, restoring the remainder of my former life gave me a buzz. I would do it somehow. Kauai, a beautiful, lush, formidable, peaceful, grand, colorful place, wasn't home.

Sophie, my dead sister, would have said, "It's like Mom used to say. 'Home is where the heart is.'"

I almost laughed. "What heart, Sophie?" I said aloud. "You mean that concrete slab in my chest?"

I snuffled back tears. "Jeez, Sophie, what a mess. Thanks a hell of a lot, sister!"

Who did I fool anyway? A hard heart was easier to live with, but the loss of my husband, sister, and career had left me with a gaping hole. What had I become? The only one who seemed to know was my dog—my freaking dog. And now she'd disappeared.

Outside, the wind came up. A shutter slammed shut, making me jump. I changed my clothes and filled my backpack. In my car, after taking another pass along the road to look for Tempest, I headed for the library.

I passed a local eatery where a new sign had popped up. "The best SPAM Musubi." SPAM in sushi? You'd never see that in Eugene. I had to get out of here. I didn't know these people, not really. I had no kinship with their culture. I cared for them, but I couldn't stay. I was definitely *haole*.

I turned on the radio. The news reported "the bizarre death of controversial activist The Grim Reaper, now identified as Steven Hastrick." He went on to say how Hastrick had been found but said little else other than the police considered it a suspicious death. Nothing about the weapon. Good.

Now I was pumped. A mystery solved. Now I could plan how to get back to my former self and Eugene.

6

As I approached the library, I slowed down. Two police cars with flashing lights were parked out front. My heart raced. What were they doing there?

A horn honked. The impatient driver flipped me off as he drove around me. Guess not every islander is laid back. I pulled over, about to call Iolana's cell, when the library door opened.

Two male and one female cop escorted Iolana in handcuffs to one of the cars. I shut off my engine. Another vehicle, a dark sedan with tinted windows, pulled up next to the cop car. The cop went to the driver's window, and a short conversation ensued. I couldn't see the person inside, but it looked like an FBI rig, not that they all looked the same. They just gave off the same vibe.

But what could they arrest Iolana for? I lit my second cigarette of the day. Her letters to the mayor and newspaper spelled out the transnationals' degradation of the island. The corporations tested tons of carcinogenic insecticides that poisoned the waters. The island now mainly grew

HMO corn seed for the Midwest. I and many others on the island considered Iolana a good citizen. She certainly didn't have anything to do with The Grim Reaper's death.

I had to do something. Iolana had helped me at every turn.

The cops pulled out and left. No one emerged from the sedan. Iolana's assistant stood in the doorway with her hand over her mouth. They couldn't have had a warrant for the library, or they would have removed the library's computer terminal. Or did they need a warrant if it were city property?

After the sedan left, I went inside to find out more. Iolana's assistant wept, and two women soothed her. They didn't know why she'd been arrested. One woman thought she'd heard one of the men mention Aisake.

I disappeared into Iolana's office, logged onto her computer, and read the latest news on the killing. Nothing new. I Google searched Steven Hastrick's name.

Page after page popped up. What the hell? He'd been a member of the Taylor Commune, the very same one Betty told me about, the one Betty's brother had been involved with before he committed suicide. My gut pinged—a connection. But even bigger—Hastrick was also the missing son of a wealthy Boston family. Betty lived in Boston. It was a big city, but I didn't like coincidences.

My phone rang. I closed the door to the office.

Aisake asked, "River? Where are you?"

"I'm at the library. They just arrested Iolana."

"I've just had a call. Cops are headed my way. I'm out of here. And you need to leave the islands, too."

"Why? Aisake, what the hell is going on? Why would they arrest Iolana?" I watched the road. Cars drove by on Rte. 50, the main thoroughfare through Kauai, but no cops.

"Take Tempest to this address." He didn't know I didn't

have Tempest. "They'll keep her until you can figure out how to get her." After giving me the address, he hung up without a goodbye.

I hopped in my car and tried to stay at the speed limit. If I found a cop at my house when I got there, I was done for.

When I pulled into the driveway, Tempest sat by the front door. I stifled a cry, jumped from the car, hurried over, and hugged her even though she was soaked and muddy, and stunk. When I looked her over, I found areas where fur was missing, odd patches around her neck. She had a cut on her ear and no collar. Shit.

Inside, I cleaned her up best I could and fed her. While she ate, I threw all of Tempest's bedding, treats, and food into the car.

Back inside, I checked my phone. A voicemail from an unknown number. It must be Iolana calling from the jail. I listened.

"Angeline, this is Gerard." I should have known I'd hear from him. My heart raced. I swallowed hard. Not now. Not fucking now.

"I'm sorry to call. I know you don't want to hear from me, but you must call me. It's about Sophie. She has a twin sister who is alive and lives in Boston." A long pause. A twin sister? "This is important. Let me know you are all right, yes? *S'il vous plait.*"

A twin sister. Rubbish. No way. This could be a ploy to get me to engage but seemed so random. And how did he get my number? Before Gerard dumped me at the hospital and disappeared, he told me to change my burner every month so no one could track me, and I did. Snoop had told me the same thing.

Although he'd told me he worked for the American FBI and the French version, I doubted everything he said. He'd supposedly been undercover, Sophie's lover, and someone I thought caused my sister's death. My lawyer brain went into overload. Now he said Sophie had a twin? How had he found out? But more importantly, what had he been doing when he found this out? What led to the discovery? If he'd used this to make contact with me, he was beyond despicable. But he showed imagination. I'd give him credit for that.

I rubbed my face, drank pineapple juice from a jug, and hurriedly threw some clothes and toiletries on the bed.

Tempest nudged me with her nose. "OK, girl. I'll hurry." I bent down and hugged her, teary-eyed. "I'm so happy to see you."

She licked my cheek.

I pulled my suitcase from the closet and now was grateful that I hadn't followed my first impulse and burned the contents—false passport, ID, and papers Gerard had sent after dropping me off at the hospital then disappearing. The documents allowed me to travel anywhere in the world as River Atwood. He'd given them to me with an invitation to meet him in Paris. I didn't go. Now I'd use them to go home. Somehow, I'd get my real identity back. How? I had no idea.

I shoved the ID into my backpack and threw my clothes into the suitcase.

7

My car stunk of wet dog, but I didn't care. At the address Aisake gave me, I knocked on the door. A sweet older woman greeted me. I explained that Tempest had lost her collar. We walked to the car, and she put a collar and leash on her while talking soothingly to the dog in Hawaiian. Teary-eyed, I grabbed Tempest's things. I would send for her when I found a house in Eugene. But that didn't guarantee I'd ever see her again. I explained to the woman about Tempest's twenty-four hours in the storm. She looked the dog over then eyed me suspiciously.

I didn't have time to explain. I hugged Tempest and whispered a few things in her ear before leaving quickly so I wouldn't upset her further.

In the car, I cried as I headed toward the airport. Suddenly my life had notched up to crazy again. I was way too emotional. I needed to stop fleeing and start fighting.

What was so crucial that Gerard had to contact me? And why would he use a ploy like Sophie having a twin? That reeked of manipulation and maybe bad news for me if he were getting that desperate. But desperate about what? I wanted to know how he'd found my number. I'd left no trail either, using only cash.

With deep breaths to lower my heart rate, I tried to concentrate on the facts. Before Gus was killed, he swore no one at the FBI was looking for me. He had worked for them and promised not to report me. But Gus died, so was that true or not? He'd given me a gun that had a microphone in the grip, giving him access to everything I did.

After Betty went over the cliff, I found Gerard where she'd left her car. I still had the gun then. When we went back to my cottage, I remember holding the gun on him. But I passed out and he dropped me off at the hospital. After I returned to the cottage, the gun was there, in with my lingerie. "So cliché" I wanted to say to him. But he'd changed the grip and left a note. "No more microphone." Good. At least I had a gun. But could I trust him? A new grip could mean a new microphone. So I threw it out into the ocean. I'd get my own gun. That would also mean I no longer had Gerard watching over me—if that were a good thing.

I knew not to underestimate the long arm of the law or greedy criminals. As Iolana said, the FBI *could* be after me now. Or they'd kept open the case of Betty and Sam's extortion racket after identifying her and Gus' bodies on Kauai. It's more than possible that whoever took over the Boston crime group wanted the money that was in the Maryland bank. That seemed petty—why go after a few million when they had bigger ponds to fish in?

Regarding Gerard, even Snoop hadn't been able to find out anything about him. My sister was the only connection I had with him. No, Gerard and I connected because of Paris.

I'd never denied his appeal, but I figured his attraction to me stemmed from Sophie.

And my sister? She'd made so many bad choices, deadly ones in fact, including the affair with my husband. That caused his death. All for the sake of protecting Gerard at first. If she'd only known the real Gerard.

I missed Hank, his voice, how he used to hold me, how familiar we were with each other. I tried to forgive Sophie, but that was almost impossible. She'd sacrificed my husband to get to our money so she could save the Frenchman. Yet when Gerard took me to my Waimea Plantation cottage, he told me she'd had the affair with Hank to get to the money in order to save *my* life. That's why, according to Gerard, she had seduced my husband.

Now I had to leave the island for my own safety. Aisake's warning seemed dire. With the killing of The Reaper and now Iolana's arrest, my gut said "getthefuckoutofhere," too. I couldn't leave without doing something for Iolana. But what? What power did I have on the island? None. I thought of our old house, felt the chair I used to sit in to read briefs or books, the bed where Hank and I cuddled. I smelled the Sumatran coffee we drank. I heard the neighbor's Chihuahua, Cognac, yapping with excitement when his owner came home.

When I reached the airport, I parked in long-term. I wouldn't be back.

8

Inside the Lihui airport terminal, I looked for the earliest flight to San Francisco. Could I still use the passport and ID that Gerard had given me?

As I stood there looking at the departure board, I figured I had nothing to lose. I called him.

He answered on the third ring.

"Angeline, *merci*. Where are you?" I told him and asked about the ID papers. "Yes, they will work. But one moment. Before you do anything, you need to know about Sophie's twin."

I set down my suitcase. "Yes, so you mentioned in your voicemail."

"A New Hampshire lawyer says he represents the twin and is trying to claim your inheritance from your husband's business. Since you've been legally 'missing,' it's been in trust."

I didn't know which surprised me more—Gerard keeping tabs on Hank's business settlement—and therefore me—or someone professing to be my sister's twin. "Sophie didn't have a twin," I said. But with our parents, how they lived, their lifestyle, how they died, I couldn't be sure. I wouldn't put this past them.

"You're not concerned?"

"It's more likely to be a scam. Plus, there are probably so many legal impediments to it—New Hampshire laws, adoption laws, me not being legally dead." I paused. "And how did you know about my inheritance being in trust? You've been checking on me." A chill ran through me. I exhaled slowly. "Never mind. I have more important things to take care of, like my safety. I need to get off the islands, pronto."

"I know. I'll tell you everything. Go to San Francisco. I'll meet you there."

I picked up my suitcase. "There is no twin, Gerard."

"Angeline, the evidence ... how you say? ... is solid."

"What's her name?"

"They call her 'Bibi.'"

"Baby?"

"No. Bibi. Her full name is Elizabeth Brackston. Her adopted name."

My mouth went dry, and the airport too loud. Hearing details like this made it seem possible. The overwhelming smell of gardenia leis made me queasy. Aloha, my ass. "I've got to go."

"Her lawyer provided documents to prove who she is."

Police lights flashed outside the airport. "OK, OK! I'll call you from San Fransisco."

"I'm already here."

Of course. I hung up, bought a ticket with cash, and raced to security. Once through, I hurried to the ladies' room, hid in a stall, and sat on the seat, head in hands, trying to control my breathing.

Once again, someone else wagged my tail, not me. I had

no idea what to expect. So what if someone professed to be my sister's twin and wanted my part of Hank's business? I'd already given up that inheritance when I disappeared. *Everyone* wanted my money. Maybe the one who had sent the note concocted this twin sham. What the fuck?

I had to leave the island, even without Aisake's warning. Yet I was torn. I should stay to help Iolana. And my poor dog, abandoned again. Was someone on the island setting us up for the fall of The Grim Reaper? I sure didn't trust multinational corporations.

On the mainland, I thought about who I could trust. Maybe my lawyer? Who probably thought I was dead. I also had no idea if anyone connected me with Sam's death in Portland. But the authorities had no way to pin it on me. Was it too much to ask that I could buy a little house in Eugene, have my dog shipped to me, and enjoy life for a change? I missed the few friends I had there. I missed waking up in the morning to fresh air, a good cup of coffee, and the newspaper. I guess my concrete slab of a heart could crack.

I'd decided I'd hear what Gerard had to say, then head to Eugene.

But now I doubted that decision. Maybe going home was just as bad as running away. I needed to stand for something. My life would continue to be tainted unless I felt good about myself again, and to do that, I needed to stay on Kauai until I helped Iolana. I also needed to stand up to Gerard. He could not call me after all this time and demand I come to San Francisco.

That damned shoulder parrot of doubt started squawking.

Would Iolana tell the police all about me? Why did I

trust her? She befriended me so quickly. Why? Would I end up in jail instead of her?

Just like that damn rooster, it wouldn't shut up until I shot it.

So I took mental potshots at it. Everyone trusted Iolana. She was nothing like Betty. Betty had acted like she cared for my dog and me, but she hadn't. Everyone knew Iolana. Everyone admired her. Betty was obsessive and skitzy right from the start, *and* she had a cocaine habit. Iolana didn't even drink alcohol. Plus, she'd helped me from the beginning, even renting my house in her name. She was also on the right side of the environmental issue. What more proof did I need? If she had an agenda with me, it seemed to come from the right place, like her heart.

My brain then flicked through pages of constitutional law, criminal law, old dusty law books. I'd done nothing illegal. Both deaths, of Betty and Link, aka Sam, were acts of self-defense. Yes, I *had* bought forged identification papers, but Gus had been the only one who knew about that. I finally breathed normally again and headed for a coffee shop.

I only wanted coffee, so I skipped the Ai Ono Cafe, ordered a Starbucks latte—a little taste of home—and sat at a small table, missing my cold-nosed dog. As far as the twin possibility, wouldn't we have heard something about this, especially with all the genealogical digging that transpired on sites like Ancestry? Maybe Gerard made up the twin to get me back to the mainland. But he could do that anytime. He had the means and power.

I shifted in my seat. Squirmed more like it. Because what if Bibi *did* exist? I'd have to face the fact that I had another sister whom my parents gave away. Our parents had been ... different. *Unconventional* didn't describe them. Outside statistical norms. Yes. So a twin was possible. Yes. But why had they given her up? And how had she found out about me and my inheritance?

I heard my flight being called. Screw it. I could find out about this so-called twin anytime. I could go home anytime. I needed to get Tempest back and help Iolana.

I took a paper napkin and wrote:

- Aisake was the one who told me to run. Why?
- What if he wanted me gone? I knew too much about the Kāne Crew.
- I knew the members' names, strategy, and planned activities.
- Maybe I had relevant knowledge that I didn't know I had.
- Maybe I had a connection with The Grim Reaper's case.

I looked up. The hair on my arms rose, a sign I was onto something. Often victims or witnesses had knowledge they didn't know they had until I dug around with questions about their experience. Hmm. I'd have to think about that one. I finished my latte and headed back to my car. No cops were outside, so that had nothing to do with me when I heard the sirens. Showed my paranoia wasn't doing me a damn bit of good.

I'd have to call Gerard. Or maybe not. What was he doing back in the States, and why the interest in this so-called Bibi twin? It couldn't be that straight forward. Something else was going on. I wanted to find out before I entered that viper's nest again.

By the time I headed back to pick up Tempest, I had a plan.

9

Tempest nearly knocked me down when I stopped to take her home.

At our house, she wouldn't leave my side. I gave her a bone and made a pot of coffee. It would be a long night. I had work to do.

First, I called Snoop. It took some time for her to try me back. We went through the same ritual as before, with a robo-voice asking me personal questions that only the two of us knew the answer to. Then her calling. I was never so happy to hear her voice.

"Hey." She said.

"Yes, I'm alive."

"I knew that, River."

"Damn! Is there no privacy?" I was awestruck that she knew my new assumed identity.

We both laughed.

"I've been waiting for you to contact me."

Her androgynous voice hadn't changed. I still didn't know if she was female, but who cared? She was a great hacker. Plus, she was loyal, and she liked me.

"Here's the deal." I caught her up on everything that had happened since I last talked with her, even about the dead left in my wake.

"Who needs reality TV? I have you." She coughed. "Sorry. Had that crud going around. No worries. What's up?"

I wondered who Snoop was. Did she live in the States? Did she have a partner? Was she talking from a sophisticated command center or a bedroom with a laptop and posters of Daft Punk?

"I need some snooping." This was an old joke between us, and neither of us laughed. I told her I wanted to know if anything on her radar came up about Gerard. She'd found nothing on him the last time, but it was worth a try. I also wanted her to find out about this so-called twin sister. If that turned out to be true, I'd need to do something. DNA tests should be run, but could the results be faked? If she was a fraud, I'd rather squash this freak and give the money to a worthy cause.

"When do you need it?"

We sorted out time and payment, but she didn't seem concerned. For some reason, I felt attached to her, like having an adopted and very smart kid sister. With me in my early forties, I figured she had to be younger. Maybe she knew I wasn't like others, and I wasn't in it for the money. I wanted justice. Maybe she liked that I was an outsider too—disbarred criminal attorney, on the lam, in disguises.

"Snoop, I have two more people I'd like checked out." And against my better nature, I asked her to investigate Iolana Ontabi and Aisake Thompson.

"OK, boss," she said, then laughed.

When I called Aisake's cell again, it was no longer in service. That raised my hackles.

I poured scotch into my coffee. What did they say about coffee with alcohol? Wide awake drunk?

Yes. I was wired. But so what? I knew the law. I knew what cops could and could not do. I called the Lihue police station. "Is Iolana Ontabi still under arrest? I'm her lawyer."

"Yeah, she's here, but so is her lawyer. Who's this?" Maybe she'd called the lawyer for the Kāne Crew. Good. I found his name in my notes. "Good. I'm his associate." Lie.

I waited. When the cop came back on the phone, he said, "The lawyer said he's got it covered."

I hung up. At least Iolana had representation.

As for me, I was done with this whole bullshit charade. I was tired of working in the shadows. My next move was to call Gerard. He needed to protect me, to tell them that I worked for him undercover, therefore the false ID. If he did that, I'd be free of any fake identity charge. I'd be untouchable. Plus, I needed to let him know I wasn't coming to San Francisco. Not yet.

When he answered my call, he said, "So you're not coming." A statement. Not a question.

I explained what was going on and why I had to stay. When Gerard said nothing, I asked, "Why are you checking up on Hank's business and my inheritance? What's with that?"

He didn't answer.

"Does this have to do with a case you're working?"

A long pause. I waited. I could picture his face—thoughtful, giving nothing away, weighing options. I liked that about him.

Finally, he said, "Angeline, I can't answer those questions. You know how this works. But I can tell you one thing." His accent was back. "I am trying to protect you."

Suddenly, it hit me. "So the Betty and Link, aka Sam, situation hasn't ended. Their little gang is still active."

Again he said nothing.

"How do you know about this so-called twin? You're still following the money, right? I get it. The money that Hank left me is bait."

His voice softened as he said, "I'd like to see you again."

Diversion tactic. Damn him. I had a fluttering in a different part of my body, and that pissed me off. No way. Not this time. Not again. Not like in Paris.

"Are you serious? You know what I went through because of you. You honestly think I'd come back as bait?" I hit the kitchen wall with my fist. Tempest moaned. "Did you forget that Sam was going to kill me? Where were you when that was going down? No way. I'm done."

Silence. I blew on my sore knuckles.

I could hear him breathing.

"*Desolé*, Angeline. I'm sorry."

I waited. "Sorry about what, asshole?"

"If you help me, I can help you. I can give you your identity back. I can make you Angeline Porter again, safe from any prosecution. You'll never have to worry. But I need you."

"And if I don't agree?"

"I will have to bring you back legally."

"You mean you'll forcibly arrest me? Who do you work for? You're French. You can't arrest me."

"I'm also a U.S. citizen."

"Then you work for or with the FBI."

He said nothing.

I shook my head and smiled. The bastard. Blackmail. But blackmail wasn't foreign to me. When I tried to raise a large amount of cash in Portland for my husband's surgery to save his life, I hooked up with dates via the Ashley

Madison dating site. I videoed the sex then demanded money from them in exchange for not telling their wives. Yes, I extorted them. But they were cheating, wives be damned.

I closed my eyes. Now that he'd killed the flutter in my pelvis, my brain came back online with a vengeance.

"I'll come back, but I have conditions. Get my friend Iolana out of jail and cleared of any bogus charges they're holding her for."

He didn't hesitate. "Done," he said.

"And I want my dog on the mainland with me."

"Dog?" He was genuinely surprised.

"Yes, dog."

"All right."

So he didn't know everything. Whatever Tempest had bolted after, it wasn't Gerard.

10

H ours later, Gerard called. "You can pick up Iolana Ontabe at the jail tomorrow morning. She'll call you when she's released."

I hesitated before asking, "Did you get her out, or was it her lawyer?"

"Her lawyer ... with a little behind the scenes assistance."

Hmm. "Did the police charge her with anything?"

"No. They want to. They think she knows where this Aisake Thompson is."

"I don't think she does, but then again, she's really protective of him." I paused before saying, "Hey, you didn't get Iolana out, right? So I owe you nothing."

"Do you want to return to Oregon?"

What the hell was he up to? I waffled. "Right now I do."

"Do you want your dog?"

I had to laugh. "Smooth, Gerard. Nice going. Even if you do get my dog to the mainland, you still owe me one more favor."

"True."

I didn't want to talk about this anymore. Aisake was gone, and Gerard probably knew where he was or could find out. I only had one more question. "Why are you doing all this? What are you getting out of this?"

I expected him to say, "It's my job."

Instead, I heard him take a deep breath. "I need you," he said.

That's something my sister would have said. What was I doing? Those two had messed up my life. Neither one of them deserved one more minute of it.

I hung up without responding.

The following morning, Iolana called me from the Kauai Community Correctional Center in Lihue. I picked her up, expecting her to be exhausted. Instead, she was pissed. Tempest licked her ear. "They kept asking me about Aisake, where he was. I told them I didn't know."

"He's gone, Iolana. His phone is disconnected. Do you know where he is?"

She looked so young at that moment, so naive. So disappointed in my question. She sighed, ignored me, and stared out the passenger window as I drove. I rolled up the windows and turned on the air. Outside was muggy as hell, and I was already sweating. Iolana kept her native cool.

A mile from her place, she turned to me and said, "My lawyer said you have a powerful friend who will make sure I'm not charged with anything."

Son-of-a-bitch. I expected Gerard to keep a low profile and let the lawyer take the credit.

"They couldn't hold me for more than twenty-four hours without charging me. They planned to charge me with obstruction of justice." She twisted her hair around a finger. "My lawyer says he got a phone call from someone who said the cops wouldn't press charges. And they didn't."

Gerard. That lying sack-of-shit. Now I suppose I *had* to go back to the mainland and help him.

I chuckled. "Iolana, make me a t-shirt that says, '*Haole* Power!'"

"Are you going to tell me who this powerful friend is?"

"Sorry. Top secret."

I sensed she didn't like it, but I was still beating myself up for sharing with her as much of the story as I had. My kind of secrets made everyone vulnerable.

At Iolana's bungalow, we drank tea and fed Tempest left-over meat from a bento bowl. I wiped sweat from my fore-head. I hated this rainy season with its thick air. Sometimes it was hard to breathe.

Iolana bent down to rub Tempest's ear. "Do you want me to take care of Tempest?" She looked up, laser eyes on mine.

I shook my head in wonder. "You blow my mind, Iolana."

"I hope not. You're going to need every brain cell." She went to the window and stared out. "So, what did you have to trade for your friend's help on my behalf?"

I knew she wouldn't give up. I gave her some of the info *and* told a small white lie. "Remember me telling you about the international extortion racket that used my sister to steal millions?" I hadn't told her they were Hank and my funds. "I guess new blood took it over. I've been temporarily recruited to help bring them to justice."

"Like bamboo. Cut it down, and it comes back, only thicker and spreading wider."

I shrugged. "Seems like the way of the world lately. Someday, it will be nothing more than invasive plants and cockroaches."

She ignored my black humor.

"So that means you're going back to the mainland. Do you know for how long?"

I shook my head. "It's up in the air right now. It's crazytown." I hesitated before saying, "I might not come back."

"Will you be safe?"

I shrugged again. I hoped that whatever I worked out with Gerard would keep me safe, but who knew? I wasn't safe the last time.

I worried I'd never, ever be safe again. I had access to the stashed millions in the Maryland bank. That money was Hank's, therefore mine. I was the beneficiary of the settlement of Hank's portion of his company, which I knew had to be substantial. The latter was what the "twin" was after. So I had two targets on my back.

"I'll feel much better with you caring for Tempest."

"When do you go?"

"Right away."

I rinsed my mug in Iolana's sink and pulled my damp t-shirt away from my body. "My contact promised to get Tempest to me on the mainland." We both patted the dog to avoid goodbyes.

Iolana looked up. "Thank you, *Haole* Power."

I couldn't speak as we hugged at the door. She felt very young in my arms. Ah, to be idealistic again. A tear rolled down my cheek, and I brushed it away. I gave Tempest a quick hug, but couldn't linger. I hurried to my car. Time to get tough.

11

On the flight to the mainland, I thought obsessively about this twin. Why did Gerard have so few details about her? He didn't even seem curious. Why hadn't he checked her out? Were the twins fraternal or identical? Did the twin have Sophie's smile or look like Marilyn Monroe too? Was she the same size, have the same color hair, walk the same way? Was she sexy and naive at the same time? Was she even real? Documents could be altered.

The longer Sophie was gone, the more she became someone I'd never known. More Marilyn than Sophie— more an idea than someone I used to help mom bathe in the kitchen sink.

The wheels on the tarmac jolted me to the present. The plane bounced, the cabin shook, and a child cried out. As we came to a stop, there was a spattering of stunned applause. We'd made the landing before fog rerouted flights. I'd been so eager to leave Kauai, I forgot how thick the fog could be in this city.

As the plane taxied, a child with Downs Syndrome whooped and waved her hands up and down. I blinked. Maybe the twin had been born with Downs or cerebral palsy. Maybe her adoptive parents were upset that their child's biological parents—*my* parents—had given her away. Perhaps it *wasn't* the Boston criminals who wanted my money. Maybe it was the adoptive parents helping this Bibi. If they'd traced her through Ancestry and found us. Perhaps that led to me, Hank, and the money in trust.

My parents—my father at least—yes, I could see him giving up a child who demanded too much. He'd gone to Vietnam a complicated man with prejudices and come back with a love of guns and wild mood swings. My mother needed love and attention, and she went along with anything he wanted, mostly anyway. He controlled her by giving or withholding love. Even as a kid, I could fathom that. They needed so much from each other.

Although conservative New Englanders in some ways, my parents lived a semi-hippy lifestyle. They moved constantly. Dad fought authority figures of any kind, from police to politicians, from doctors to bosses. I think his PTSD made him paranoid. In eleventh grade, I nicknamed my parents "hippy John Birchers." That really pissed off my father. Still—give up a child and never let that drop all those years? Not a hint, not an overheard, whispered conversation? I couldn't wrap my head around that one.

The plane pulled up to the gate. Whatever was at work here, whether the twin wanted money or it was the adoptive parents, I would deal with it. If she was deserving of the something from our family, let her have the stash in the Maryland bank. It wasn't important to me.

A sense of relief flooded me. What I needed was to get

my old self back, my true identity. I was tired of pretending and hiding. This sister thing, if real, well, I don't know how I'd feel or react. Right now it wasn't real. Best left like that.

I stood and filed out with my fellow passengers. Inside the terminal, the smell of West Coast coffee welcomed me home. It was different from Hawaiian coffee. I needed a cup. I didn't miss the scent of gardenia, tropical fruit, and coconut sunscreen. Too cloying. I couldn't wait for fresh Northwest air.

On the way to baggage claim, the idea that I was still being hunted hit me hard. I was back with Betty, hearing the gunshots that killed Gus, being led to the cliff, seeing Betty go over the edge.

My mouth went dry. The airport crowd suffocated me. Pushing through toward a wall, I stumbled but caught myself. My heart beat so hard, I couldn't swallow.

I hurried to the nearest restroom, locked myself in a cubicle, sat down, and held my head until it passed. "Come on," I said aloud. "You didn't go through all this shit to have Betty's ghost cripple you."

There was a soft knock on the cubicle door. "Are you OK?" someone asked.

"Yes," I said a little too loud. "Just a little motion sickness."

I searched my pack for Pepcid. My hands trembled, and I dropped one of the pills, popped another.

When the dizziness passed, I splashed cold water on my face. Had I eaten? I couldn't remember.

Finally, at the carousels, I found my flight number. People crowded me. As I was putting my pack over my shoulders, someone tried to yank it from me. I whipped around and smacked the guy with my bag. Stunned, he stumbled backward and ran off. A sunburned couple wearing Hawaiian t-shirts nodded at me. The guy said, "Nice move."

When I saw my bag, I reached out, but an arm reached over mine and grabbed the suitcase. Expecting the thief again, I turned, about to throw a kidney punch, but found myself face-to-face with Gerard.

He backed up, hands in the air. "Whoa, Angeline. *C'est moi.*"

"Screw you!" I said between my teeth.

He nodded. "Yes. Fine. Can I carry your suitcase?"

"No." I pulled up the handle. "Leave it alone." I headed for the exit.

Before we reached the door, I stopped and planted my feet. I shook. It was all I could do not to punch him. "What are you doing here? We were supposed to meet at the hotel." He smelled like cigarettes and the cologne he wore in Paris, a smell that sent signals to the wrong places. "I need a smoke."

"*Moi aussi,*" he said. At least he agreed with me.

When we reached short term parking, I said, "Where are you taking me?"

"To a hotel downtown. I didn't want us too close to the airport. Besides, we need to make a plan and strategize. At least we can do it in comfort."

That sounded all too rational. "Do I have a separate room?"

"*Bien sûr.*"

"Knock it off with the French. We're in the States now."

He chuckled. He acted like he was happy to see me. Oh, sure.

In the car, we buckled up.

Gerard lit two cigarettes and handed me one. "You have a new perfume."

I took a deep, relaxing drag. I wasn't wearing perfume, so I said nothing.

"I believe they call that scent *crabot humide*."

"That sounds like a humid crab," I said, having no idea what it meant.

He laughed, started the car, and headed out of parking.

I rolled down the window and exhaled smoke into the consuming mist. The cool air felt good on my face. I glanced at Gerard and reluctantly said, "OK. I'll bite. What does *crabot humide* mean?"

"Wet pooch." He grinned.

"Oh, just great. I smelled like a wet dog all those hours on the plane? That's a hell of a way to break the ice."

"I didn't think there was any ice to break."

I suppressed a laugh.

"It's good to be with you again, Angeline."

This time I did laugh. "You do remember I tried to kill you, right?"

"It's a risk in my job." His smile spread slow and sexy.

I turned away. "So tell me. Are you in disguise for a reason? The beard. The glasses." He even looked good in those.

"I needed the glasses. I wanted the beard."

"Monsieur Hipster?" The glasses were a throwback to fifties intellectuals.

"Trying not to be afraid of change."

I rolled my eyes. "Right. Good for you."

But he still hadn't answered my question of whether he was in disguise or not. I let it go. As the city came into view, he skirted around traffic like good French drivers do. He stayed quiet, concentrating on the road.

I picked up a very used copy of the *San Francisco Chronicle* and checked all the latest news.

When he stopped, he said, "Here we are."

I looked up over the paper.

My mouth dropped open.

12

G erard checked us into the Palace Hotel. Even when I was an attorney making decent money, I never stayed here on trips to San Francisco. It earned its name. I waited for Gerard to say something about its history, the way he'd introduced me to the Paris Opera House, but he remained silent.

As he checked us in, I stood in the foyer and gawked, hopefully not noticeably. Why had he chosen a place that was so much like Paris? Maybe it reminded him of home? Maybe he just loved luxury. What did I know about him personally?

But what I did know was everything with him was calculated. Hadn't he taken two rooms, one with a suite so we could "strategize"? He had a plan. I knew that.

At our rooms, he handed me the key card. "Get some rest."

I stepped between him and the door. "I want to know about this new sister. Is she disabled or—"

"Listen, we need to discuss what you're willing to do for us. You'll understand after we talk."

"I understand that you're blackmailing me."

"It's not what you think. It's complicated."

"Fuck complicated. I'm in no mood for a nap. I want to know everything. Now."

"Let's unpack. Then come to my suite in fifteen." He paused, studying my face. "I'll order a bottle of scotch."

Of course. Gerard remembered. He was a pro.

I hugged myself, hoping to pull off a defenseless-woman kind of thing so he'd relent. "You're scaring me a little."

"Nice try. I'll see you in fifteen." He smiled and walked away.

In my room, I paced. He called the shots, and it was pissing me off.

After ten minutes, I walked down the hall and banged on his door. He opened it. "You didn't give me enough time to dress," he said. He wore one of the hotel's robes, and his hair was wet.

"Well, at least you're not naked. Thanks for that," I said and pushed past him.

The modern Art Deco suite featured a fireplace, couch, chairs, and minimal art. A bottle of Macallan scotch sat on the glass coffee table along with two crystal glasses and cloth napkins. An end table included a built-in chessboard. A knight had been played. Obviously, wet or not, Gerard could not resist a game. Was I expected to make a move?

I poured a drink and sat on the couch, taking the bottle with me. Gerard settled into a chair, wrapped the robe around his nether region—not that I'd noticed.

I tipped my glass toward him. "So tell me, what do you want, and who is this twin?" I was ready for whatever he had to dish out.

Or so I thought.

13

Gerard wasted no time.

"Do you know how much your late husband's share of the business is worth?"

"How would I know?"

"Around fifty-seven million."

I almost spit out my scotch. "Fifty-seven? How do you know that?"

"It was written up in Buzzfeed. Quite a story. Husband dead, a big inheritance sitting in trust. Couple had no children. Wife, a disbarred attorney—missing. Her sister, deceased, suicide. The missing wife used Ashley Madison to financially extort married men so she could save her dying hus—"

"What the hell?" I shot up from the couch. "No one knew that!"

He half grinned. "True, but someone *might* find—"

"Stop messing with me," I hissed. "If you want my help, out with it." I stood over him, glass in one hand.

He looked up, saw my face, and the grin disappeared.

I filled his glass and mine and waited.

"Would you sit down?" He sounded weary. "*S'il vous plait.*"

I sat.

"With Betty and Link dead, we're dealing with a couple that took over their game, two people, Ralph and Rena, we refer to as The Boston Duo."

I laughed. "'The Boston Duo?' That's the best you could come up with?"

"It works for us. We're the FBI, not an ad agency."

I snorted. "Sorry, but that's pretty lame, even for the FBI."

He sipped his Macallan and ignored me. "This Duo? They're good, very good. They research their marks, find the mark's vulnerability, then match a trained 'family' member to shake down the target. They're thorough. They put time limits on the jobs." He sat back and crossed his legs. "If a job gets sketchy or overly complicated or too many people get involved, they back out. If something looks like it could jeopardize the job or botch the deal, they cancel the operation. They run their extortionist racket like a business ... unless someone screws up. Then we find a body washed up in the bay."

"So, that's why you're restoring my identity? So I can claim the money and be a mark ... a target ... the bait?"

He rubbed the back of his neck. "Like I said, it's complicated, more so than what we even know. This Duo? They just seem to be carrying out orders and keeping the business running smoothly. We think someone else is at the helm. Someone else is the big ... what do you call it, head honcho?"

I huffed at all this. I hated long explanations.

"Are you asking me to be a mark or bait, or what? You didn't answer me." Was this his idea, or did it come from a superior? Damn. Did he even have a superior? Talk about head honcho. Who *was* this guy? I wanted to go home. "Why didn't you leave me on the island? I was happy on Kauai."

"No, you weren't."

That pissed me off. How did he know I wasn't happy?

"You said I'd have nothing to worry about if I did this job. You forgot to add, 'If I survive the job.'"

"We'll stay close. We won't let anything happen to you."

I snorted. "Oh, sure. Like you saved my ass from Betty?" I put the empty bottle on the glass table with a clunk. "In less than seven years, they'll declare me legally dead. I could have waited them out in Kauai."

"You can't go back. They were going to kill your dog and deliver her in pieces, just to show you what they'd do to you if you didn't cooperate."

My cheeks burned. "How do you know that?"

"We were watching your house when we saw two men nab your dog. We followed. When we found them, your dog had been quickly hoisted up on a tree limb, was choking, but fighting hard." He locked eyes with me, making sure I had this image in my head. "One of the men had a knife and was about to butcher her. We fired a warning shot, and they fled. We cut her down just in time. When we knew she'd be OK, we left her on the steps of your house."

Heat filled my face. My jaw clenched. Through gritted teeth, I said, "Did you catch the thugs who did this?"

"No. It was either save the dog or chase after them."

"I have to call Iolana and let her know, tell her to—"

"They'll be safe, Ang. Don't worry. We have someone watching her place."

I was so tired. Now I owed him for saving Tempest.

The ice in my glass had half melted. I'd kept the scotch

watered down because I really, really wanted to get drunk, but I couldn't. I needed to stay on the case.

I sighed. "I haven't even heard the whole story, and we've already polished off the bottle."

"I have a bottle in the bedroom."

I didn't know if that implied anything. I couldn't read his face, that attractive chisel-cheeked face. I was such a cliché finding a Frenchman attractive, not handsome, just so, oh, hell, full of that *je ne sais quoi*. Something Hank never had. Hank had been like a teddy bear, a WISIWYG as Sophie called him. I needed a hard heart to get through this. I swirled the remainder of the ice in my drink until it was gone.

"Angeline," Gerard said, popping me out of my musings. He leaned forward. "Remember I worked with Sam for a year. I did nothing but trail around with him to learn what he knew. He was using me for bait, too." He paused. "Sam finally did what I'd hoped he would. I needed evidence against him. When he set me up with your sister, he said, 'I want you to get your *hands* on her, then her money.' I knew what he meant. But I fell in love with her and everything changed. Everything."

Get your hands on her? That bastard. I was glad I killed him.

"When do I get to be Angeline Porter again?" Saying my name aloud startled me. "How fast can that happen?"

"By tomorrow."

I sat up and took a deep breath. "What do I need to do?"

He rolled his glass between his hands. "Here's the plan. You go to your lawyer's in Eugene. The shock of losing your sister and your husband under such tragic circumstances. PTSD. Deep depression and grief. The fear of this extortionist outfit catching up with you." The French accent was thick again. "You were emotionally exhausted and scared. Kauai was an island. That sounded safe. Sounded like you could lose yourself there."

"How do I explain why they couldn't find me? I'm sure they used a PI."

"Just tell them you have no idea why they couldn't find you."

"Then what?" He didn't answer. "What? I get a massive inheritance, buy a house, and bury the money in the back yard?"

"Put it in your Maryland account."

"How do you know about *that*?"

"Remember? I taught Sophie how to hide the money she stole."

"Oh, right. And you caused her suicide."

"I *loved* your sister. I wanted those bastards stopped, no matter what." His face hardened. "When you poisoned Sam and pushed Betty off the cliff, I cheered. That was justice in my book."

Now it was my turn to be shocked. "You can't know I poisoned Sam."

"Toxicology report."

"You can't prove it."

"We have video of you getting into the car with him. You came out. He didn't."

I didn't bother asking where the video came from.

"Why wasn't I arrested?"

"You were considered an asset."

"By whom?"

"By me."

I was still a pawn in this whole FBI operation—*if* Gerard was indeed working with the FBI. But what else could he be? To me, it sounded as if he had plenty of evidence to arrest the ... the Boston Duo ... and put these people away. So what was he looking for? What more did he need?

Now it hit me—he wanted the head honcho.

I still had a choice even though he thought he owned me. But I needed a strategy and some time to think. I stood, picked up my shoulder bag, and said, "I'm going to the bar. I need time to think. Don't follow me." And I knew he wouldn't. He was still in his bathrobe.

14

The dark bar in all its classy, wood-encased glory was just what I needed. I passed up the comfortable seats and intimate tableaus for the drinking crowd, took a stool at the bar, and ordered a Manhattan.

I'd been so fixated on the twin, I hadn't considered the ramifications of being a pawn—again. Gus had been FBI, and he died trying to defend me. But he never told me that Gerard was involved in their operation. There were, however, many divisions in the FBI, and they could have been working the same case for different reasons. Gerard needed to tell me what Gus had been up to.

As I sipped my Manhattan, I considered a plan. Lack of control was hard for me. Always had been. Now, as I sipped, I considered how to get it back. I stared at a mural of the Pied Piper above the bar. That had to be a Maxfield Parrish painting. The bartender came over and leaned against the bar, following my gaze to the art. Sophie had introduced me to Maxfield Parrish. She'd once gone into a long explanation of how his colors were so vibrant because he painted one color at a time between layers of varnish. The bartender was talking, but I'd missed half of it.

"... and the twenty-seven faces? They include those of his wife, his mistress, two sons, and Parrish himself as the Pied Piper. Imagine getting away with that?"

He had no idea. Parrish was a slacker compared to what I'd gotten away with. When I didn't respond, he said, "Let me know when you want another," and walked away.

Now I was enthralled. The fairytale took on new significance with its theme of old-world justice. *If you don't pay me for ridding your town of rats, I'll get even by stealing your children.* The Pied Piper was a seriously vengeful prick.

But the scales of justice were never equally weighted, not when money was involved. I sipped my drink. Maybe Gerard, after losing my sister, was in revenge mode, wanting to finish off this Boston crime group once and for all. I do think he loved Sophie. Even he admitted to cheering me on when he found out Betty and Sam were dead.

What I needed was to build a file. Snoop found out that Gus worked for the FBI, but she couldn't find anything on Gerard. Perhaps when an agent goes undercover as he did, the FBI took down anything pertaining to the agent's personal ID on the net. All the info I'd given Snoop—Gerard's address in Paris, his phone number, his position with the French government—vanished after I tried to poison him in Paris. Maybe I *was* out of my depth, but I wanted my life back. If I had to make a deal with the devil, so be it.

Tired, I mindlessly looked around the bar, watching couples talk. Why the hell did I leave Kauai? I *hadn't* been happy there. I'd been bored out of my mind. Those twenty years as an attorney were some of the best of my life. It kept me sharp, it kept me in the game. Gerard had put my life at stake again. But this time, I'd do it my way. I needed Snoop still.

First, I'd have Snoop find this so-called twin Bibi. I needed evidence as to whether she really existed or was part of a scheme to get my money in trust. If it was true and she was my sister, what could have possibly made Mom give up a child? One person who might know something was my mother's closest friend back then, Kathleen Glanville. *If* she was still alive. She would be around Mom's age if Mom were alive, maybe seventy? Snoop could scope that out for me, too.

If there were a twin, how would I handle that? I rubbed the goose bumps from my arms. Would I even like her? Would she like me?

A sister. I had another sister. I tried to imagine meeting her, but without a photo I couldn't.

Then it hit me—she could be in danger too. Whoever wanted me as a conduit to the trust could be using her as a conduit also without her knowledge. Speculating in legal terms, however, a blood relative adopted by a Boston family might not have any legal claim on an Oregon trust. I'd need to check Massachusetts' law about that.

Second, after Gerard restored my identity, I'd meet with my lawyer in Eugene. I'd give him a brief rundown and permission to keep my money in trust until I knew what was going on. I could also find out if anyone else had laid claim to the trust besides a biological sister.

So now what? How to handle Gerard?

I paid for my Manhattan, and when I spun around on the barstool, he stood there in casual clothes, looking relaxed, as if we were a couple headed out for a walk before dinner.

"Would you like to go for a walk?"

"Were you reading my mind?" I didn't wait for an answer. "OK, a walk sounds good." Maybe now he'd tell me about the twin. "Let me hit the lady's room first."

In the swanky women's room, I called Snoop. The call went to her robo-voice, but she didn't call back. I figured I'd ask her to look up my mom's friend too. It was taking too long waiting for her, so I shut off my burner and rejoined Gerard.

Gerard took my arm. We walked Market Street with its steady stream of traffic, towering buildings, and retro-fitted gas lamps. Fog horns blew in the distance. So far from Kauai and so welcome. I had no idea how he felt about me personally, but at that moment, I almost felt sorry for him. Something in his body language said he found our closeness both comforting and sad. We didn't talk. I still found him sexy, but I smelled trouble. My gut told me Gerard was holding out on me, at least for now. He'd tell me the whole story, even if I had to seduce it out of him.

Back at his suite, Gerard brought out the second bottle of scotch. He probably *wanted* me drunk, but I was pretty damn good at holding my liquor. I'd noticed, however, that he'd drunk as much as I had, maybe more, and he showed no signs of it. He held out a glass and squinted at me as if daring me to drink with him again.

"No, thanks." I stood and looked for bottled water. That was my trick, drinking water between the alcohol. I found one in a cabinet. I drank half the bottle and wiped my mouth on the back of my hand.

It was time. I faced him across the glass coffee table. "Let's talk about the twin. Tell me what you know. Every detail."

"First, you willingly agree to help me with the Boston Duo?"

The water must have been clearing my head because I said, "Why is this Boston Duo so important? You said they took over Betty and Sam's racket."

"It's a family organization. Ralph is Sam's brother. Rena

is Betty's first cousin. Let's agree to refer to Sam by his nickname, Link, from now on."

I nodded. "So this criminal group is like the Mafia. An organized crime family."

"Yes." He answered the questions like he was on the stand being cross-examined. I could appreciate that, but I wanted more.

"How would you know about the twin unless she's somehow connected to this brother-sister crime outfit?"

He sipped his drink. "Yes, something like that."

Asshole. "What does that mean?" I practically spit the words. He didn't answer. He wanted me to pry it out of him for some reason. What the hell was his reluctance? "Did this 'family' get to the twin like they did Sophie?"

He stared into his drink. I sat down and folded my hands in my lap. Time to spell it out for him. "If you know the twin has a legal right to my trust, the brother-sister duo will go after her, and you don't need me. But if she can't legally access my trust, then they'll come after me, so you *do* need me. So why be concerned about the twin at all or even tell me about her?" I couldn't get my thoughts out fast enough. "Say something, damn it. Tell me what the fuck is going on."

He blew his cheeks out, exhaling as if he had nothing. I was about to call him a few choice names when he took a photo from his pocket and pushed it across the table.

"That's Bibi," he said.

So he did have something. But why the nervousness? I was almost afraid to look. Here it was ... or she was. The twin. I reached across the table, slid the photo toward me, and looked down.

I did a double take.

I picked up the photo. "What is this? A joke?"

"No joke," he said. "I have copies of the adoption papers."

I blinked a few times while staring at a beautiful woman —a beautiful *black* woman.

16

I didn't know what to do. Or say. I examined the photo as if I could find answers. Finally, I said, "But she's black."

He nodded.

"She can't be Sophie's twin."

"Believe me, no one was more surprised than me."

I snapped the photo at him. "You?"

"OK, I'm the second most surprised person," he said.

"First of all," I said, taking a deep breath, "how is it even possible to have twins, one white, one black?"

Gerard tugged at his shirtsleeves. "It's extremely rare but indeed possible. A woman in her fertile cycle needs to have sex within a five-day period with both a white male and a black male ... ah, not at the same time, or I suppose—"

"Relax. I get it." I felt rather smug with him acting so uncomfortable. "Well, you'd never mistake the twins for being identical." My bit of humor fell flat. I cleared my throat, the reality hitting. This was my *mother* we were talking about ... my mother, who had screwed around with two men, Sophie's and my father and an unknown black man within a five-day fertile period.

I picked up the photo again. On further examination, the woman did look like Sophie with her sleepy eyes and a beautiful smile. Bibi was enjoying whatever she was doing at the time the photo was taken. "Who took the photo? How'd you get it?"

"I will get to that in a moment. Right now there is something even more surprising about this twin." He hesitated on the word *surprising*.

"I doubt it." I needed a cigarette.

Gerard sat back and crossed his legs. He looked tired.

"Bibi was adopted by a well-to-do white Boston couple with one child, a boy. They couldn't have more children and wanted a girl, so they adopted. Unfortunately, they unexpectedly died when Bibi was in high school. From what I understand, they never had a chance to change their will, so Bibi received nothing. The brother hated her and kicked her out. She was on the street for a few years."

I stood, unable to sit still, and walked a tight circle by the fireplace. Then I sneaked a glance at the photo as if it would change.

"Bibi is an artist and was picked up by a woman who would become her lover."

I glanced around the room, looking for cameras that might be filming this for a reality television show. Then I dropped into the chair, head in hands.

When I looked up, he leaned forward, hands clasped together, and locked eyes with me. "Angeline, I know this is a lot to comprehend." He said the last word in French.

"Comprehend? This is way more than that. This is ... is. ..." I couldn't think of a word. I picked the photo off the glass table. Why did I have to hear this from Gerard of all people.

He was responsible for my sister's death. He didn't tell her the truth about his job or his disappearance for a month. He could have told her that he could only protect her by pretending she meant nothing to him so the extortionist gang wouldn't suspect their relationship. He assumed that she would be secure in their love. What a fool. What ego. I wanted to hurt him, hurt him bad.

"So, let me get this straight. I have a black, bisexual sister, *twin* to my straight, nymphomaniac white sister."

"Nymphomaniac?" he said, his voice suddenly animated and edgy.

"Sophie loved her sex. So what?" She was no nympho, but he didn't know that.

His face flushed. I watched him squirm and fight for control. I crossed my arms over my chest. I did *not* like the pained look on his face, but tough. My sister hung herself, and there was no bringing her back because of his mistake.

I waited for him to say something, but he didn't. I knew there was more, but how bad could it be. "So what else is there?" I said this like I was bored, like nothing else could shock me.

Gerard's face tightened, his eyes narrowed, and he simply and quietly said, "Bibi was Betty's lover."

Stunned, I examined his face. "What? Say that again."

"Bibi was Betty's lover."

"No way." My voice cracked. "No, no, no."

Shit. I covered my mouth to stop from screaming a long, loud vomit of expletives. God, how I wanted to smash and pound him into a pulp.

I pressed my palms against my closed eyes. Betty's face flashed before me as she fell from the cliff, an expression of surprise, then fear, followed by a sneer as if she were saying, "You just wait. You have no idea what's coming."

Was that how it really happened? Had she really sneered? Or was I—

"Angeline?" Gerard stood, walked over, and touched my arm. "Are you OK? Do you need anything?"

"Need anything? Like what? For you to say, 'April Fools?'" I pulled away. Now I *really* needed a drink—and not water.

I poured scotch into his glass and gulped half of it. A pleasant warmth flooded me. When I felt steady enough, I perched on the arm of the chair he'd been sitting in. "This really sucks, you know that? You're going to explain everything—how, what, when, where, and why. Everything. Every little detail. And I'm going to cross-examine you until I'm satisfied that I know everything. Got it?"

He looked relieved as if he had expected me to go ballistic. He was lucky I hadn't.

I swallowed hard. It had been a long time since I'd been an attorney. I was out of practice. But I managed to clear my head. I needed to be detached as if this were happening to someone else.

I tapped the photo. "How did you get this?"

"It was with Betty's possessions when we raided her house. There was more than one photo of Bibi, but this one was on her desk in a frame."

I sighed. So many questions ran through my head I couldn't keep up. I wished I had paper and pen to make a list. Wait, I did.

"Just a minute."

Near the room's telephone, I grabbed the hotel's pad of paper and pen and made a quick list while standing there.

- Did Bibi know she was adopted?
- Did she know about Sophie and me?

- Was she in cahoots with Betty and the extortion?
- Did she know I killed Betty?
- Where was she now?
- Why the hell did my parents give her up?
- Did my father force my mother to give her up because Bibi was black, and the whole world would know Mom had been unfaithful?

I chewed on the pen, walked to one of the windows, and looked out, processing as much as I could.

Mom had loved us girls, protected us from Dad. She kept the peace by *not* showing her true self. I always felt there was a side to my mother I never saw. But when you're a kid, as long as your mom hugs and kisses you, cooks meals, gets you to school (no matter what town you now lived in), it didn't matter if you moved all the time and had the bare necessities. It didn't matter if your father seemed distant and brooding and scary at times as long as your mother loved you. But I'd witnessed the messy times, usually overhearing Dad's accusations about her fooling around. Even as a kid, I'd thought mom deserved better. Maybe that's why she'd had other men—to get the attention and love my father withheld when he felt his control slipping. Perhaps we moved so often because of her affairs.

But dad had been a bottomless pit of expectations. Sophie and I could never please him no matter how hard we tried. He wanted us to perform perfectly—when he was paying attention. And no matter how much my mother gave, it was never enough. She gave up her love of piano because they couldn't cart one of those around in a van. She left gardens that were ready to harvest. He wouldn't let her visit her folks in Maine, but she did, even when she knew she'd pay for it later with drunken assaults, often of the sexual kind. Sophie and I would hide in the kitchen pantry. He scared us into submission. Then, after, he'd come home, all teary-eyed and sorry, kneeling on the floor in front of Mom, begging forgiveness. Now it's all so cliché, but back then, it was us four, living with something that was too complicated to understand or know where to get help. We never had support because we moved too often. All Dad wanted was his wife, children, and guns. And that meant the rest of us had no one except each other.

"Angeline," Gerard said, pulling me from my mental storm. "I don't know if Bibi knows about you or her birth. We are not sure Bibi's the one after your trust or if it's the Boston gang. Betty and Link's cousins are now in charge. Perhaps they are secretly acting on Bibi's behalf via an attorney to claim your trust. We don't know yet if she was involved with the extortion racket or how much she knows."

I returned to the couch. "You need to find out more."

"We're working on it. But we couldn't do anything until after we had proof that Betty was either alive or dead. Her remains weren't found for a month after she died."

That visual turned my stomach. I could have been those "remains." I blew out a long exhale and clutched my stomach.

"Are you all right? Can I go on?"

I nodded.

"The police investigated Betty as a missing person, but found nothing. Bibi hired a PI on Kauai to find Betty, but the PI found nothing."

"Why did Betty go to Kauai? Her story to me is that she and her deceased husband spent their honeymoon there, and she was there to relive the memories. At the end, I assumed she was there to find me, force me to turn over the money, or kill me."

Gerard poured more scotch, held it up to the light, then sipped it, moistening his lips with his tongue. "We know that Betty had her assistant Mike tail you from Portland to Kauai. Maybe that *is* why she went, to confront you. But why would she use an alias and take professional fake IDs?"

"I knew her as Karen." I paused. "What other reason could there be?"

He set his drink down and rubbed his hands on his slacks. "I think she had a second reason for being there, but we're still looking into that."

I waited, but he obviously wasn't ready to tell me what it was. "Where's Bibi now?" I wondered what this twin was like. If she was anything like Sophie.

"After Betty's memorial service in Massachusetts, Bibi retreated to a house Betty had purchased for her on Lake Winnisquam in New Hampshire. From what I know, she's been in seclusion there ever since."

"Winnisquam? No way. That's too coincidental. That's near to where Sophie and Bibi were born and where we lived for a while."

My hand went to my chest. I'd used both their names, together, as family. This was becoming real, along with my past and my parents. The last time I'd been to New Hampshire was for my parents' funeral. Now I knew that's where I'd go. I covered my eyes, groaned, and for some reason, blurted out, "Do you know anything about The Grim Reaper's murder?"

Gerard grimaced. "*Quoi?*"

I had no idea why I said that, but something bugged me. "I said, what happened to—"

"Not now." He paused. "Did we forget to eat?"

Not now? Why not now? But my brain wasn't working. No, we hadn't eaten. No wonder I was fading.

"I'll order room service." Gerard picked up the phone and ordered.

Both of us were beyond words or answers or any more questions at this point. I headed to the bathroom where I leaned against the wall, smelled his aftershave, squeezed my eyes shut, and stayed for I don't know how long.

When I returned to the living room, Gerard stood at the window looking out over the city. His arms hung limply by his side, Bibi's photo dangling from his left hand.

I coughed slightly to let him know I was there.

Without turning around, he said, "I was going to bring your sister here after. ..."

His voice trailed off, so full of sorrow. I was tempted to put my arms around his waist, to let him know that I knew his pain. Instead, I slipped Bibi's photo from his hand. Then room service knocked at the door with our order.

17

That night at the hotel, I couldn't sleep. I'd eaten too late. Lights flickered through the curtains as a foghorn bellowed intermittently. Street traffic created a loud white noise. Compared to Kauai, everything was louder, bigger, faster. What energized me earlier now gave me a headache.

Being alone made me miss Tempest. And worry about her. At least the light supper Gerard and I ate restored my energy and thinking. He told me he'd look into the death of The Grim Reaper, now identified as Steven Hastrick. But I had a hunch he was already doing that. Somehow Hastrick's wealthy, Boston family and his death plugged into the mission of the Boston Duo in extorting wealthy people. Was Hastrick one of their victims?

But that was not my concern. Bibi was. Her connection to Betty seemed so random that it didn't fit. Could Betty have had Bibi sign up on Ancestry, then happily discover that Hank and I had a tidy sum coming in from his business? That would have been a no brainer.

Sleep evaded me. I opened a window wide enough to

lean my upper body through and not set off the alarm when I lit a cigarette. The night was chilly, the fog a mist on my face. Noises drifted up. Someone crying, maybe laughing. A wave of delicate, sorrowful violin music. Oddly, I could hear my heartbeat, not from the outside, but from inside my head.

When I finished my smoke, I wrapped the butt in toilet paper and flushed it. Gerard's room was next to mine. I pressed my ear against our adjoining wall but heard nothing. What did he sleep in, or did he sleep naked? Was he a light sleeper or a deep sleeper? Did he snore? Did he need an alarm to wake him? I could picture his mussed-up hair and hooded eyes in the morning, and I hugged myself. I missed a man's arms around me, his kisses, the body rubs, and the hot breath of his words on my neck, among other things.

The next morning, Gerard called. "Meet me in the lobby in an hour. We need to catch our flight."

"We?"

"I'm going to Eugene with you. I've booked a room for you at the Inn at the 5th."

"Where are you staying?"

"I prefer not to say."

"Yeah, I bet, Mr. Secret Agent Man."

He chuckled.

"If you're not going to tell me, why go at all? It's going to take some time for me to get through the legal paperwork." I didn't want him with me. "What about my ID and papers?"

"I have everything you need."

"You'd better." At that point, I didn't care what he did. In Eugene, after I had my life straightened out, I'd lose him and follow my own plan. I wished Snoop would call. I needed that info.

Forty-five minutes later, I met Gerard in the lobby. A valet delivered the car.

Just before we got in, Gerard handed me one of those large mailing envelopes. In the car, I pulled out my Angeline Porter Oregon driver's license, passport, and birth certificate. They looked like my original ones. I dug in the bottom of the envelope and found a credit card in my name, one-thousand in cash, plus two phones, one an iPhone, the other a burner.

"What? No protective vest?"

"Do you want one?"

"That was a joke. But if you took it seriously, maybe I *do* want one."

"If you like."

I threw up my hands. "Damn, Gerard. If you're offering, then I *want* one."

As he drove, buildings flew by in a blur, horns honked, sirens blared, loud music escaped aggressive cars. My spine straightened and my pulse quickened. I held the envelope to my chest and lifted my chin. I was once again Angeline Porter. I glanced over at Gerard. No more being a pawn for someone else. I would do things my way.

18

Gerard flew with me to Eugene, but we didn't sit together. That gave me time to put together a plan. My brain seemed to have cleared. If there was going to be any justice, I'd have to pursue it. I still didn't trust Gerard. There were too many unanswered questions.

I started a list.

- The FBI raided Betty's house. They found photos of her and Bibi. What else did they find?
- Did Bibi inherit any of Betty's holdings? Or did the FBI freeze all assets?
- What does Bibi do for a profession? Or did Betty pay for everything?
- Is the lake house Betty's or Bibi's?
- What does Bibi know about Betty's death?
- Who was Gus? Was he FBI? What case was he working on? He said he was there to protect me.
- What does Gerard expect from me? Is he using me as bait? How far will he push to capture the Boston Duo and shut down the extortion ring? I

need a specific strategy from him before I do
anything.

- Who else is Gerard working for?
- Why didn't Gerard do more to save my sister?

I underlined that last question. My body heat rose. My
jaw clenched. That bastard. He could have saved my sister.
I'd find out more. I'd grill him some time and find out why
he'd screwed up so badly.

I couldn't do much more and was dead tired. I needed
my wits about me when I got to Eugene. So I put away the
notebook, closed my eyes, and concentrated on the noise of
the airplane engine, a white noise that flooded my brain and
washed out everything I'd been thinking.

When the plane landed, I woke with a jolt. We pulled
into the gate at the Eugene airport. As we filed out of the
plane, I tried to get Gerard's attention, but he hurried away.
Inside the terminal, I tried to catch up. On the escalator to
the ground floor, I caught a glimpse of him. Past security, he
looked at his phone and rushed out of the terminal door.

What the hell?

At the carousel, while waiting for my bag, I tried calling
him. It went to voicemail. I texted and waited. No reply.
Screw him. I'd take care of him later. I grabbed my bag,
nabbed my Uber, and headed to the Inn at the 5th. Gerard
was full of shit. I wasn't safer working with him. I was in
more danger. He loved my sister, but look at what happened
to her. I was so done with him. Besides, I was home, on my
own turf. A large amount of money waited for me to claim.
Without him around, I could carry out my plan.

In my room at the Inn, rain pelted the roof, a steady
drumming. He'd reserved a place for me on the top floor.
Only one entrance. Some of the other rooms had entries

onto the European patio, but those weren't safe. At least he'd considered that. The room was upscale but comfortable and made me sleepy. The rain made me sleepy. Life made me sleepy. So different from my life as a lawyer when I slept only four to five hours a night. I'd never thought of "home" much, but now I felt its comforts, its happy memories.

I knew this place like no other. I belonged here. This had been my home with Hank and Sophie. I knew the owners of my favorite restaurants. I knew the lawyers and judges, the city council people, the mayor, the baristas at Starbucks. While in Kauai, I thought I'd never be able to return without being killed. Once I understood I could never return, I missed it more than I ever had. At the time, I was relieved, but I think that was just me fooling myself.

As I unpacked, I worried about Snoop. She hadn't called back. I hoped she was all right. She must have been telepathic because my phone rang.

"Sorry. Ended up with the flu," she said.

"Snoop! Oh, shit. I was worried about you."

"You were?"

"Of course."

Silence. I waited. I was almost ready to ask if she were OK when she launched into her findings.

"Bibi owns the house on Lake Winnisquam ... it's in her name ... free and clear. This is the address and her cell number. She's legit ID. Nothing unusual."

Snoop talked so fast I had to have her repeat it.

"I haven't had time to track the other people. I'm still pretty sick."

"Forget the other two. That's history. Take care of yourself. Are you drinking plenty of liquids? Resting? What about zinc? Elderberry? My sister told me it's antiviral."

"Damn, Mom, chill."

And I did chill, or at least I had a chill run up and down my back. No one had ever called me "Mom" before. Not even when joking.

"OK, Snoop. I'm chill. Get back to me when you can. And thanks."

She hung up.

I checked the address on Google maps. It was a mile from one of the lake houses where we had lived as a family for a few years. At least that place held a few good memories. How weird it would be to be back there. Nothing like a walk down memory lane. More like a walk down nightmare lane. Living with an untreated bi-polar war-vet father was no rubber raft float on the lake.

I looked out my window to get my bearings in relationship to Fifth Street Market. Down below, a cafe-style patio. Across from my room, Marche Restaurant, and a red vintage phone booth barely visible in the Oregon post-rain-gray. So quiet. I unlocked the door to the private balcony. The sound of cars passing by on 6th Street rushed in. People parked and hurried into the market. A dog incessantly barked. Tempest never barked like that, only when it was necessary. When I closed the door, all sound stopped.

I needed caffeine and a smoke, and headed downstairs. I missed my pooch. After buying a latte and warming my hands on the cup, I pulled out my iPhone and called Iolana to see how Tempest was doing. She was fine, but the police had been to her place, asking about me. Who was I? Where had I come from? What had I been doing there? Why had I disappeared?

"What did you tell them?"

"I told them I knew you as River Atwood, that you had very powerful friends, and that I thought you could possibly be secret service."

I rolled my eyes. "How'd they take that?"

"They stopped asking questions, thanked me, and left."

"You rock, Sistah."

"That doesn't sound like you, River. You smoking something?"

We both laughed.

After we hung up, I tried Gerard, but the call still went to voicemail. I threw the phone across the room.

19

The next day, I walked downtown to my lawyer's office. He looked at me and spit out his coffee. "I thought you were dead," he said as he dabbed his hankie at the coffee on his shirt. He flushed, stammered something, but quickly regained his composure. Then he shook my hand so vigorously I thought he'd break a few fingers. "Sorry, I really thought something dreadful had happened to you."

I reassured him that I understood his concern. Then I gave him the story that Gerard and I agreed to: in extreme grief, I'd fled to Hawaii, kept a low profile, and stayed there until I felt strong enough to come home. No, I had no idea why the PI hadn't been able to find me. Keep it simple, stick to the script, I reminded myself. The same advice I used to give to my clients. He asked many questions. He told me the Portland police had suspected me of having something to do with the poisoning of Lincoln "Link" Stillwater III but later dropped the case. I feigned shock. (Gerard was probably responsible for that.) In the end, he shook his head, still somewhat stunned, and welcomed me home.

I left his office with the trust reinstated and protected from anyone else claiming it. My lawyer *had* heard from a New Hampshire lawyer who said he represented a sister who claimed the inheritance in the trust, but that was bullshit. As I thought. A scam. As to Bibi, she couldn't claim the trust. Massachusetts law didn't allow her access to it as she'd been legally adopted. So how did Gerard think the trust money would be bait to the Boston family of crooks? Unless they kidnapped me and forced me to turn it over. Would they dare? I wouldn't put anything past them. What was *Gerard's* game plan?

I walked six blocks to get some air and stretch my legs, then slipped into Perugino Café, ordered a house coffee to go. When leaving, I glanced behind me. As a criminal defense attorney, I'd been stalked before, threatened even, had to change my cell number once. I couldn't say for sure this time, but to play it safe, I walked to Kesey Square, lit a cigarette, and kept an eye on people coming and going. Nothing suspicious. A homeless vet in a wheelchair, displaying his ribbons and pins from the Iraq War on a fatigue jacket, asked me for a smoke. I lit one and handed it to him, along with a twenty.

As I headed back to the Inn, I tried Gerard one more time on my iPhone with the cracked screen. I'm lucky it still worked after throwing it last night. I didn't like that I had no idea where he was staying or what he was doing. Better to know than not know. I finished my cigarette. Now at least I'd stop getting dirty looks from people who passed me. A lot of non-smokers in Eugene. At least non-tobacco smokers.

In the lobby, Gerard sat in a chair waiting for me, his face devoid of expression.

"Let's go to your room." He strode to the elevator. I hurried after him and grabbed his arm.

"What the hell is wrong with you?"

He shook off my grip and pressed the button. "We need to talk."

When we entered my room, I turned on him. "I'm tired of your attitude and you directing this show. I'm tired of not getting answers. I'm tired of—"

"Stop using the hacker."

"Huh? What did you say?"

"Stop using the hacker."

My mouth opened, but nothing came out. Now he looked angry. Why should he be angry? I let it rip. "You son-of-a-bitch. You use people. You set them up. They die. Don't tell me what to do."

"Angeline, please listen. We've had your hacker under surveillance. You two popped up last night in a communication about the twin. Now my superiors are ... *fâché*. They are pissed that I've allowed you two to communicate, pissed that I've given you so much freedom."

"Allowed?" I said it under my breath. "You asshole. With all you've done? With all the shit you've pulled on me? With all the—"

"*Arreté*. Please, stop. Let's talk. We need to firm up our plans."

"*We* don't have any plans. You can't continue to use me and put my life in danger. You can't use my money as bait. Why are you bothering? Bibi can't legally go after it. The only card you hold over me is that the Boston Duo family might try to physically force me to turn it over to them."

He sighed and sat down in a chair. I waited. He rubbed his brow, leaned back, and stared at me. I glared back.

"What's going on, Gerard? What aren't you telling me?"

He continued watching me as if weighing the consequences of exposing what he knew. Exhaustion lined his face. Finally, he entwined his fingers and said, "Please sit. I will tell you."

I sat across from him.

"When we raided Betty's house and found the photo of Bibi, I had the team take DNA from Bibi's bathroom. Before the DNA results came back, we learned from her public records that she'd been adopted. But more curiously to me, personally, was she had the same birthday as Sophie's and was born in the same hospital. Even though she was African-American, I had a gut feeling. That sounds crazy, I know, but this is what makes me good at my job."

"Mr. Intuitive. Yeah, right."

"I have a heart, too, Angeline."

Seeing the pain on his face grabbed my stomach. We were still both in pain over my sister. I said, "OK. Continue."

He pushed back against the chair, crossed his legs at the ankles, and tried to look relaxed, but he wasn't. "Bibi was adopted right after birth. New Hampshire was very 'white' back then, and few people of color resided there. If a young white woman became pregnant from a black man, the public humiliation and shame would have been overwhelming. That would explain the baby being given up at birth. After Bibi's DNA test came back, I had something of Sophie's tested. It was a match. That's how I found out they were twins."

"OK, but not much of that is new. I figured it went something like that. What's so damned important that you have to hijack me and force me to my room?"

"Remember earlier I told you an older white, wealthy Boston couple adopted her?"

I didn't remember.

"That older white couple had a son who was a few years

older than Bibi. As forward-thinking parents, they were held in high esteem for adopting a black baby."

He stopped.

"And?"

"Bibi, from what we could ascertain, was well cared for and loved, except by her older brother. The couple had problems with the son. He acted out against anything he disagreed with." Gerard shrugged, like this was just a common problem. "But then he was arrested for hitting his mother. They had him on medication, but he often refused to take it. I don't know what happened in that house between him and Bibi, but I'd guess she endured plenty."

"Doesn't sound good."

"Just before Bibi graduated high school, her adoptive parents were hit by a drunk driver and killed. The son had already moved away. But when he came home after inheriting the estate, he had his lawyers instruct Bibi to vacate the house and take only her personal belongings. He gave her a thousand dollars. That was it."

"That poor girl."

"I agree."

"Why wasn't she left anything in the will?"

"The parents never updated it. Their deaths were sudden and unexpected. Plus, from what I know about mental illness, the son took up so much time and effort that they were constantly engaged with him and therefore distracted."

"She didn't get a lawyer?"

"She was only seventeen."

"What happened to her?"

"She stayed with friends for a while. When the money ran out, she was on the street selling small paintings to stay alive. That's where Betty found her."

"Do you think the son had sexual relations with her?"

"No idea."

"Is the son still alive?"

I sipped my now cold coffee. Out the window, a crow sat on the balcony railing, cawing, either swearing or laughing at the world.

Gerard leaned forward and ran his fingers through his hair. "Here's the issue. You need to stop using Snoop. You're interfering with our operation."

"How about telling me about your operation? It won't help to keep me in the dark."

He stared at his hands. The guy was really at a cross-roads here. He was probably not supposed to tell me, but I knew he would.

He looked up. "You cannot give anyone this information, Angeline. Do you hear me? No one."

"Get on with it, Gerard."

His face softened, and his eyes met mine with what I can only describe as kindness. This was so unlike him. This had to be bad news. I held my breath.

Finally, he said, "Bibi's brother? The one who inherited everything? That was Steven Hastrick, The Grim Reaper."

I stood so fast, I had to steady myself on the arm of the chair. Images from Kauai flashed by. Hastrick. Iolana. Aisake. The Kāne Crew. My little house. Tempest. I turned back to Gerard. The crow on the balcony flew off. Gerard waited for me to say something. So I did.

"Fuck."

20

I guess I shouldn't have been surprised the way life had been lately. But this rattled me on several levels.

"So, I'm guessing that Steven Hastrick wasn't killed because of his activism."

"We don't know at this point, but we think Betty originally planned to go to Kauai to arrange to have Hastrick killed. Her only motive seems to be for Bibi to inherit his vast estate. But her henchman, Mike, told her that you killed Link in Portland. He followed you to the airport where he learned you were going to Kauai. So now she had two goals for Kauai—kill you and Hastrick. She didn't succeed with either."

I needed a smoke. My mind was spinning. "So Betty's primary motive for killing Hastrick was revenge for Bibi and gaining access to the inheritance."

"*C'est vrai.*"

"So the two that took over the Boston Duo? Ralph and Rena? They had Hastrick killed."

"We believe so. We do not have the evidence yet, but we will."

"That means Bibi is in danger—if she's not part of the extortionist racket."

"If she was not involved with having Hastrick killed."

"Do you know if she inherited anything from Betty?"

"Betty left her a sizable inheritance. The Feds have frozen the estate until they sort out what's legit and what's not. But all of her computer financial files look legit. So we don't know where the money from the extortion is, probably on another computer somewhere with Ralph and Rena. Even then, it will be moved around in the usual shell game. So we can't go after Ralph and Rena yet."

"What are Ralph and Rena like?"

"They are much smarter at this than Betty and Link. Plus, they approach it like a big business."

"But Bibi will now inherit the adoptive parents' estate and whatever Hastrick had now that he's dead."

"He left no will. But yes. As she is legally entitled to it. That, too, will take time. We also need to eliminate her as a suspect."

"For what?"

"Having Hastrick killed. We do not know if or how she's involved with the Boston Duo."

I understood. Bibi had motive and means, especially if she were part of the extortion racket. Remove Hastrick and she'd have access to her adoptive parents' legacy. But Betty was taking care of her, so why kill Hastrick at the risk of being found out? What if Bibi were involved, though? Not just a kept woman. She *was* part of the "family." Betty found her on the street, fell in love, sent her to college, bought her the house, and helped her become ... what?

"What does Bibi do? Does she work? Does she own a business?"

"She's an up-and-coming digital artist in Boston."

"Computers."

He nodded.

She had that in common with Sophie. Computer savvy. But digital art? I had to admit to having no appreciation for the form. Call me old fashioned, but I liked paint on canvas.

"Gerard, what exactly do you want me to do? What's your plan? Let's do it and be done with it. I want a home with my dog. No more crazy-town. End of story."

"First of all, agree to no more communications with your hacker."

Snoop? No way.

"OK," I lied. "What else?"

"Settle back here in Eugene, maybe pay rent for the time being, use your money, get back into life."

"Life? So I'm bait to all those fishing for my money?"

"Do I have to remind you that you have your legal ID back and will not be prosecuted for Sam?"

"Oh, gee, thanks for reminding me. I almost forgot." I scowled at him.

"Also, you will not be extradited for trying to kill me."

I took a deep breath. "May I remind you that you don't exist—anywhere? My hacker couldn't find you. So how can I be tried for attempting to kill someone who doesn't exist?"

"Touché." But he wasn't smiling.

"So you want me to stick around here, make myself visible, spend money like a drunk gambling in Las Vegas to get their attention? What do you think they'll do? Hold and torture me until I sign over my trust?"

"They have time on their hands. They've been clever. We've seen them send handsome, intelligent men to target women of means. Some have even married these guys. Then on a romantic vacation or another getaway, the women mysteriously die. The favorite is by drowning while on a yacht. Nothing ties these men together. They're hustlers. They don't know each other or know about each other."

"That wasn't the plan with my sister. You forced her to steal the money. You threatened her family."

"Link and Betty weren't patient. They wanted the money as fast as they could get it. They had no qualms about how they did that. Ralph and Rena are different. They're in it for the long haul. Getting caught is not an option."

"So, you think they'll send some handsome guy like you to sweep me off my feet?"

"So, I'm handsome?" He chuckled and continued. "I don't know what they have planned for you, if anything. We're waiting on information."

I didn't know if Gerard was flirting with me or not. Half the time, I liked him. Half the time, I hated him. No in-between. But screw him. He killed my sister.

Then I looked at him again. I'd always thought he was attractive. But handsome? No, not in the traditional sense of the word. But my sister? She'd been a knock out. She was insecure and often thought that men only wanted her for her looks. She always told me in detail about the guys she dated sometimes to the point of disgust, disgust usually about the way she let them walk all over her. But I never heard much about Gerard, and that was unusual. She could have told me what was going on except I'm sure she was guilty and ashamed that this time she'd robbed my husband's business. I guess she felt she had no other way out after she figured Gerard had used and ditched her. The gang had threatened to kill Gerard unless she stole the money. She made a terrible mistake. Two terrible choices. She had sex with my husband for access to his bank account, and she stole the money, all for the sake of Gerard, not for me, but for a man. Then she killed herself.

So why was I always blaming Gerard? Or anyone else who happened to be part of her choices? She'd been an adult who acted like a child. Like our mother.

Gerard jerked me out of my misery.

"I must warn you. Someone is keeping Ralph and Rena informed about you and the trust. I have no idea who it is. Someone clever with computers, perhaps?"

"Wait. Do you think Bibi is their hacker? And she's monitoring me?"

He shrugged.

I chewed a cuticle. I needed a drink.

"You know there will be media people coming after you for your story. Give them a version of it. The sooner the Duo hears about it, the sooner they'll make a move."

"Right," I said. I'd had enough. I needed to stand up to these pricks. Let them come after me. I'd buy a house and run around, waving my hands, saying, *Come get me!*

"What are you thinking?" he asked.

I swallowed hard and tried to keep from crying, but I had to ask. "Who was Gus? Who was William Augustus Martin?"

"He was one of ours."

"Did you know him personally?"

"*Non.*"

"Were you told anything else about him?"

"I was told he was on assignment to cover you, protect you."

"From what?"

"From Betty and Link."

"So you don't know any of this for certain? Interesting that you were an undercover asset to gather evidence on Link and his operation, and you know nothing about Gus."

"Not unusual." He leaned forward, alert. "What is it, Angeline?"

I locked eyes with Gerard. "Was Gus dirty?"

Gerard paused a moment before answering. "I do not know. Why ask that?"

"Never mind. Just something he did."

"We know about you and the Ashley Madison men. You were forced to raise money quickly to keep your husband alive. To make that 50K, you blackmailed your Ashley Madison dates, each one for five to ten thousand."

"And?"

"One of your dates was Gus."

"What the *fuck*? I should have known." I walked to the mini bar, found a bottle of whiskey, and poured it into a glass.

Gerard walked over and stood behind me. "Angeline, we weren't after you. We were trying to keep you alive. Link and Betty wanted your money, and they would do anything to get it, as you soon discovered."

I closed my eyes, rubbed the back of my neck, and turned to Gerard. "Something was wrong with that date with Gus." I slugged back half the drink. "Do you know about the date?"

He shook his head.

"Gus arrived, dressed like Mick Jagger from the 60s. He called me his 'bird' using a fake English accent." I couldn't help smile. "I thought that was weird, but when we went to the room, my gut told me to run. It wasn't his costume or his lousy accent. Something didn't feel right." I swallowed hard and drank the rest of the whiskey. "When I told Gus this, he gave up the pretense and told me I could leave. He wasn't angry, just disappointed. Even offered to get me another room for the night."

"But you *didn't* leave." Now he sounded accusatory.

"No, I *didn't*. He'd already ordered food and a bottle of Macallan 12, my favorite single malt. How he knew that, I don't know. He invited me to stay, just for the companionship. We ended up laughing and getting drunk."

"And having sex."

The son-of-a-bitch.

Gerard remained silent, a good ploy to get me to talk, to either admit or deny it. Was he jealous? I decided instead of giving him nothing, I'd give him everything. "Yes, we had many drunken attempts that were great fun." I actually couldn't remember if it was "many." To twist the knife, I added, "Sorry, I didn't video our tryst so you could enjoy watching it."

Gerard flinched. Good. But then he asked, "Then? In the morning?"

Oh, my god! He wanted to know if we had sex in the morning. But when I remembered what *did* happen, my bottom lip trembled, and I hugged myself.

"In the morning, Gus was gone. He left five one-hundred-dollar bills on the coffee table like I was a cheap hooker."

"*Salaud!*"

I assumed he was calling Gus a nasty name.

Then he said, "You didn't deserve that, Angeline." He took my wrists, pulled me forward, and kissed me.

I tried to wrench free, but couldn't. When he pulled me by the waist and pressed me against him, I wanted to resist. Instead, I let my arms stay limp as the heat melded us together. Then he kissed me again, a long, intense kiss.

I was close to crying, angry at myself for allowing this and suspecting that all this sex talk had turned him on. Now I felt even cheaper.

I shoved him away, and he stumbled backward. I wiped my mouth on the back of my hand. "And to think my sister died for that."

He looked stunned.

"Please leave," I said and walked over to the window.

"I didn't mean to—"

I threw my glass at him, and it smashed against the wall. He quickly left.

I sat on the edge of the bed, head in hands, and cried.

21

The day after the kiss, I withdrew money from the trust, procured a credit card from Amalgamated, and bought a new phone with a new number and a few burners. After buying a plane ticket to New Hampshire, I packed.

Then I called Gerard so he wouldn't suspect what I was going to do.

"Look, I'll forget about what happened yesterday if you do. This is business, and we need to keep it that way." He didn't sound too convinced, so I added, "I'm going to look for a new place today, either a house or condo. So I'll be busy for the next few days. I'll talk with you later."

I left the two phones Gerard had given me in the hotel room. I didn't check out. It was his bill. I called a taxi.

The taxi came, and I caught my flight to New Hampshire to find Bibi.

PART II

22

After driving to Portland and taking the red-eye, I landed in a gray, cold Manchester airport around noon. People chatted with excitement as we disembarked, the New Hampshire accent sending me back to childhood. When had I lost that? As I headed for car rentals, I said, "New Hampshire," out loud saying each syllable correctly. Then I tried saying it like the natives: "Na Hampsha." It sounded forced. Would that be a detriment or plus? Sometimes it was best not to stand out.

I rented a car and set my GPS for Bibi's house. Had Gerard discovered I was gone yet? After last night's kiss, I'd hoped he'd unraveled for at least a day. He'd find me. Eventually. He had powerful resources. But I had passion and a head start. He could also send someone from his agency in Boston or New Hampshire to track me down. Maybe even arrest me. I doubted it. The man had enough ego to go it alone. He wouldn't like others knowing he'd underestimated me. Or did he? What if he didn't? What if he knew all along I'd take off?

As I deposited a dollar at the Interstate 93 tollbooth, I

thought about Bibi, what I wanted to say to her, what I wanted to find out. It didn't matter what color she was, or gender, or that the twin was somehow tied to Betty.

Elizabeth "Bibi" Brackston, her adoptive name, could be a purple leprechaun with a love of unicorns for all I cared. If she was Sophie's twin, she was my sister.

And that's why it was more important to meet her before anyone else got to her. Like Gerard's people.

Then there was the damn Boston Duo and "family." If Bibi wasn't mixed up with extortion and killing, she was in danger. Could she really *not* know about it? I figured I had a better chance of getting a bead on her before she headed back to Boston—*if* she headed back to Boston. I also wanted to meet her to see if there was some kind of instant bond, something instinctual, some kind of gut recognition. I nailed Gus when I met him, saw past his costume and fake English accent as more than just a fantasy he wanted fulfilled. I knew something was wrong, and I'd surprisingly been right. I rarely used my gut for anything, not when being a lawyer demanded adherence to connecting the dots and proving a case with evidence. But Gus *had* turned out to an FBI agent. Score one for instinct.

I also wanted a chance at a relationship with Bibi, to meet her before all the crazy shit hit the fan, before the FBI dirtied up our fledgling, vulnerable sisterhood.

A relationship with Bibi hinged on her never finding out I'd killed Betty. But all it would take was Gerard opening his mouth. I doubted that killing her lover would make me sister of the year.

The sky turned dark around Concord. I'd forgotten about the quick change of weather here. The rain came in a downpour. Thunder sounded in the distance. I needed coffee. Again. Hank once teased me that I should have it hooked up intravenously.

Thirty minutes from the airport, I took the exit to Laconia, Rt. 3.

Everything had changed. What had I expected? The turnoff to Winnisquam and Laconia used to have a sand and gravel business at the intersection. I didn't remember what was across the highway. Now a large shopping outlet and big box stores covered the area. My energy flagged. I needed food although I wasn't hungry. Heading directly to Bibi's might not be the best idea. On the plane, I'd debated that. I'd decided not to call ahead of time and give her an excuse to either bolt, hide, or shoot me.

I needed a bathroom. I needed a smoke.

I pulled off outside the Tilt'n Diner, a throwback to the 1950s, a relief from the mall feel. Outside, I leaned against the car. The rain had stopped, leaving the air heavy with humidity. A mosquito buzzed around my face, and I swatted it, reminding me of summers here when the humidity brought mosquitoes, no-see-ums, and horseflies. The only relief came from a day at the lake. Sophie never got bit. She once told me I didn't have enough Vitamin K in my system to keep them away.

"Guess I still don't," I said as if she were next to me. "What's Vitamin K anyway?" I laughed.

A couple passed by paying no attention to me, alone, talking, laughing. One good thing about cell phones and Blue Tooth—no more crazy looks from people passing by when I spoke out loud.

I stayed near my black Jeep Renegade and lit up. The smoke would keep the bugs away, and the cigarette relaxed me. After stubbing it out, I threw it in the trash and went inside.

While waiting for a coffee to go, I studied the photo of Bibi I'd stolen from Gerard. I may have underestimated her. What if she were dangerous like Betty? What if she had no qualms about hurting or killing someone? Bibi looked tall, taller than me. I had to consider that Bibi might be badass and violent, even more so in grief. Choosing to love Betty, however, said something about her character, didn't it? That smile, though. So like Sophie's.

As a former lawyer and a white person, I had to check myself for prejudice. Boston was a tough city. Still corrupt in many ways. Still a city of villages known by ethnicity. Was a black woman from Boston someone to fear? Would she kick my ass? Dig my grave? Betty had been white, and she wanted to throw me off a cliff. So what did color have to do with greed and revenge?

It was painful thinking of Bibi possibly being like Betty. Did she have a screw loose like her twin when it came to men? Did she lack common sense and self-protection? What about loyalty? Maybe Betty had protected Bibi like I'd tried to protect Sophie.

I had to stop thinking and projecting. I grabbed my coffee, paid the bill, and, inside the Renegade, put Bibi's address into the GPS.

23

A weak sun filtered through the birches, and a fierce wind blew, creating white caps on black water as I drove the winding secondary road along the lake. The Renegade shuddered from the gusts of wind. I'd expected blue skies and a sparkling lake. So much for that.

The radio station turned to static, and I shut it off.

Many of the familiar landmarks still survived. Over a rise in the road, I passed the Lord Hampshire Hotel, a remnant of the old days, a place where my mother had worked for a summer as a housekeeper.

I thought of the kiss with Gerard and wiped my mouth again.

The landscape changed. Some cottages remained, but the area was now built up and across from where I thought there'd been a farm was an outdoor recreation area. I almost missed the road where we used to live. The pines that had once surrounded our place were gone so the house was visible from the main road. I remembered playing in the pines with the neighborhood kids, all boys, who taught me to swear and take no crap. I pulled over near the house.

Our dusty salmon home was now painted a garish blue. Sheets hung in the windows instead of curtains. The grass had grown knee-high. A peeling white picket fence lay in the grass. Part of the garage door was mangled. My hand covered my mouth as I groaned.

"Oh, Dad, you would hate this."

He may have had problems, but he'd been great at fixing things. A smell came back to me, of freshly drying clothes and sheets that Mom hung on an old-fashioned outdoor clothesline.

I shook off the memories, turned the car around, and pulled out onto the main road. I knew this would happen, that the past would flood and distract me, so I forced myself to focus on the here and now. About half a mile up the road and across from a small market, I made a left turn, then a right. When Siri said, "In five-hundred feet, your destination is on the right," I started to shake.

I pulled into a driveway. I was here. With a quick glance, I noted no garage and one nearby house. The area was heavily wooded, dark. The driveway side of the house had one window. I jumped out of the jeep, ignoring the shakes, battled the wind, shielded my eyes, and ran to the door. I knocked several times and rang the bell. When no one answered, I walked around to lakeside. A light was on over the door of the glassed-in porch. Sneakers sat near one entrance to the house. To the left, a wicker chair and couch, and to the right, a book laid splayed on the café table next to a red mug. Someone was here.

I pulled my thin raincoat around me and walked to the corner bank of windows that looked in on an open dining room. I put my nose to the window and shielded my eyes. A bank of overhead spotlights had been left on. A long harvest table draped in batik cloth held a laptop, printer, and stacks of books and files. Digital art hung on the walls along with a painting of what looked like African musicians. On the hutch was a framed photo of Betty.

Betty. That face. That damned woman. The woman who had deliberately sliced Tempest's leg to make a connection with me. The woman who had killed poor rock-'n'-roll-fantasy-driven Gus. She'd ripped off millions from unsuspecting people. That dead woman.

I walked back to the jeep. How could Bibi, twenty-five years Betty's junior, love a woman like that? How could she possibly have no idea?

I backed out of the driveway and parked along the dirt road so I had a vantage point to see if, and when, Bibi came home. I rolled the windows down and lit a cigarette, missing the times when Hank and I shared one on our back porch steps. He'd say, "You sure grew a beautiful garden." Our little inside joke. I hired a professional to do that. Left to me, all those plants would be dead. I didn't know a daisy from a dandelion.

After I put out the cigarette, I swatted a mosquito full of blood—my blood. I started the jeep to roll up the windows. Just then, car lights flickered through the trees. I slumped down. The car passed me and continued on up the dirt road.

Screw this. I started the jeep, jammed the gear into drive, and pulled out, throwing dirt and gravel up behind me. What I needed was a drink and food, in that order.

Tomorrow, I'd do it again.

24

My cabin at Paugus Bay was about ten miles away, and I had no idea what I'd find in between. Then just a few miles up ahead from Bibi's, a sign said, "Shooters." This was so close to her place maybe I'd overhear some locals talk about her. She was black in a state still predominantly white.

I swung into the parking lot. Inside, a lively crowd drowned out the piped-in music. I sat at the bar, ordered a Manhattan and burger without looking at the menu. The anonymity felt good. I drank the first drink before my burger came and scanned the room. Near me at a big table, a group of friends were downing shots and getting loud. Good for them.

But when I glanced their way again, one of the women stared at me while whispering to another woman who looked at me over her shoulder. Maybe they thought they knew me. We looked about the same age. Something felt familiar to me about them, too.

Stevie Nicks came on, singing "Dreams." I remembered my mom playing the "Rumours" album over and over when

Dad wasn't home. I'd always wondered what significance the album had for her. She would dance around and sing while making supper or cleaning the house.

My burger came, and I ordered another drink. The bartender lowered the lights, and now it felt like any other sports bar in the States. I could be anywhere. I ate small bites of burger and sipped my second drink, my nerves mellowing a little. *Mellowing?* I never said that. My dad did. He also said, "Cool it," sometimes laughing as he tickled us, then other times at the top of his lungs when we were bothering him.

As I ate, I watched a couple play pool. I'd learned the game from an Indian named "Bunky." He was from Oregon's Grand Ronde tribe. Easy-going bull rider. I'd gone to the Sisters Rodeo once to watch him. This was just after I'd graduated from law school in Eugene and just before I met Hank. Bunky was short and rugged, easy to hang with, never hit on me, but he taught me a mean game of pool, how to make bank shots, and put English on a ball. I loved letting the men underestimate me before I wiped their asses. I thought about challenging the table but decided against it. I needed to get to the cabin.

After I finished my burger and was paying, I caught the woman to my right as she nudged her friend and motioned toward me. When I locked eyes with her, they both looked away. I tried to ignore them, but when I glanced back, the woman said something to the group and pointed toward me. They all burst out laughing. What was their problem?

High school rushed back. A popular clique of weed-smoking, sports-loving students called me "egg head" and "ass kisser." They had an attitude about school, that if you liked school, there was something wrong with you. I loved school, especially debate. I just didn't fit in with my classmates.

So, unlike high school, I walked over to this group. They turned away as if they'd never noticed me. But one woman chuckled, and that did it.

"Hi," I said, sounding cordial. "Can I help you?"

The leader of this pack gave me a defiant look as if she was not used to being spoken to uninvited. "Gosh, I don't think so." She faked a smile.

The chuckler now smirked. One of the men said, "Excuse me," and headed to the men's room. Smart move.

"Oh," I said, still cordial. "I thought maybe you knew me."

"No. Can't say that I do." She sat back, cocky, sure of herself.

"I'm sure I recognize *you*." I paused until I had everyone's attention. "Oh, that's right! I represented you in a criminal case. So glad you avoided jail."

"Whoa, Linda!" her friend said. "Boom!"

Nervous laughter.

I smiled at everyone around the table. "Have a good time, and stay out of trouble."

When I walked out to my car, years slid off me, like I'd shed an old, nasty skin. I wished I'd done that back in school or some form of it. Better late than never.

Outside, the muggy darkness enveloped me, and the satisfaction drained away. What was that? I'd learned long ago that engaging like that didn't bring satisfaction, just a sense that I was no better than them. More than anything, righteous injustices sent me to law school.

I needed to get to my cottage and concentrate on the twin and Kathleen Glanville, my mom's best friend. I wanted to piece together what happened to my parents and the twin all those years ago. When I turned on the jeep, I tried the radio again, and the song "Tainted Love" played—again. It was like my sister was haunting me.

I flashed back on all the times I'd tried to make Sophie choose a different song for her life. But like Mom, she somehow couldn't change the song of her life. She and Mom might be more alike than I'd ever considered. How much, I didn't know, but I intended to find out.

25

On the way to the Paugus Bay cottage, I stopped at the grocery store. The air, still thick with humidity, felt physically heavy. Back in the car, I put on the air, and, as I neared the area called the Weirs, I heeded the signs that said, "Caution. Potholes." Around here, potholes could wreck a car's alignment, never mind rattle your teeth.

I found the cottage, put away the few groceries I'd bought, and sat outside under the gazebo with a glass of water. I'd never understood people who loved summer. I loved autumn in New England when the air was fresh, the hillsides filled with color, and the bugs were gone. Plus, school started in the fall. I'd repressed the past for a reason. Now I was afraid everything would come flooding back.

As if I needed more drama in my life, thunder rumbled, followed almost immediately by lightning. I put my hand down to pet Tempest, something I did back in Kauai when a storm hit, and she trembled next to me. I missed that dog. I missed my life in Eugene when I was blissfully ignorant of what was to come. I raised my glass to the dead. "To you. I hope you're happy wherever you are."

That came out snarky. But I'd been betrayed by the two I loved the most. Since they were both dead, however, I had to imagine that they'd either paid for their betrayals or been forgiven—if there was an afterlife. I'd tried not to think about that after my parents died. That was way too painful. But the idea that there was nothing? Well, that was also too painful to consider.

I fell asleep in my clothes, and woke the next morning with a pounding headache. The clock read six-thirty. That was three-thirty on the West Coast. I groaned.

After popping two ibuprofen, I made a pot of strong coffee. What did that t-shirt on the waitress at the Tilt'n Diner say? "Where the wait staff is strong, and the coffee has personality." I liked that.

My burner rang three times then stopped. It rang again. Snoop, my hacker. Shit.

I didn't dare pick up. Didn't she know the FBI was tracking her?

The call ended. A few seconds later, I had a text.

download app called SIGNAL ... ok to talk and message over it ... they can't track us this way

That was Snoop—all lower case and smarter than the FBI. But then I wondered how someone outsmarts the FBI. Even more to the point—why do I trust this person?

But I once remembered a cop telling me that he had friends in the Hells Angels that he trusted more than some of the cops he worked with. I was startled that he admitted that. "But how do you know to trust them?"

He said, "They come through for you. It might be instinct at first, but you know it, feel it, and their actions proved it."

I downloaded the app. A few minutes later I received a call on the app. I picked up.

"I found your mother's friend."

Not a person to waste words or explain how she knew about the FBI or how she'd outfoxed them, she gave me the info.

"Any history on her?" I asked.

"Pretty normal life. Except she lost her daughter to smack."

"Heroin. Ow."

"Her only child."

"Double ow."

"She seems to be on a crusade to turn the town of Tilton around. She bought a historic building downtown and is trying to bring it back to life. The nearby outlet mall ruined it. Lots of drugs. But that's everywhere."

"Thanks, Snoop. You're beautiful."

"Yeah, so they say." She laughed. I'd never heard her laugh before. Female? Trans? Should I ask? No.

We hung up.

I drank my second coffee on the deck. The wind blew strong enough to make whitecaps on the bay. Oregon had lakes but not like this. Oregon lakes were either dam reservoirs or so out of the way, you had to hike to them. Besides, I'd learned to love the ever-changing Oregon rivers, the dynamism, the lively beauty, and sometimes their treachery. Rivers, like people, had to be respected or they'd turn on you if you weren't careful.

I slugged down the coffee and headed to Tilton.

26

I don't know what I expected when I reached my old town, but I should have had some idea. After all, times had been tough on small factory towns everywhere. When I was a little kid in the early 1980s, small New Hampshire towns still felt like Norman Rockwell land. We lived outside Tilton up in the hills of Sanbornton. Mom would take us to town for groceries at the A&P, and sometimes we'd get ice cream at the soda fountain in Rexall's pharmacy. Rexall was gone, and so was Achbers, where the town kids bought their school clothes unless they ordered from Monkey Wards, what we called Montgomery Wards. When I saw the Catholic church, I remembered going through the rummage-sale piles for our school clothes, the intense smell of used items that never quite lost that smell. The jeans that were never in style. I once wore a top from the rummage sale, one that was cool and looked good on me. Someone at school recognized it and made a comment to her girlfriends within my earshot. I spilled mustard on it so I'd never have to wear it again.

My stomach hurt and my chest ached. It was literally painful to be back here.

As I drove down the main street, the only places left from those times were the Bryant & Lawrence Hardware Store and the Tilton Prep School that sat on the hill above the town. The "preppies" hung out downtown to ogle the "townie" girls, or used to.

One day Mom bought us ice cream cones from Rexall's. As we walked down the street, three preppies came out of Tony's Pizza and stopped in front of Sophie, wide-eyed and smiling. One bent down. "Hi, aren't you beautiful! What flavor of ice cream are you eating?" They totally ignored Mom and I. Even though Sophie was only four, she seemed entranced with the attention. Ice cream melted down her hand. Mom tried to shoo them away, but they ignored her.

I stepped between the preppie and Sophie. "Go away. Leave her alone."

He stood, hovering over me, and said, "Why? Just because your sister is a doll and you're ugly?"

I stomped on his foot, took Sophie's sticky hand, and dragged her to our rusty Ford Econoline van. Behind us, the preppies were laughing.

In the van, as Mom drove, she said, "Sophie, you are beautiful. Boys will naturally be attracted to you. You need to be careful. Boys aren't always nice."

Not very helpful, Mom. What four-year-old would figure out that cryptic shit? I'm certain the only thing my sister heard was "you are beautiful." Unfortunately, Mom never gave us the tools we needed to survive. We had to acquire those on our own. She loved us, but keep us safe? That's when I took over keeping a watchful eye on Sophie. She needed a protector, and I was it.

I sighed, rubbed my stomach, and wished Sophie hadn't

been so beautiful. But there was nothing I could do for her now.

Driving down Main Street, I looked for numbers on the buildings, but someone behind me honked. I picked up speed and headed to the East end of Main Street to see the train station, my favorite place in town. I used to fantasize about boarding that train and setting off to another world. I'd loved trains when everyone else loved airplanes. Sometimes I'd do my homework there when the weather was good.

When I reached the end of Main Street, the station was gone. In its place was a parking lot—an ugly one. Who the hell was responsible for that? I stared and remembered another song my mother loved, a Joni Mitchell song about paradise and parking lots.

I pulled over and checked the info Snoop had given me. I did a U-turn and drove along, searching for numbers on the buildings. Kathleen's was an 1875 brick building with an empty store below and apartments above. Lights were on upstairs. I parked, called her number, and held my breath. She answered. Would she remember my mom?

"Hi, Kathleen?" A pause. "This is Angeline Porter. I'm Annie Avery's daughter."

This would either be a shock, or she could be trying to remember who my mom was, so the long pause didn't surprise me. Finally, she said, "Angie? Is that really you?"

I exhaled. She remembered. After Mom and Dad died, I only had one conversation with Kathleen just before the funeral. Then I flew back to Oregon, wanting to forget everything and everyone in my former life. Strangely, I remembered nothing about what we talked about. In fact, I remembered nothing about the funeral. Nothing. I didn't even remember if Sophie was with me or even there. I guess I'd done well at erasing at least that part of my former life.

"Is this a prank, because if it is—"

"Kathleen, it's really me. It's Angeline. Are you busy? I'm downstairs, parked across the street."

The curtains in one of the upstairs windows pulled aside, and a face looked down at me. I waved up at her and said, "I need to talk with you."

"Yes, of course." The curtain fell back in place. "Go to the storefront door. I'll come right down and let you in."

Was that fear in her voice? When she opened the door to the empty storefront, she looked behind me, then at me. Eyes wide, she said, "You look just like your mother."

I wasn't sure what to say. I didn't look like Mom at all. I didn't want to look like Mom.

Kathleen pulled me into the empty store, locked the two bolts on the door, re-set an alarm system, and motioned for me to hurry and follow her as if the town were under siege. This seemed a little overly dramatic, but I'd bet drugs had moved in as they had in so many once-vibrant, now run-down towns. I hurried after her up the stairs.

Her apartment was a stark contrast to the empty down-stairs. It was like stepping into a different world. She had style, modern mixed with Asian touches. From the way she dressed, Kathleen had obviously traveled. She wore a blue silk sari over black tights, and her shoes, flat, pointed, and colorful, looked like something from Thailand. Her place reminded me of an article about the New York City Chelsea Hotel apartments where the artists lived, so different from minimalist, neutral spaces with no color or soul. Eugene had its share of what I called bohemian bungalows, living areas created from vintage shop purchases.

"Please. Make yourself comfortable. I'll make tea. What kind do you prefer?"

I asked her to choose as I didn't know anything about tea.

I sat on a green velvet settee and took in the numerous Asian artifacts—buddhas, a three foot tall statue of Quan Yin, a small, handcrafted Persian wall hanging, a South African batik of three dancers, and what looked like a collection of colorful Oaxacan wood-carved rabbits. Everything around me was plush and exotic, including the vintage furniture and brass lamps.

When she came back, I said, "I like your place."

"Thank you."

She seemed nervous and not happy to see me. Yet the few times I saw her as a child, she was warm and loving, eager to hug and squeeze us and cover our faces with kisses. Maybe she was just in shock or worried about why I was there. Perhaps she was upset that she'd never heard from me after Mom died. Now I felt terrible. But the only way I could move forward after my parents died was to cut all ties to the past. Now I regretted that. But what was done was done.

I couldn't sit. I wanted a smoke. At the window, I peeked through the space between the curtains and froze. Parked behind my car was a black SUV with tinted windows. I'd seen plenty of black SUVs since I'd arrived, but this one gave me chills. If it was FBI, why would they park right behind me? Wouldn't they want to keep a low profile? This felt more like intimidation, so it could be the Boston Duo. They might want to scare me. I couldn't see into the SUV, so I couldn't see faces. Damn.

Kathleen came back with a tea tray and assorted cookies.

When she caught my eye, she said, "Is that black SUV down there?"

I whipped around. "What?"

"The black SUV with tinted windows."

"Yes. How long have you noticed it?"

"Since yesterday. At first, it was just another black SUV. But today, it appeared again."

No wonder she seemed nervous.

She took a chair near the round, teak coffee table. I sat across from her on a velvet divan. She poured tea then held out the cookies. "Would you like a biscuit?"

I took one even though I wasn't hungry. "Do you know who they are or what they're here for?"

She picked up her dainty teacup and saucer, looked over the teacup's rim, and said, "Do you?"

Smart woman. I decided to be honest. "I think they're looking for me."

"And who are *they*? Are you in trouble?"

I cleared my throat and leaned forward, no longer wanting the cookie. I placed it on my saucer. "They could be FBI."

Kathleen thought about this for a moment. "It's a New Hampshire license plate, and in this state, you're not allowed to have tinted windows like those. So I'm guessing only the FBI could get away with that. Or maybe some other arm of law enforcement."

She was observant and no fool. Good. "Look, Kathleen, you deserve the truth. I'm a lawyer or used to be. Could they be checking on you for some reason?"

"No, not that I'm aware of. But, who knows?" She nibbled a cookie, sipped her tea, and sighed. "So what brings you here, Angie?"

That was some segue. I wanted to know more about the black SUV from her viewpoint.

Instead, I took a deep breath and focused on what I'd come for. "You were Mom's best friend. I'd hoped to find out more about my parents' relationship."

Kathleen set down her teacup, crossed her legs, and said, "What was your impression? Being a child, I'm sure you formed some of your own ideas about them." She held up her hand. "Excuse me. Do they still call you Angie?"

"No. I go by Ang or Angeline."

"Thank you," she said as she studied me. "How is your sister Sophie?"

That shocked me. Of course she didn't know. I inhaled and exhaled and looked at the high ceiling. My teacup rattled on the saucer, so I set it down. When I could talk without choking up, I said, "She died. A year or so ago." I knew she'd ask how, so I added, "She committed suicide."

Knowing Kathleen had a daughter who died from a heroin overdose didn't help. Too close to home. Both were forms of suicide. Kathleen, however, kept her composure. "I'm so sorry," she said. "That's tragic."

I said, "I was sorry to hear about your daughter."

Kathleen nodded. "Thank you. It was a difficult time. May I ask? Do you know why Sophie did that?"

Damn. Did I really want to go into all that? I tried to keep it simple. "Heartbreak. She loved someone who betrayed her badly."

Kathleen picked up her teacup, sipped, and again studied me, this time with compassion. I could tell she understood why I didn't go into it more deeply. I said, "It was very complicated."

"Yes. Their reasons are never simple."

We now both seemed to be on equal ground. The tragic loss of a loved one and a black SUV.

I decided to dive in. "I know my parents were troubled. I know about Dad's PTSD and being bi-polar. But I also know they loved each other. Not in a healthy way, of course."

"True," she said. "Another complicated story."

"Can you tell me about your relationship with them?"

She stared into her teacup and cleared her throat. "I won't give you my opinion. I can give you an example of what I experienced."

I nodded. Good.

"Before you girls were born, we double dated once. Your mom was so excited and happy that Bob and I—he became my husband—agreed to go to the Weirs with them. They had very few friends. You know the Weirs Beach with its arcade games and the Mt. Washington boat that takes you around the lake?"

I nodded again.

"Bob and I bought four tickets to go on the boat. We did it under the guise of giving them a gift for their first anniversary. We had a blast on the bumper cars and having our fortune told by one of those mechanical fortune-tellers. We shared a pint of onion rings and fries, then smoked while watching the summer tourists go by. Everyone smoked back then."

God, I wanted a cigarette. I ate my cookie instead.

"Your father had a flask of whiskey and kept handing it to Annie. She hated whiskey, but she sipped anyway. Your Dad loved pinball, and by the time he played my Bob, he was drunk and aggressive, so I led Bob to another machine so he could play me. Ron pushed Annie into playing him. She was a lousy player, and Ron made fun of her. Annie said, "Play by yourself, then." He grabbed her wrist and wrenched it. When she cried out, Bob confronted him. But Annie shook her head and took off down the boardwalk. I stepped in front of Ron and said, 'You're a real bully, you know that? It's only a stupid game.'"

No surprises yet. "Then what?"

Kathleen looked toward the window, her arms tight to her sides as if she were in pain. "Your father said, 'From now on, stay away from Annie, you bitch.'"

I felt my face go hot. "Then?"

"Bob punched him."

After an awkward silence, she said, "I saw your mom a few times. One time she had a black eye. Your father just wouldn't get help, and neither would your mom. She told me that while you kids were still at home, she wouldn't leave your father."

I groaned and stood. With my back to her, I said, "I've seen so many women do that. Some don't make it out alive." I wanted to add, "including my mom," but was that true? I left home and moved three thousand miles away so I didn't have to deal with our dysfunctional family life. I turned to Kathleen. "I just couldn't protect her."

"You were a kid. It wasn't your job to protect her. It was her job to protect you."

"Do you know that Sophie and I never talked about the three years she spent alone with Mom and Dad?"

"I don't know much about that period of time. Your folks had gone up north. Or was that when they went to Vermont? I don't remember. Your mom did call a couple of times. She called me from a payphone when Sophie left at sixteen." Kathleen looked down at her hands. "She missed you girls terribly."

Ouch. I'd always tried to stuff that guilt, to forget I'd left my sister with Mom. "We both called her whenever we could or whenever she had a phone. Every once in a while, Dad would get on and say a quick hello and add, 'When are you coming home?' Mom and I wrote occasional letters to each other. I sent photos. We pretended that everything was fine, normal." I paused. "If only she'd divorced him."

We looked at each other. Kathleen's eyes watered.

The past had caught up with both of us.

I went to the window. The SUV was gone. I should have felt relief, but I didn't.

27

I returned to the divan. We gave each other a look of "What can you do?" I rubbed my chest.

Kathleen asked, "Are you all right?"

I tried to get comfortable. "Yes, fine."

Kathleen poured more tea then scrutinized me. "What made you come here now, Ang? It's been a long time."

I took a deep breath. "It's something about my family." Kathleen waited. I watched her now neutral face. "Did you know about the twins?"

"Twins," Kathleen said with no inflection but her cheeks flushed.

"Yes, twins. Did you know about them?"

Kathleen pulled her legs up under her and looked away. What if she *didn't* know? I waited. And waited. New Englanders are notoriously close-lipped about what they know. The idea is to keep up the perception of a perfect family. But I didn't expect Kathleen to be like that. She seemed worldly.

Finally, she said, "Yes, I knew."

It took me a second to grasp this before blurting out, "You did know? Really? About the twin?" I set down my tea, leaned forward, and braced myself. Goosebumps ran up my arms. She *knew*.

Kathleen folded her hands and held them to her mouth as if praying. I didn't know what to say. Shit. I chewed my lip to keep from asking her a thousand questions. I tried to remember my training, to stay silent so that the other person would have to talk. But damn, it was hard.

"Your mom had a home birth. It was that back-to-nature lifestyle for them then. Also, Ron's distrust of everyone, including doctors. Luckily, with you, your mom had a short labor and no problems." She paused and stirred her tea, but she hadn't added anything to it.

"Did you hear about the twins' birth from Mom?"

"No, Angeline. I was there. Your mom called me when she went into labor."

I scooted forward to the edge of the divan. "What? Really? You were there for the birth?"

"Yes. Your father was in the kitchen, drinking a beer with you snuggled up on his lap. When I walked in, I was sure he'd kick me out. Instead, he said, 'Annie will be OK, right?' I assured him she would be, but I didn't know."

Kathleen wriggled in her chair and turned a ring on her finger, round and round. I didn't dare push as I could see the conflict on her face of whether to tell the story or not.

"Your mom, bless her heart, had an easy labor. Sophie came first, all plump, beautiful, and shiny. But the second baby? That was a shock. Who knew you could have twins from different fathers? I certainly didn't at the time."

"I know. That shocked me when I heard."

She continued on as if I hadn't said anything. "The midwife, cool as a cucumber, laid the second baby in Annie's arms along with Sophie. Annie didn't flinch. She kissed her and held her mouth against the cool brown skin.

She loved them both immediately. Your mom was always stronger than Ron or any of us gave her credit for."

"What did you do?"

"I freaked. I told the mid-wife not to tell Ron yet, that I needed to talk to Annie. I asked Annie what she wanted to do, knowing Ron would go ballistic. I even offered to adopt the girl, take her home right then." Kathleen was now looking at me, but still twisting that ring. "Your mom pulled both babies to her and said, 'No. They're twins. They're supposed to be together.' I tried to reason with her, but she was determined."

"What did Dad do when he saw the babies?" I held my breath.

"He acted as if he didn't notice. It was weird. He sat down on the edge of the bed and kissed both of them. Then Annie smiled and thanked me for coming. Ron thanked me too. I was dismissed. It was all too strange. I reluctantly left. What could I do?"

"What happened to the twin?"

Kathleen fidgeted with the ring again. "Annie called me in hysterics a few days later. She woke to find Ron and the twin gone. I drove down to Henniker again and begged your mom to call the police. I was scared that he'd kill the baby. Your mom insisted he'd never do that. When he returned, he told her he took the baby to Massachusetts and left her swaddled in a box at a fire station in a black area of Boston. He told her he had left a note saying the baby's name was Bibi. Ron cried. She'd never seen him cry before."

"Wasn't he upset that she'd had an affair?"

"No. They both fooled around. What he didn't know is how many different men your mom had been with. Her pattern was to have flings after your father was violent."

"But dumping her baby at a fire station? That had to be worse than anything before in their relationship."

"I think it was the beginning of the end. No mother could deal with that situation. She started to have problems —stomach, headaches, weight loss."

"Did she take drugs to escape?"

"No. She wouldn't do that while breastfeeding. But her milk dried up. She was now left alone with the baby and you for long stretches because Ron was rarely home. She'd call me when he was gone, said because his bi-polar swings were getting more extreme, he didn't want to be around her and you two kids when he was manic and could get violent. Then your father discovered her talking to me one day on the phone. I guess he stood outside the door and listened. I have no idea what we were saying, but he moved the family to a place up north."

Kathleen wiped tears from her eyes with the hankie she stashed up her sleeve. I waited, wanting to hug her, to have her hug me.

She looked over at me as if to see if she should go on. I tilted my head slightly and said, "That must have been hard for you."

She half-smiled. "Yes. I didn't want her isolated. I did try to stop her from going. I tried to get your mom to leave him, but she wouldn't. She said if she left and took the children, he'd kill himself. She recognized his mental health issues and tried to get him to go to the VA to get help, but he wouldn't."

"Mom told me it was because of Vietnam."

Kathleen huffed, dismissing this idea. "I met people who knew him from high school. At the time, they called him a rebel. It was popular to be a rebel back then, you know the James Dean type. He got into trouble. He got into an accident with his girlfriend, who died in the wreck. He walked away with scratches. When he left school, he joined the Marines."

"I didn't know about the accident." This was my dad she was talking about. I felt like a child again, as if this were time travel. It seemed surreal.

"He had a few veteran friends who told him the VA was understaffed and useless, so he refused to go."

I'd also heard that from wives of Vietnam veterans, so I understood the dilemma. But I also understood the ego of some men who thought they were fine.

"I know this question will be hard to answer, but did he love my mom?"

"Yes, he did."

She didn't hesitate and said it so assuredly that I felt enormous relief. I hadn't wanted him to be a sociopath or misogynist. I had to believe Kathleen. I needed to.

Kathleen sighed, long and sad. "Your mom adored him and said she understood the pain he was in. She thought love would change him, but it couldn't, not with his untreated bipolar disorder and PTSD."

We were silent for a bit, not even sipping our tea. I was on the fence about whether the VA could have helped him. I'd heard positive and negative stories. The VA at home in Eugene seemed to do a decent job with their vets. But sometimes it wasn't enough. And could it ever be enough? The vets had complicated mental and physical health issues. One client of mine, an Iraq veteran, *had* gone to the VA, and the doctor prescribed meds that caused a type of schizophrenia in rare circumstances. He ended up shooting up his house. No one was home. He hadn't hurt anyone. He'd only scared the cat.

With a deep breath in and out to calm myself, I struggled to be objective and gather this info like a lawyer, except I could also use a shot of whiskey. But this was my father, the man responsible for me being born, the man who loved my mother, a complicated man I loved and hated. My stomach clenched. I wanted to cry. I wanted my parents back so I could talk with them. Their deaths shut the door on memory and memories. It kept them at a certain age that would never change. It was like reading a novel that was missing the last half. What happened to these two people?

I hugged myself, wondering if Kathleen had told me the whole story. I searched her face, needing to know everything, but doubting that I ever would.

28

While Kathleen made more tea, I mentally ran through everything she'd told me. What I'd learned seemed to raise more questions than answers. Besides being so hard to grasp, I didn't even know what to ask now to get to the truth, the full story.

The pounding and sawing from the downstairs renovation acted like white noise. I shut my eyes and tried to empty my head of "monkey mind." I focused on the back of my eyelids, and a dreamy state took over. A memory surfaced.

"Are you all right, Angeline?"

I opened my eyes. Kathleen stood over me with the teapot.

"I just remembered something."

Kathleen set the teapot on the table and sat down. "Yes?"

I shut my eyes again. "Sophie and I were in the living room, playing on one of the rugs Mom had braided. Mom gave us little boxes of raisins to eat. It was late. Mom had kept the meatloaf and potatoes warming in the oven. When Dad came home, he was happy and silly. He'd found a job at a resort with good pay and benefits. He'd also gone out and bought a used four-wheel drive to replace the old, rusted van. Grabbing Mom, he danced her around the kitchen. Dad gave us girls horseback rides. At bedtime, in our pajamas, we went for ice cream in the new car."

I covered my face with my hands, smelling the meatloaf, Dad's cigarette smoke on his shirt and in his hair, and the pine smell of the air freshener in our new car. I hugged myself as the rest of the memory poured out of me.

"The next night, Mom made a special meal. She sang and laughed in the kitchen. When she called us to the table, Dad said it smelled yummy. He tickled me when he said it. Mom brought out the mashed potatoes first. Then she proudly brought out a small plate with this tiny piece of meat on it, covered in a sauce and pierced with cloves, like a ham."

I cleared a tickle in my throat, remembering my mom's eager look, her wide eyes and half smile. Now, in retrospect, I also recognized the hands wringing her apron in fear.

"We'd been so happy the evening before that I expected Dad to sweep up Mom again in one of their silly dances. But Dad said nothing as he stared at the meat, his face turning a furious red. He scooped his hand under the platter and heaved it against the wall, barely missing Mom. Then he grabbed his keys and left."

I stared at Kathleen. She returned a look of sadness and resignation.

"Later, I figured Mom must have served him SPAM. Veterans had it in their C-rations. But why wouldn't she know that?"

"According to your mom, your dad never talked about Vietnam. She probably didn't know about SPAM either. But it was cheap. Annie didn't have much money to work with to put meals on the table."

I wasn't about to tell her that Dad came home drunk that night, started to beat Mom, and I threw myself between them, knocking Mom down, covering her, screaming at him to stop. He did. Then he sat down on the floor and cried. Mom crawled over to him and held him. I waited for a bit, angry at them both, confused, upset, wanting one of them to include me. But they didn't. So I went to bed.

I held my cramped stomach, tasting bile at the back of my throat. "Kathleen, do you really think their wreck was an accident?"

"Such a terrible day." She stared at her hands then vehemently shook her head. "No." She swallowed audibly and blinked back tears. "I'm sorry, but I'm sure it was no accident." Kathleen's face looked ten years older.

One of my eyes twitched. I felt nauseous and shifted on the divan. I really needed a drink. But I also ached to find out about that day. Not knowing was worse.

Kathleen's cheeks had lost their color. Her hands were clasped, her knuckles white.

In almost a whisper, I said, "Aunt Kathleen, I really need to know about the accident. Please tell me. What happened that day?"

She stood and pushed her thick, white hair away from her face. She gripped the back of her chair as if to give herself support for what she was about to say.

"On the morning of the accident, your mom called me. Ron had bought her flowers, and they were taking a romantic ride up into the White Mountains. After, they were going out for clams and onion rings."

"Really? That sounds nice." I was hoping it was an accident, hoping that they'd died in love on a romantic date.

Kathleen looked at her hands and then up at me. "Did you know your mom had a fear of heights?"

I shook my head. "No." Now was not the time to tell her I had a fear of heights, too.

"One time, your father tried to take her to Tuckerman's Ravine to watch him ski the headwall. She threw up even at the idea and refused to go. They fought."

"So she did stand up to him on occasion. But what does that have to do with taking her on a romantic drive?"

She moved over next to me on the divan, took my hands, and said, "Angeline, he drove her up a steep, winding mountainside road, wide enough for only one vehicle. To get to the top, you had to cross a deep chasm." She rubbed my hands as if to make this easier. My hands turned icy cold. "That meant driving across the chasm on two logs. The logs were just far enough apart for a vehicle to straddle. There was nothing to protect a car from going over." She paused. She held my hands tighter. "At the log crossing, your mom tried to get out. A man in a vehicle on the other side waited in a turnout for them to cross. That man told the police your dad was shaking your mom, and he thought he heard screaming. He wanted to do something, but if he crossed, there was no way to get around them. Then suddenly, the four-wheel-drive lurched forward, your mom and dad were still struggling, and somehow the vehicle took a sharp turn and went off into the gorge."

Tears rolled down Kathleen's cheeks. When a tear dropped onto my hand, I wiped mine away.

My mom. My dad. It didn't seem real. It felt like it had happened to someone else. But it hurt. I could hardly swallow. I pulled my hands away and shakily took a sip of my tea.

Kathleen pulled the hankie from her sleeve and blew her nose. "That piece of shit." She glanced up at me. "Sorry. I said I'd be objective."

"Did the police suspect ... you know?"

"Hon, I'm sure they did, but how could they prove it? And what could be done? Your folks were gone, and that was that."

"Was there a police report written up about it?"

"Yes. The police wrote it up as an accident. There was no suicide letter. They questioned me, and I had to tell them what Annie told me about the romantic day her husband had planned. But I *did* tell them about her fear of heights. She would never have crossed that chasm."

"Was there ever a newspaper report about it? I mean, did anyone investigate it?"

"There was nothing to investigate. The police deemed it an accident. Case closed."

I chewed on my lip. There had to be something else. "Did my dad have any friends that he would have talked to?"

Kathleen just cocked her head as if to say, "You're really asking me that?"

I couldn't let it go. "I suppose if it had been someone important, the cops would have investigated. But with my parents, just some hippies living on the edge. ..."

"Angeline, even if they had investigated it, what good would it do? There was no evidence one way or the other."

"They had a witness who—"

"Who eventually said he wasn't sure what he saw."

"Oh."

We both reached for our tea at the same time and sipped even though it was cold.

A small memory returned. "Did you once tell me they found something wrong with the four-wheel drive?"

She rubbed the back of her neck. I felt bad for dredging this up, but she was the only one who could help me.

"Ang, you girls were still young. I knew the funeral

would be rough for both of you. I wanted to tell you something that would give you some peace before the funeral."

I wanted to yell at her for that. Then I realized she was just being kind. I would have done the same thing if the roles had been reversed. "I just don't understand why Mom agreed to go with him. It doesn't make sense." I wanted to curl up next to her like a little kid. It felt like an eternity since I'd had that warmth and comfort.

"Oh, sweetie, it makes perfect sense. Your mom was finally leaving your father. And I was helping her."

"What?" I jerked upright, jumped to my feet, and walked around the divan. "Why then would she fall for the romantic day?" I was almost yelling.

I shook my head, stuffing tears of frustration. This was too much, even for me. I had wanted to keep a level head no matter what I heard. I told myself that this couldn't be worse than some of the horrible shit I'd been through.

Kathleen pushed herself off the divan and faced me, her hands out as if offering this explanation. "I think she thought she had to go. If she turned down this romantic outing, he might suspect something was wrong. He had the ability to sense things before they happened."

She poured us more tea. I didn't want any more tea.

Kathleen's expression changed to one of determination. She had such a beautiful expressive face I could almost feel her emotions. This time, I knew I was going learn what she thought was true, what she suspected, and something more accurate than anything I'd heard so far.

"Do you know what I think? I think he felt her pulling away. I think he saw something she'd done, like saving money in a secret place. I think he knew he'd lose her once you kids were grown."

I waited, suspecting what she'd say next.

"I don't think your father ever forgave your mom for Bibi. He was a proud man, too much ego. He couldn't have dealt with the shame. A black daughter would have proved to everyone that your mom fooled around. Giving Bibi away probably tore at them both and especially their relationship. I know your mom never forgave him."

"I don't understand why Mom didn't just take me and the twins after they were born and go stay with her parents. They hated Dad. They would have taken us in."

"Would they? A black child? I think they would have drawn the line at that. I knew them. They were conservative Baptists. They didn't even come to the funeral."

"They didn't?"

"You don't remember?"

I shook my head. "I always thought that if we lived with grandma and grandpa, Sophie and I would no longer have to be scared when Dad came home from work, wondering which daddy we'd get—the fun daddy or the scary one. So to me, it seems like he always came first. And I guess he did, even over Bibi, her own child."

Kathleen got up, came over, and hugged me. "I'm sorry you had to go through that."

The hug was comfort and warmth, one hand on my back, the other on the back of my head, pressing me against her. She kissed the side of my face. Her hugs were the best. The few times "Aunt Kathleen" visited, Mom would be so cheerful. When I reluctantly pulled away, Kathleen said, "Is there anything I can get you?" I shook my head. "Even after all these years, I still miss your mom. I miss you girls."

I snuffled and tried to smile.

"I think we could both use something a little stronger. I'm going to have a vodka on ice. How about you?"

I swallowed hard and took a deep breath. "I'd love a scotch, neat, if you have it."

She went to the kitchen for ice and returned to fix our drinks at the liquor cabinet that opened into a small bar. After she handed me the drink and sat down, she said, "So what about the SUV? And why else are you here?" Now her voice was concerned and maternal.

I sipped the drink, relieved with the liquor warming my chest and with the change of subject.

"I found the twin." My voice cracked.

"You what? Really? That's incredible!"

I told her the story, a redacted version.

Kathleen shook her head in disbelief. "Then she's alive. Oh, my. Thank God. Where does she live?"

I told her about the house on Lake Winnisquam.

"She's that close? Why did she come here? That's strange. This state has always been racist. Did she come alone?"

I didn't want to tell her about Betty yet or the Boston crime family until I'd talked with Bibi. I need to protect this new sister, and I didn't want anyone, even Kathleen, knowing the danger she was in.

"The woman Bibi lived with, Betty, had a vacation home in Wolfeboro on the lake. She was a wealthy Bostonian and Bibi's, uh, patron. They probably knew the area. But from what I gather—Bibi's an artist—she wanted a retreat away from the city where she could work. The woman she lived with bought the house for her."

"You're using the past tense when speaking about this woman. Is she dead?"

My stomach cramped again. "Yes."

"Well, that's sad, but I'm glad this woman cared for Bibi

so well. It's just a little uncanny that she now lives so close to where she was born."

I nodded in agreement. It *was* uncanny. Or did we all come back? Were we all so haunted by this place that we returned to it, even unconsciously? I had to add, "But I'm not sure she lives here full time. Not sure if she inherited the house in Boston."

Kathleen looked tired. "After you meet her, will you call me?"

"Of course." I knocked back the rest of my drink and stood to go.

"Thank you for coming, Angeline. And I'm so sorry about everything. You girls deserved better."

I sucked back tears.

"Look at us," Kathleen said. "Both crying. Two weeping Ada's."

We both laughed. I had no idea where that saying came from, but I'm sure she said it to keep us both from sobbing. As we said good-bye, Kathleen hugged me again and held on a little longer. Her daughter would have been much younger than me, but I'm sure she was thinking of her as she held me. Then she kissed my forehead. "Please come back," she said.

I nodded, unable to speak. In a small way, it was like hugging my mom.

When I reached the car, I looked back at the storefront, reluctant to leave. Kathleen waved. I waved back.

As I unlocked the Renegade, I glanced up and down the street. The black SUV sat parked where the train station used to be. It pulled out when I did.

29

I adjusted my rearview mirror. The black SUV couldn't be more obvious.

It gave me renewed energy to take on these assholes.

"OK, City Boys. Let's see if you can keep up on country roads."

When the rain started, I knew I could lose them. This time I blessed the downpour. I had plenty of experience with driving on Northwest rain-soaked roads.

Black clouds turned day into night. I took unlit back roads around Sanbornton, and surprisingly, remembered most of them. The SUV followed until I rounded a corner and took a route that split. I darted left. They kept going straight. I took another left to circle back toward the main highway. That would bring me to a dirt road that led to Bibi's.

The downpour stopped as suddenly as it had started. Typical New England storm. That was OK. I needed a vantage point. Instead of parking along the road, I backed into the driveway of the summer home next to Bibi's. You could always tell a summer home. The curtains were pulled, all the boats were stored, no lawn chairs visible, and no parked cars. Plus, the place had a feel of hibernation. With this vantage point, I could look left to see if anyone was coming and look right through the trees to Bibi's back door

I slumped down a little and went through the papers in the envelope Gerard had given me—Bibi's adoption papers, the DNA test Gerard did that proved she was my sister, including one that confirmed her mother had been white and dad black. Time passed. I slipped the papers back into the envelope. When a silver BMW came into view, it slowed, pulled into Bibi's driveway, and parked near the back door, I checked my watch. An hour had passed. My hands shook. This was it.

A hooded figure slipped from the car. When she unlocked the back door, I figured it had to be Bibi. She opened her car's back door, and a dog the size of a small pony jumped out and ambled into the house. Bibi unloaded bags from the trunk. She walked around to the driver's side and swung a handbag over her shoulder. All her motions seemed so normal, yet I fought tears. That was Bibi. My sister. I had another sister.

My insides twisted, and I clutched my stomach. Yes, I had another sister, and with that a new worry. A new vulnerability. Something to lose again.

But I was getting ahead of myself. I hadn't even met her. I didn't know if she would mean that much to me. My emotions quickly lost out to the practical. My chest loosened and my face relaxed. I had to remember we had no history together. She was Betty's lover. She was East Coast. I was West Coast. I did, however, find the dog reassuring. We both had dogs, so how bad could she be? Stupid question. I had Tempest as a companion. Bibi probably had this one—

Pitbull? Mastiff?—for protection. By the looks of it, the dog could definitely rip me apart.

Before going inside, Bibi turned to look out toward the road then over to where I was parked. Did she know I shouldn't be here? Did she instinctively feel she was being watched?

She went inside a little past four o'clock. I started the car, drove into her driveway, and sat there, but couldn't get myself to move or stop shaking. That framed photo of her and Betty I had seen yesterday bothered me in ways I could never have anticipated. I imagined what Betty looked like after they found her remains at the bottom of the cliffs and shuddered. Had Bibi seen the remains? Had she been the one to make arrangements for cremation and a memorial? How horrible for her. For a second, I felt guilty about Betty dying, but only for a second. She'd killed Gus. It had been either Betty or me over that cliff. There were no suspects in Betty's death, so Bibi couldn't connect me with it.

Then again, I had no idea what Bibi knew. Why had she fled to this house in New Hampshire? Was she part of Betty and Link's crime group? If she were, wouldn't she stay in Boston? Why was she acting afraid, and who was she afraid of? Maybe I could help her. Maybe she needed my help.

I shook myself. I wasn't sure I had the emotional strength for this meeting. Maybe this was a mistake and I should go back to the cottage and come here in the morning.

No, now that I've seen her I had to meet her. After talking with Kathleen, I was full of family fever, full of longing, and the possibility that I would have a sister again. I'd already regained a little of what I'd lost by finding Kathleen. I wouldn't know if this sister would accept me or even believe me by sitting here in this car.

30

I knocked on the back door then rang the bell. I knocked again. Her dog barked and growled. I hadn't considered that she might not answer. I was so off my game.

When it comes to protecting others, I am a she-devil. I can keep my head on straight and fight like there's no tomorrow. But when it comes to me, I've locked up my emotions.

I didn't realize they'd someday riot for freedom. And here I am, standing at the door of the house where my new sister lives. I forced myself to knock again. Did I dare go around front?

The dog continued barking, its sound loud, then receding, then loud. It scratched at the back door. Shit, maybe I should have sat in the car and called her. I was making amateur mistakes. And it was raining again.

I took out my phone. My fingers flew across the phone's keyboard. "Bibi, my name is Angeline Porter. I'm from Oregon. I need to talk with you." I wiped the rain from my face and pushed back my hair. I tapped in another message, "It's about your biological family."

I waited. Maybe half a minute passed? Then the door opened. Bibi stood there, pointing a gun at me. "Is anybody with you?"

I expected the door to get slammed in my face. I didn't, however, expect the gun. It took me a few seconds to respond. "No. I'm alone." I stepped away so she could look behind me.

"What kind of joke is this? Who are you?"

"My name is Angeline Porter. It's a long story, but I just recently found out we're related." I was dripping wet. "I'm sorry if I scared you. I have papers in my—"

She grabbed my arm and pulled me into the mudroom. As she did, she also looked outside. "Did anyone follow you?"

"A black SUV. I ditched them."

She swung around, slammed the door, and locked it.

"How do you know the SUV was following you?"

"I've been followed before. This time it followed me from Tilton."

She muttered something under her breath. With the gun trained on me, she handed me a towel and told me to take off my shoes. The dog was nowhere in sight. I did as I was told, hung my raincoat on a hook, wiped my face and hands, and toweled my hair.

"Show me ID."

I pulled out my wallet. She inspected it.

"Are you packing?"

I nodded.

"Hand it over."

I did.

"In the kitchen," she said, motioning the gun at me

like a gangster in a film noir. She looked pretty comfort-able with the weapon, so I assumed she knew how to use it.

In the kitchen, I laid my shoulder bag on the counter, took a barstool, and placed both hands palm down on the countertop. The dog growled and snarled from an adjacent room. Without yelling, Bibi sharply said, "Quiet." The dog stopped.

Bibi never took her eyes off me. Still pointing the pistol, she stood across from me at the peninsula counter. She wore designer jeans, a yellow blouse, and gold hoops. Her long, black hair was in cornrows. She had eyes like Sophie's, only brown.

"How could we possibly be related? And how did you find my place?"

I couldn't take my eyes from her. "As I said, it's a long story."

"Then get started."

"I was a lawyer until I was disbarred for putting away a serial rapist. But that's another story. I just wanted you to know that." God, I'd lost my train of thought. Why did I say that?

"OK. Now how did you find me?"

"You lived with Betty. Her cohort, Link, shook down my sister for a lot of money. The FBI got involved."

"So what? You know that I lived with Betty. Not hard to find out."

"I went after Sam. I mean Link. Another FBI agent went after me. As I said, it's complicated." I paused. "I'm sorry. I'm not making a lot of sense."

"Link was a schmuck. Betty wouldn't have died if it hadn't been for him."

Oh, god. What story was she told?

"Yes, he was a schmuck. He swindled a lot of people. What do you know about his death?"

She hovered on the edge of a stool and looked tired. "No, I ask the questions. How do you know about Betty and Link? Are you FBI?"

"No. The FBI keeps me informed because of the extortion. But I had to go underground and change my identity because of people involved with the crime group who wanted the money my sister had stolen. That's when I met Betty on Kauai."

"So you met Betty," she said, raising an eyebrow.

"Yes. She saved my dog. We did a few things together. Was she on Kauai for vacation?"

"I think you should tell me your story before I tell you anything. *If* I tell you anything. You do know Betty was murdered."

"I thought she fell off a cliff."

"She was pushed off a cliff."

She could have run off the cliff. No one could determine it was murder, except two bodies were found nearby, and they were murdered. So one *could* draw conclusions, faulty or not.

I kept my voice soothing as I lied. "I was supposed to go to lunch with her that day, but she didn't show up at the cottage. She didn't answer her phone. The FBI found out from the manager at the Plantation that we knew each other, so they asked me about her activities."

"Interesting that you had that connection with Link then Betty in Kauai. Did you kill Betty?"

I almost choked. "Why would I kill Betty?"

"Good question. You tell me."

"I didn't kill Betty." I gathered my wits. "Look, it's been a rough time. Sam, I mean Link, threatened my sister and forced her to steal millions from my husband's business account and transfer it to another account. If she didn't, Link said he would kill her and me. I've kept in touch with one of the FBI agents. That's how I found out about you."

She didn't say anything but kept the gun steadily pointed at me.

"Bibi, I found out about you when the FBI investigated Betty's death. Plus, I was involved with the activist group that knew about The Grim Reaper, Steven Hastrick, your brother."

She flinched. "He wasn't my brother. He was a prick. I'm glad he's dead."

That was my first clue to her character. But hadn't I said things like that about the schmucks Betty and Link? Whoa. Careful. It would be easy to make a mistake right now, let down my guard, and blurt out the wrong thing—if I hadn't already.

"I found you because the FBI took your twin's DNA and cross-referenced it for any other links. The FBI agent who was working undercover fell in love with Sophie, and when he found out about you, he told me."

"How convenient. And why did he tell you."

"Because I'm helping him with a case."

"What case?"

"The extortion crime group, the one Link was involved in." I shouldn't be telling her all this. Hell, I didn't know if or how deep she was involved with Betty and Link's racket. But I had to draw her out. Besides, what if she were involved? Would I be able to turn my newly-minted sister into the authorities? What if they found out and arrested her? Another sister gone because of Betty and Link? I couldn't let that happen.

Bibi stared at me so intensely I had a hard time keeping eye contact. Maybe I'd said too much already.

Finally, she said, "Betty had nothing to do with Link's shit. He used Betty. Betty was no angel, but she was a good person."

I asked, "How so?" and hoped it sounded innocent enough.

"Why should I tell you? When I told the FBI what I knew about Betty, they didn't believe me."

"If the info is in her favor, why not tell me? You knew her more intimately than anyone."

Her expression changed from suspicion to confusion back to suspicion. "Yes, I knew her. So? Why tell you?"

"Because all I have is the FBI's story. I've been used and I was afraid you'd be used. I lost one sister because of it. I don't want to lose you. I want to protect you. We're in this together. Like you, I'm suspicious of the FBI's motives."

She snorted. "Right. So why wouldn't I be suspicious of *your* motives?"

"Because I'm here as family, that's why."

"Well, I don't need protection."

I didn't say anything.

"So, how am I supposedly related to you?"

"You're my sister."

This time she guffawed. "Oh, right, white girl. I'm *your* sister."

"You're my younger sister Sophie's twin ... and she's white too."

She waved the gun at me like a wand. "And, poof, my twin is a white girl, too." Then she jabbed the gun at me. "What kind of stupid bitch do you think I am? Why are you fucking with me? Just because I'm black? Betty warned me of cons like you who'd be at my door as soon as they found out I had money."

I didn't blame her for seeing this as a con. "Look, I know it sounds like a con, but it isn't. Got your phone? Google twins of different colors. You'll see that it is possible. Rare, but possible. I didn't believe it at first, either."

She switched the gun to her left hand and picked up her phone with her right. Her fingers played the keyboard so fast, I was impressed. Then she looked up. Now her face drained to a lighter shade of brown.

"What?" I said.

"I don't like this." She held up the phone so I could see it. "Twins *can* have different fathers. It's extremely rare though to have one black and one white."

I nodded. "Yes, it is. Like I said, however, I didn't believe it at first either, but I not only have the DNA results, I also have the entire story from a reputable witness."

"Oh, I'm sure you do." Her arm came down, but that gun was locked in her hand. "What witness?"

"Bibi, I'm not here because I need money. I have all I need. I'm here to make sure your safe."

"Right." She leaned her elbows on the counter. Her arm was getting tired from holding the gun. "Money doesn't have to be about need either. You could be greedy."

"True, but in the state of Massachusetts, I have no right to your inheritance. And more importantly, what possible motive could I have to tell you this other than we're sisters, and I want to get to know you. Even though it sounds far fetched, it's true, and I have proof." I pulled out a sheaf of papers, copies of the DNA results from Gerard, and pushed them across the counter.

Bibi stood and glanced down at them. Then she looked up. "These can be faked, too."

"I know, but they're not." That put a seed of doubt even in my mind.

But I went on to explain what I knew about what was in the papers. She listened, still gripping the gun. I was tired of *her* asking all the questions, so I asked, "Did you ever try to find your biological parents?"

She filed through the papers with a glance at me every few seconds while holding the gun on me too. No clumsiness as if she'd done this before.

"No. My adoptive parents died. Betty took me in and said that most people who find their biological parent or parents wish they hadn't."

I had no idea if that were statistically true or not. In her case, I'm sure it would hurt to hear the truth. But I held hope that she would, after the shock, see me as a sister who wanted to help her. Shit, I hadn't even got to that part yet. I wanted to keep her safe. I could do that, even if I had to make a deal with the devil, namely Gerard. Besides, I liked this woman. She was tough.

"I was left on the steps of a Boston fire station with a note that my name was Bibi. Who the hell would do that? Give me a name then leave me? I could have died out there." The color rushed back to her face.

Mom must have given her the name and Dad, needing something to make him feel better, wrote her name on the note. At least he'd done that.

"I do know who left you there. My father."

31

"Your father?" She leaned forward. Now I had her attention.

I shifted on the stool. "He had bipolar disorder and PTSD from Vietnam. He was troubled, racist, and paranoid."

"So, your mother got it on with a black brother."

"Yes. Somewhere around Boston, I think. Don't have a clue where or with whom. She left Dad for a time, but I don't know for how long, where she stayed, or with whom."

"Where are they now?"

"Both dead."

She exhaled like blowing out a lung-full of smoke. "So you came all the way from Oregon to tell me this? Thanks."

"I'm sorry. But I wasn't told the truth either, about you or their deaths."

She searched my face. I held her gaze. "How did you know where I was?"

"A friend told me."

Otto scratched at the door and woofed, saving me from an explanation.

"I've gotta let Otto out. You OK with dogs?"

"I have a dog."

She slid both guns into the back of her jeans' waistband. After she opened the door, she took Otto by the collar, squatted, and ruffed his head, whispering something I couldn't hear. I can't say I wasn't frightened of this dog. I got off the stool and hunched over in a passive position. When she let go of him, he barreled over to me and stopped short, teeth bared. I slowly put my hand out palm up. He sniffed it, sat, and looked at me with big dopey eyes. His tongue hung out, and he breathed heavily. He drooled.

"Hi, Otto."

He gave me his paw. I shook it.

Bibi looked on, surprised and amused. "He likes you. Cool. I trust his instincts."

That seemed to rid the room of some tension.

"I need a drink," Bibi said. She didn't ask me what I wanted, just reached behind her in a cupboard and pulled out a bottle of Glenlivet, not the best, but not bad.

"You have good taste," I said, pointing to the bottle.

She poured us two fingers in tumblers and knocked hers back. "OK, here's my story."

I sipped and listened. The switch in her demeanor had thrown me, but I was ready. When she gestured for me to sit, I eagerly complied.

"Steven Hastrick was the biological son of the couple who adopted me. They couldn't have any more children, so they adopted me six years later. He gave them trouble. I didn't." She sipped and licked her lips. "They showed their favoritism to me, making him jealous. He used to try to hurt me. But as you can see ..." She ran her free hand up and down her body. "... I'm pretty solid. He was a runt." She grinned, almost a smirk. "He could never get his revenge.

Mother and Father were older parents who thought they'd live a lot longer. After their accident, Steven took over the estate and kicked me out."

She paused, trying hard to keep it together. I'm sure all of this took a toll on her. I could tell the gun weighed heavy in her hand.

"No one protected me. Nobody would take my case because I wasn't named in the will. The lawyer said my parents had discussed an inheritance for me, but didn't get to the legal work before they died."

She poured another scotch for both of us.

"That must have hurt."

She didn't respond. I wanted to say more, but it was the wrong timing. We sipped our drinks.

I glanced sideways, out toward the lake. The rain had quit, leaving a low-hanging fog. This was the lake I used to swim in, boat on, loved. The lake held only good memories. Mom loved the lake too. I turned back to Bibi.

"What was your relationship like with Betty? That must have been a painful loss."

Bibi held tension like a stretched rubber band. She was quite beautiful. I tried not to stare. This would be tough on both of us. Her eyes pooled.

"I'm so sorry about Betty," I repeated. "I lost my husband in an accident. It's so tough to lose a partner, a lover."

Her head jerked up. "Lover?" Her face scrunched up, and her nostrils flared. "You don't know anything, do you? What do you want?" She pulled the gun and pointed it at me again.

Shit. This is not the way I'd dreamed our meeting would go. I thought I'd tell her who I was, show her the papers to prove it, then she'd throw her arms around me, and we'd both cry. But I suspected Bibi was more like me, neither a hugger nor a crier.

"Look, Bibi, I *don't* know anything. Obviously, I assumed wrong and didn't check." Now I *did* sound like an amateur. I'd been away from the law game for too long.

"Betty was the only honest person in my life. She told me to be careful and suspect everyone, that they usually weren't who they said they were."

I tried not to laugh. Of course she told her that. I tried to regain my old attorney composure. "So if she wasn't a partner or lover, what was she?"

After a disgusted exhale, Bibi said, "It's none of your business, but Betty was my godmother."

I must have looked surprised because she said again, "Yes, Betty was my godmother."

"I'm so sorry," I said. "That must have been a terrible loss." Now I was stumbling along, repeating myself. "I don't know what to say."

"Yes, no shit," she said. "You certainly don't." She walked around the counter and looked out toward the lake.

I kept my mouth shut. I'd messed up. Her godmother? Damn. Thanks, Gerard, for the faulty intel.

She turned. I sat on the stool, and she looked down at me. "How can you be an attorney?"

"My only excuse is I don't practice anymore."

Bibi grimaced. "Oh, that's right. You were disbarred."

Now I was angry. "Look, I made a choice." I stood, she stepped back, and we locked eyes. "As I said earlier, I chose to put a serial rapist away, even when I knew it would cost me my profession."

I sat down and took a sterner tone.

"Bibi, I just talked with Kathleen Glanville who was Mom's best friend. I wanted to know about my parents, what they were like. I also wanted to know if she knew about you and the birth. She did. She was there when you girls were born. But Kathleen didn't know who your father was, whether Mom stayed with him or if it was a one-night stand. Mom never told her about that. Kathleen said she was shocked when you were born. She thought Mom told her everything."

Bibi didn't say anything.

"At some time, when you're ready to talk with Kathleen, I'm sure she'd love to meet you and tell you about your mother."

Still nothing.

"So tell me. How did Betty find you? How did you become her goddaughter?"

Otto growled, barked, and ran for the back door.

Bibi turned and followed the dog, gun in hand, my gun still in her waistband. I thought about grabbing it as I followed her, but I didn't want to break any trust I'd built so far. Otto snarled and scratched at the door. Then he turned and raced to the lakeside door. Bibi had to be afraid of something to be armed and have a dog like that. The dog jumped at the door. Bibi flipped off the inside lights and turned on the outside lights. Two men, one medium height, the other tall, both in raincoats, stood there. One knocked on the doorframe and said, "Put the gun down and restrain your dog."

Bibi yelled, "Show badges or get the fuck off my property!"

I walked over to stand next to Bibi. The dog paid no attention to me, but he was ready to rip these guys apart. Bibi put her hand on his head and said, "Otto, at rest." Otto sat but kept growling under his breath.

Both men pulled out their flip FBI badges and held

them against the screen. We couldn't make them out through the glass and screen door.

"I'm a lawyer," I said. "Tell me your names, why you're here, and what you want. We're not opening the door until you state your purpose."

The tallest one said, "Ms. Porter, you're no longer a lawyer, and, even if you were, you wouldn't have any jurisdiction in this state."

Shit. "Did Gerard Duvernet send you?"

"We need to speak with you."

"Need to talk to whom? Me or Bibi?"

"Both."

Bibi looked over at me.

"This is bullshit." I pulled out my phone, hit the button for the traffic report, waited, and said, "Hi, Gerard? Yes, it's me. Two men at the door say they're from the FBI, and—"

The men looked at each other. One made a motion with his head that they needed to leave, and they did.

Bibi checked the locks and headed to the kitchen. I followed. We watched the black SUV disappear down the road. Otto sat between us, quiet now.

"What the hell?" I said.

Bibi exhaled. "Assholes."

"Really. I wonder if those two *are* FBI. But they recognized Gerard's name. That could mean they are or they aren't."

Bibi put her gun on the kitchen counter and finally started unpacking the groceries. I noticed her hands trembling. "I'm making a pot of coffee. Want some?"

"That would be great."

"So who the hell is Gerard?"

32

As Bibi made coffee, I told her about Gerard.

"He's an FBI agent who fell in love with your twin while undercover in ... Link's gang."

She stepped back like she wasn't ready to acknowledge any of this. "Then the agent knows all about me."

I shrugged. "He's the friend who told me about you."

"Yeah, but why is he telling you all about me? Those guys don't do things from the bottom of their hearts. There's always a motive."

"He gave me the info so I'd play nice. I'm bait for the two who took over Link's crime ring." She didn't need to know about his suspicion that there was a dirty FBI agent involved in this.

A tremor flicked at the corner of her mouth. "All that means is he'll be tracking you, and you've led him here."

"He already knows where you are. Who do you think told me? But he better not show. I'll hurt him."

Now she laughed. "I'm messing with you anyway about the two Feds driving the black SUV. They've been tailing me on and off, even before Betty died."

"*If* they're feds."

"If they are or aren't, good luck, motherfuckers."

Now we both laughed.

She poured us two mugs of coffee. "So this Gerard told you that Betty and I were lovers?"

I nodded then sipped the coffee.

"Why should I be surprised? They've been wrong about Betty all along."

I had a hard time keeping my mouth shut about that one.

Bibi gave Otto a rawhide chew, and we settled at the counter again, this time with coffee and the gun between us.

I said, "Do you know that I grew up on this lake?"

She cocked her head. "Really?"

"I loved it here. Those were the best years with my parents."

Whoops. I shouldn't have said that. One of those parents was hers.

As if she hadn't heard me, she said, "Why do you suspect those two might not be FBI agents?" She squinted at me as if to read my expression. Now that she was a little more relaxed, she looked younger, her age, instead of the tough city gal.

"They could be FBI, but I'm not trusting anyone at this point. Same as you. When I say they might not be FBI, I mean they *might* be FBI, but on the take with Link's criminal group. If they're after me, they would know who Gerard Duvernet is. I have no idea why my mentioning him scared the bejesus out of them. They took off pretty fast. Maybe they had orders. I honestly don't know. Have they approached you before?"

Bibi's hand trembled as she set the mug down. She shook her head, and her cornrow braids swung back and forth. "I saw the black SUV two days ago, and I thought it was following me. But there are so many black SUVs around here, I thought I was being paranoid." She inhaled and let out a trembling breath as if she were trying not to cry. "I'm sorry. I'm shaken because of everything I learned in Boston. Now I'm afraid of what I know."

"Can you talk about it? We'll be stronger together if we both have all the information." I needed to show her that I was no fool, and I would share info with her. Hopefully, that would gain her trust. "Look, you're smart, smart enough to outwit these people. While Betty was alive, she protected you. But now, the criminal group might want to shut you up. I can help keep you safe."

Her look of suspicion quickly morphed into a glare. "Do you know about them? Are they after me?"

"No, I don't know. But I'm making an educated guess. They've been trying to get me because I have the money my sister stole. Gerard used me for bait to try and bring them down the first time. I want justice too, but I'm tired of being used. And I'm doing this alone."

"Do you trust Gerard?"

"It's complicated. When Gerard was undercover, he buddied up with Link. Link had Gerard sweep Sophie into a relationship so she'd steal millions from my husband's business account. She did it because Link told her he would kill Gerard if she didn't. She was madly in love with him so she did." I wasn't about to tell her that Sophie also slept with my husband to get his passwords.

My chest filled and tears threatened. I slurped my coffee to get a grip. When I looked up at Bibi, her eyes and mouth had softened. I sighed.

"But Gerard also fell in love with Sophie. Before they could form their own plan to get out of their situation,

Link told each of them lies about the other. So my sister thought Gerard had played her, that he didn't love her. I thought he'd used her too, and after he went back to Paris, I blamed him for her suicide. I wanted revenge, so I went to Paris."

"What for?"

I nodded at the gun. "To kill him."

Bibi's eyes widened. "Whoa. And now you're friends?" She tapped her fingers on the counter.

"I got to know him. He didn't even know she was dead." I swallowed painfully. "I could see why she'd fallen for him. But honestly? I'm glad I didn't kill him. He did love her, but he'd screwed up. Anyway, we're not friends. Let's just say we try to work together." It was lame, but true.

Bibi sat back, studying me. "Did you fall for him too?"

I spit out my coffee. Bibi laughed and threw me a towel. We sat in silence for a minute. I'm glad she didn't ask that question again.

Finally, she said, "I don't know why Betty couldn't see through Link. And I don't understand what they found in Kauai. It doesn't make sense."

I liked the way this conversation had turned, like we were two sisters just sitting here drinking coffee and catching up.

Bibi squinted as if trying to figure out something. "I thought maybe Mike, Betty's bodyguard, killed Link in Portland because he threatened Betty in some way. But the Feds said no. Somebody poisoned Link."

I'm glad I didn't tell her that I tried to poison Gerard.

She fingered an earring. "And near where Betty died, they found the bodies of Mike and another man. From ballistics, they determined Mike killed the FBI agent, and Betty killed Mike. But I don't believe that. She admired

Mike, and he not only protected her, but he also respected her."

I wasn't about to tell her the truth.

"So excuse me if I can't trust you," Bibi said, eyeing me, waiting for a reaction.

So much for "just two sisters catching up." That did it. I was sick of trying. I straightened my back, lifted my chin, and put on *my* best tough girl expression.

"Look, Bibi, I've been in hiding for a year. My sister's dead, my husband's dead, I have no home. I don't have my dog, and I want her back. I'm being used by the FBI in a case they would have cleared up a long time ago if my sister and Gerard hadn't fallen in love. And I'm being pursued for the money my sister stole. Now that I'm out of hiding, I'd like to not look over my shoulder all the time."

Bibi pulled the adoption papers over toward her and scanned them again. Her expression turned cold. Damn it. I shouldn't have lost my temper. I needed to engage her again. Plus I wanted to hear her story.

"How did Betty find you?" I asked.

I could tell she was wrestling with whether to tell me. She looked over the adoption papers for much longer than it should have taken. When she did speak, she seemed young again, fragile, tired.

"I was living on the street and crashing at various friends' places." She tugged at the sleeves of her blouse. "My art kept me going, and I did everything possible to keep working. A friend let me use his computer and printer when he wasn't using it." She held up one of the papers to the light, probably to see if it was legal. "What I earned bought frames for the miniatures, and I sold them near the North Market at Faneuil Hall. A friend had a kiosk where she showed a few local artist friends."

A glimmer of a smile passed over her face. "One day, Betty came by and bought all my miniatures, ten of them. That was a good chunk of change. I was able to invest in more frames and get a motel room for the night." She looked up at me. "A few days later, she came back and said, 'You're talented, young and black, and you need a patron to break into the art scene here. Let's talk.'"

Bibi took a deep breath and struggled not to cry. Then she walked over to the dining area, pulled a few of her pieces from a file, and spread them out on the counter in front of me. The miniatures were of black faces and bodies: one of an angry crowd holding sticks and signs, another with naked people dancing, and the last one of stacked, dead, black bodies. That one made me shudder.

"They're powerful."

I'm sure she'd heard this before.

"And you did these digitally? They look like miniature intaglio paintings."

She picked them up to return them to her file. I walked over to the dining room cabinet where her framed photos stood and picked up a picture of an older white couple with a young white boy and a black toddler. "Your adoptive family."

She turned, took the picture from me, and put the photo back on the cabinet.

We were now facing each other, only a few feet apart. Bibi had a scent, amber and woodsy.

"When Betty approached you about being a patron, what did you think at first?"

She eyed me like I was a dimwit. "What do you think I thought? Was this woman hitting on me? Was this woman trafficking? Was this woman serious?"

"How'd you determine she wasn't a predator?"

"I didn't, not for a while. Betty was way too eager. But eager in one of those innocent kinda ways, ya know? She seemed excited. I never had anyone be excited about me and my art. But that could be faked. So I took a male friend with me for our first meeting at her house. She sent a limo to pick me up. When the driver saw my friend, he called Betty, and she said it was fine, let him come."

"What kind of meeting was it?"

"She'd invited some of her wealthy friends to look at my art. I had no idea she was serious about this patron thing."

Bibi directed me back to the kitchen. I sat down. Bibi's shoulders sagged, and her face lost its vibrancy, probably from exhaustion and grief. I felt for her, not just because of her loss, but for what she didn't know about Betty.

"I'm sorry for your loss, Bibi. I wish there were something I could do."

Then I thought of something I could do for her, something that would stand up in court in case the Feds dragged her into the extortionist ring.

"Look, here's a tip to deal with anything that comes up about you with the FBI."

I waited to see if she were listening. She was. "I had clients keep journals of everything that was happening daily. This will be accepted as documentary evidence in court cases or even before it goes to court."

She waited for more.

"Here's the reason. If someone keeps a journal of what has happened to them, it shows their seriousness about their situation, plus it's very hard to fake."

"I doubt it."

"No, it is hard to fake. If it's done on the computer, there's a time stamp associated with it. If it's done by hand, it's easy to see how entries have been written at the same time. A good forensic analysis can tell."

"So what are you saying, start keeping a daily journal?"

"Yes."

"What about what I've been through? That's the important stuff."

"Reconstruct what you can remember and make sure you note that's what you're doing. Believe me, it will help."

She didn't say she would or wouldn't, but I suspected she was considering it.

Bibi pushed a loose hair over her ear. "I'm hungry," was all she said.

From the fridge, she grabbed sandwich fixings, including a bottle of pepperoncini. As she laid out everything in front of me, she asked, "Want a grinder?"

"Sure. Thanks."

She put both guns on the counter behind her. OK, so she didn't trust me yet. Good. She shouldn't, because I didn't trust her fully yet, either. But I was getting there.

33

Finally, we were doing something Sophie and I used to do—stand in the kitchen while we ate and talked. As Bibi told me about her art, I thought of a neuroscience study that found women, when faced with danger or adversity, were all about "tend and befriend," not "fight or flight," and that's what we were doing. For the first time, I felt hopeful.

Then Bibi's phone rang. She stared at it until she wiped her hands on a towel, put both guns back in her waistband, and took the call in the room where she'd kept Otto.

When she came back, she seemed flustered and distracted and pushed the remains of her sub aside.

I asked, "Everything OK?"

"Yeah. Fine." She sure didn't look fine.

To keep her mind off of the call, I returned to our conversation. "Having Betty must have been wonderful for you as an artist. What as a mentor did she expect from you?"

She stumbled through disjointed answers. "To get a degree from the Boston School of Fine Arts." She picked a small piece of onion from the sub and put it in her mouth.

Her mind was clearly not on what she was saying. "I had to learn to drive ... ah, oh, and elocution lessons. We went to plays and museums." She stared off into the distance. "I also had chores—I had to clean my room." Her chuckle turned into a sniffle. She whispered, "I miss her."

"Why elocution lessons?" I wondered if the phone call had something to do with Betty.

"Betty had big plans for me. She wanted me to lose my Boston accent, the rough stuff. She said art collectors would have more respect for me and that I'd be more acceptable to the upper class where the money was."

I had my doubts about that. I'd bet Betty just wanted Bibi not to embarrass her. The woman always had her own agenda.

"Betty sounds like she cared a great deal about you," I said, hoping Bibi would see that I respected how much their relationship meant to her. Maybe she would confide in me, not that it would happen this soon. I was building trust as I did with former clients.

Her gaze came back to me. "I told her I didn't want to refer to her as 'my patron,' so *she* suggested I call her my godmother. I could go with that. But she had big expectations for me. She wanted me to become 'a great artist.'" She laughed, one of those sad laughs. "No pressure."

This time I could hear my mom in that laugh, and I choked back a sob.

"Yeah, no pressure there," I said, chuckling, feeling she was opening up to me.

"Right? That did nothing but scare me." She turned to the condiments cupboard, took down a bottle of olive oil, and drizzled it along her sub. "Surviving on the streets gave my art an edge. With all of Betty's luxuries and support, I was afraid I'd lose that edge. But she seemed to need me as much as I needed her. She used to pull me to her and kiss my forehead. She was quite lovable when she wanted to be."

That was hard to believe. Betty? Lovable?

Bibi pulled back her shoulders. Her mouth hardened, and her eyes narrowed. She must have noticed the disbelief on my face.

"I'm not naive about her weaknesses." She shot me a sideways glance. "She attracted the wrong kind of people, Link being one of them. He was there before me. It was still hard to keep my mouth shut."

She took another bite of her sandwich and licked mustard from a finger.

I leaned back against the counter. "What was Betty's business or profession?" I needed some inkling as to how much Bibi knew.

She hesitated. After glancing at her cell again, she said, "You mean, how did she get so rich?"

"No. I don't care about that." I ate the last bite of my sub while watching her face. "I was just curious as to what she did. As a woman, I'm always curious as to how we live and what we do. It's tough out there."

Bibi picked up our plates and put them in the sink.

When she turned around, she sat on the stool and leaned on the counter. "From what I understand, Betty had family money that she put into investments and working international money exchanges. Do you know what that means? Those are code words for putting investments and business gains into tax shelters. Good ol' corrupt Boston."

"Good ol' corrupt world."

She smiled.

Betty had done a decent job at covering up the real "business" venture. At least in Bibi's mind. But was Bibi really kept out of the loop, or was she covering?

"I was so busy going to school I had little time to pay attention to what was going on at home with Betty. It didn't matter anyway. It was none of my business."

I found that hard to believe, but as my—our—mom would frequently say, time would tell.

"So you're certain Betty wasn't involved with the extortion scheme."

She almost choked. "How the hell would I know?"

"Listen, I'm just trying to get all the info I can. This whole thing, all the connections, the damned FBI—I didn't ask to be in this movie." I stopped. "But then again, if all this hadn't happened, I would have never found you." I smiled, trying to show how much she could mean to me.

We were both wound up tight, and I didn't want that. I wanted us to start building a relationship. I wiped my sweaty palms on my slacks. Bibi hadn't even asked where her twin was yet. I dreaded that.

Another phone call. This time Bibi didn't answer.

"Are you sure you're OK?"

"Whether this whole thing is real or not, everything— and I mean everything—comes with a downside."

Damn. Had she read my mind?

"What was your downside?" I asked.

This time her face took on an expression of what I can only describe as fierce hatred. She tapped her phone. "Betty's new girlfriend. Real. Bad. News."

She sucked in air and blew it out through her teeth. Whoa, a new piece of info.

"Who was she? Is that who called you?"

"A piece of shit, that's who. After she came on the scene, they were in bed all the time. I mean *all* the time. And they made a lot of noise. I get it. I understand being crazy about someone." She rolled her eyes. "But after a week of not seeing her, I came home early one day, hoping to talk to her, and caught them snorting something off the glass coffee table. Then I saw the brick of coke next to them. I lost it. I yelled at them both, called Shawn a cunt, and told her to get out. She just laughed at me. I appealed to Betty, but she just looked at me, glassy-eyed, and said I was overreacting."

"Was she selling?"

"With a brick sitting on the table? What do you think?"

"Maybe that's why she died," I said, happy to have something else to explain Betty's death.

"No doubt. After Betty died, I found out that Shawn had given her a phony name. I tried to track her down, but couldn't. The bitch disappeared."

"But she's back again?"

She nodded and pulled at her earring again. "That was Betty's housekeeper who called. I kept her on as I'm not sure what I'm going to do with the house. She told me Shawn had showed up looking for me."

"Shawn doesn't know about this place does she?"

"No. Only Betty's big house on Winnipesaukee. But I know that cunt. She'll find out."

"Then you need to get to a safe place."

Shawn sounded like bad news. No wonder Betty had so much coke with her in Kauai. She'd been getting sloppy with it too, like offering it to me.

"Did you have a falling out with Betty before she left?"

"No. She left me a note saying she'd be back in a week or so."

"Where was Shawn while Betty was gone?"

"Don't know. Mike told me that Shawn didn't go with Betty. That's why I thought Betty might have gone there to dry out."

Behind Bibi, out the back window, headlights scanned

the driveway. The black SUV was back. It parked along the road. Shit.

Bibi didn't notice as she had her back to the window. "Even Link tried to get her to stop," she said. "A few days before she left, I overheard him say to her, 'You'll lose everything if you keep putting that shit up your nose.'"

"So he knew about it?"

"He was her financial manager. I figured he was worried that Betty and Shawn were snorting the profits. Then she started keeping her bedroom door locked, even from me."

Bibi was a tough, but she'd been through a whole lot of crap. I had to admire her.

"Was it Betty's idea to buy this place for you?"

"No. She wanted to give me the house on Winnipesaukee. We'd go there in the summer like lots of city people do, but it was too massive and not my style. Plus, I didn't want to live among all those wealthy white people. I told her I'd rather have a small house on a small lake so I could escape, do my art, and be left alone."

"What do you mean 'be left alone?'"

"When Shawn and the coke showed up, the Winnipesaukee house became a party house. Too much traffic was going on at Betty's house in Boston. It was impossible to be alone and quiet, and I didn't want to be around the drugs. I'd seen too much of that on the street, not coke as it was too expensive, but meth."

Since this girlfriend Shawn was not only into drugs but had used a phony name, she'd been up to something else besides the drugs. Maybe Gerard could turn his attention to *that*.

"Betty once told me if anything happened to her to come here. The cops and feds would want to talk to me about her business dealings. She said not to worry, just let her lawyers deal with it."

"Did you go to Kauai?"

"Yes, I tried to find her."

Funny. I hadn't heard that from Gerard. Thankfully, Bibi and I never ran into each other.

"Was that before or after Hastrick was found murdered?"

"How do you know about that?"

Her eyes were puffy and bloodshot. The coffee had gone cold. I repeated what I told her earlier. "I worked with an environmental activist group on Kauai. We knew about The Grim Reaper, but he wasn't part of our group."

I checked the black SUV. Still there. Son-of-a-bitch.

"Bibi, excuse me a minute. That black SUV is back. I've had enough of this shit."

I grabbed my raincoat, walked out the back door, and approached the SUV.

34

I motioned for the driver to roll down the window. He did. It was Gerard.

"So what the hell do you think you're doing, Ang?"

I looked past him. He was alone.

"Take a wild guess." I shoved my hands into my jacket pockets. "Were those your thugs who came to the house?"

"They're FBI, yes. But there are two others posing as FBI."

"So what are you doing here?"

"You and I had a deal. You broke our agreement."

I snorted and rolled my eyes. "Gerard, does everything have to go your way? This is my sister. My *sister*. Get it? Could you just back off and give me some time with her?"

He put two cigarettes in his mouth, lit both, and handed one to me. It tasted good.

"Look, Ang, I know what this sister means to you. I get it. But honestly, you don't know if she's clean or not. Even we don't. Get in the van. You're getting wet."

I hadn't noticed the light rainfall. Back at the house, Bibi was standing at the window. I waved and made a motion that it was OK. But if she locked me out, I wouldn't blame her. "What do you want, Gerard?"

"I want to make sure you're safe."

I took a deep drag and weighed my options.

"I'm going back in the house. From what I've heard from Bibi, I don't believe she's involved or knows about the extortion. I think she believes it has something to do with cocaine. You need to check out Betty's girlfriend and coke buddy, Shawn. I only have her first name. Bibi hated her and said she really messed up Betty. I know Betty was into coke because she used it in front of me on Kauai."

Gerard didn't say anything. His expression didn't change. He continued to smoke.

"Did you know about Shawn? Have you tracked her down?"

He didn't answer. So I came in with the one-two punch.

"By the way, Gerard, you got it wrong. Bibi wasn't Betty's lover. Betty was her patron. Bibi considered Betty her godmother." I paused. "And did you know that Bibi went to Kauai looking for Betty?"

Now I had his attention.

"That's it," I said. "You're welcome."

He shook his head as if I didn't understand. "Watch your back."

That did it. "Fuck, Gerard!" I blew out a plume of smoke. "How am I supposed to watch my back if you're not clueing me in about what to watch for? Look, no more goons bothering Bibi. You'll find out soon enough if she's involved."

"Yes, but will you? You're acting pretty sure of yourself."

"She's spooked. She's scared. Quit sending white males to check on her." My voice lowered. "Don't you have a few people of color to do surveillance?"

"If we put two colored men in a black SUV here in New

Hampshire, it would draw attention, and not the right kind of attention."

I snorted. "Then mix it up, you dope! Put a person of color and a white guy in a tan Prius. The black SUVs are nothing but an ego crate for you guys."

He reached out to me, but I backed up. "Ang, you don't know everything that's going on. We're doing our job. Please, go back inside," he said. "You're getting soaked." He finished his cigarette, squeezed the lit portion out the window, and threw the filter into something in the cab. I noticed the smokes were Canadian.

When I reached the back door, Gerard drove off. I knocked on the door. Bibi opened it, gun in hand. Otto growled.

35

"Inside. Hurry up." She waved me over to a stool. "Who was that?"

I'd lost any fear, probably because I was tired of being understanding. I was just plain pissed off.

"That was *the* Gerard Duvernet, the FBI agent whom I've been helping. He's upset with me for coming here and not doing what we agreed to. I told him I don't care, that finding my sister was more important than his mission."

"How do I know that's what you were—"

"Bibi! I *am* your sister. I can use Gerard. He told me those goons who came to the door *were* FBI, and they're responsible for your safety. But you do have two other men posing as agents and trailing you."

"First, you don't need to protect me. And if you're so good at protecting me, why'd those *goons* come to the door?"

"They saw my rental car in the driveway, ran a check, and came to the door to identify me and make sure you were safe. Then they reported to Gerard." Now Gerard's words of caution made me ask, "So you knew nothing about Link and the organized crime group?"

Bibi banged her fist on the counter. "I told you. I knew nothing until after Betty died. She told me he managed her business affairs. But with her dying and Mike being shot and an FBI agent killed—"

"His name was Gus, Bibi. William Augustus Martin. He was a good guy. He got killed so that I wouldn't."

"You knew him?" Her voice lowered. She held the gun on the counter, but now she pulled it closer.

"Gerard put him on my tail to protect me." I wasn't sure it was Gerard who did it, but why complicate things even more?

"That didn't go well, did it? Another FBI fuck-up."

Now I wanted to slap her. "Look, lighten up. You have protection. Gerard doesn't want anything happening to either of us."

She squinted at me. Maybe that was the wrong thing to say. It *did* sound like I was in cahoots with him. I figured she needed to know more.

"Link's crime group had my sister steal millions from my husband's business. But instead of giving it to them, she stashed it someplace only she could access. Even after Link died, Gerard said the crime group was still active and wanted their money. *Their* money. Ha." This time I smacked the counter. "So do you see why I'm a little upset too?"

I could tell Bibi was having a tough time keeping it together. I couldn't blame her. It was horrific and, if she weren't involved, she'd be wondering what was real and what wasn't. Why would she take my word for anything?

"OK," she said. "So we're both in similar situations. They're after you, and whoever killed Betty is probably after me."

"Have you met with Betty's lawyer yet?"

She pulled on an earlobe and the earring dangling

there. "I thought Betty went to Kauai because she needed time away. I hoped she'd gone to get off the coke. Then she disappeared. Maybe Ralph and Rena, the two people who took over the business, killed Link, Betty, and Mike."

"Do you know them? The Boston Duo?"

"The Boston Duo? Who calls them that?"

"The FBI."

"That's pathetic."

"That's what I told Gerard."

Bibi poured her cold coffee down the sink and poured more scotch. "Yes, I knew them. They were at the house on and off. Betty told me they worked for her. They were relatives. They'd been with her for a long time. So I guess she lied about not being involved." She thought about that for a moment. "But I *knew* everything she did wasn't kosher. You couldn't do business around Boston without being somewhat ... you know."

"Crooked?"

She shifted from leg to leg. "Betty said she wanted to make as much money as possible for my sake. She wanted me to 'make art 'til the sun don't shine.' I laughed, thinking how cute she was. I guess that was selfish, not wanting to think about what that meant or where the money came from." She looked down at her hands.

"Were you involved with any part of the crime business?"

She hesitated, and that made me watch every move, every facial muscle, every shift of her eyes and hands. What I saw was resignation.

"I know they suspect me of being involved."

Interesting. She didn't answer the question. I pushed. "Were you?"

She pulled back her shoulders and looked me in the eye. "If you have to ask that, you can leave."

When she picked up her scotch and downed it, I noticed her hand trembling. Shit.

"Right now, I don't trust anyone, not even you." She sounded defensive.

"I get it. I don't trust anyone either. With me, it's something that has to be earned." That wasn't true, of course. Sometimes I went on my gut, like with Snoop and Iolana.

Her eyes welled with tears. I needed to be more sensitive. Maybe she did know about Betty's activities and chose to ignore it. Still, right now, I cared more about keeping our tenuous sister bond. I waited to see what she'd do next.

She moved toward the gun, and I froze. But then she pushed it to the edge of the counter. She poured a shot of scotch for me, another for her, and lifted her glass. "Here's to Betty." I had no choice but to join her. "To Betty," I said. I downed the brown liquor and wiped my mouth with the back of my hand, feeling every bit the Judas.

36

Enough had been said about Betty, Link, the FBI, Mike, and every other piece of shit business.

Then the inevitable bomb dropped. "So are you pissed off at Sophie for getting you into the mess and stealing the money? Is that why she didn't come?" Bibi asked.

"No." My voice cracked. I cleared my throat. "She died."

Bibi clutched her throat. It was if she was feeling her twin's pain from hanging, and she didn't even know yet how she'd died.

I stumbled over my next words. "I ... I'm so sorry. I feel rotten giving you this, then having to take it away. Well, not all of it. I'm still your sister. But Sophie, your twin, was ... I don't know what to say." My mouth felt dry. I slugged back the scotch.

What a cruel joke.

Bibi covered her face. She gulped as if she were choking. I closed my eyes, hoping I wouldn't fall apart. Watching Bibi's struggle made me physically weak like I hadn't eaten in days. She clutched her throat again. Finally she said, "What happened?"

So I told her.

"Do you have a picture of her?"

I looked through my phone's photos and sent Bibi a few. She sat down, and as she looked through them, tears fell. She kept swiping them away, struggling to see Sophie's pictures. When she was done, she dabbed her face on a kitchen towel and turned her phone over on the counter, as if to shut out the pictures.

"I don't think I ever had one of those twin things, you know, the feeling that something was missing in me, a sense that there was another me out there." She laughed. "Oh, my god, how could I? She's white!" She looked through the photos again. Finally, she said, "She's beautiful. Did she know she looked like Marilyn Monroe?"

I shrugged. "Beauty isn't always a gift."

Bibi rubbed her arms and snuffled. "Do you have videos?"

"Of course." I started to send one, but Bibi stopped me.

"Don't. I can't take anymore."

I thought about how much loss she'd experienced, how much I had given and taken away within a minute. But how else could I have done it? "I'm so sorry, Bibi. Really. It's been horrific." I paused. "I can empathize. I lost my profession, my sister, *and* my husband. Then my home and identity. All I can offer you is an older sister who will stand by you and help you any way I can."

But that nagging little voice inside muttered, *Hypocrite.* Could I really keep her safe? I hadn't for Sophie.

I could feel her emotionally pulling away and wanted to go over and hold her, but I knew it was too soon. "What can I do?"

Seconds passed. Then Bibi said, "I'd like you to go now. I'd like to be alone."

My gun was still on her side of the counter. I pointed to it. Bibi pushed it over to me. I put it in my bag. Bibi looked empty, exhausted. I walked over to hug her, but she backed away. Otto growled. I said goodbye and headed to the door, but stopped and looked back. She had squatted down and was forehead to forehead with the dog. My chest filled, my eyes watered, and I wondered if I'd ever see her again.

37

The ride back to Paugus Bay was a struggle. After I passed Shooters, the booze hit. I leaned forward, gripping the steering wheel, drunk and flooded with memories of calm nights by the lake, the smell of bonfires, the call of loons, the twinkle of fireflies. During the day, mating dragonflies would crawl up my arm, the lilacs would over-power me with their scent, and Dad once guided us in a canoe on the quiet water just after dawn. Mom and I used to walk the old woods, the ground soft and spongy. She taught me not to pick the wild, endangered Lady Slipper.

When I was little and we camped out by a lake, I once saw her and Dad go skinny-dipping when they thought I was asleep. They seemed to be so much in love. Mom giggled, and Dad kissed her. Their bodies were young and lit by the moon.

A melancholy came over me. So many people lost, gone. I could empathize with Bibi. I wondered if knowing about and finding Bibi was worth it. I often thought of what Dad used to say: "Ignorance is bliss." What if I'd never heard about Bibi?

I took the new highway that cuts through dense woods like a scar. My heart felt like that, surgically divided between the old and new. Driving this road in my state of inebriation, feeling what it was like here during my childhood, made me long for the life I'd made in Eugene. But that no longer existed either.

Maybe, if I could spend time with Bibi at her house, our feet dangling from the dock, sun on our faces, the lake laid out before us, I would remember, and she would be part of those memories. We could tell each other stories, share our histories until they melded and we had a past together.

My hands gripped so tightly to the steering wheel, I had to shake them out one at a time. This visit was taking a toll. Maybe I shouldn't have come. Perhaps it was selfish of me to show up and disrupt Bibi's life. What had Bibi gained by knowing she had a sister who died? Had I told her Sophie had hanged herself? I couldn't remember. And what about me, a stranger, claiming to be sister who wants to get to know her? I mean, what the hell?

Wait, where was I? I pulled off onto the shoulder. Somewhere I had made a wrong turn. But I hadn't turned, had I? Around me, the woods kept an unbroken line. Not a single light shone. My heart raced. Sure, I was drunk, but now I felt sick.

When I looked in the rearview mirror, I saw headlights approaching. I locked the car and slipped down in the seat.

But the vehicle drove past.

I shook myself and smacked my face, then fumbled for my phone, found it, and GPS told me my mistake. I gave it the address of my cottage, and when I was steady enough to drive, I followed the directions.

When I pulled up to the cottage, I almost cried. So what if I took a wrong turn? I struggled up the stairs, my mind racing, and unlocked the door. My hand shook as I poured a glass of scotch. No, I couldn't drink anymore. As I tried to pour it back into the bottle, the glass slipped and dropped onto the counter, not breaking but spilling the liquor everywhere. After mopping it up the best I could, I grabbed a blanket and flipped on the TV.

"Please let me pass out," I said to the room.

Curling up on the couch, blanket to chin, I clicked through the channels. The more I surfed, the worse the programming.

I stopped at an ad for a new series about three women. The theme music was "Tainted Love."

"Can you believe that? It's your song, Sophie," I said aloud.

"It's OK, Ang," she said. "We'll watch it together." She held a glass of wine and pointed to the screen. "Look! It's a comedy about women who kill. That should be fun."

I turned to face her. She wore that damn blue dress. "Hey, Sis, are you all right? Are you happy wherever you are?"

"Of course. Why wouldn't I be?"

Then she was gone, and I was stinko. I clutched the blanket. Now my sister's song would be everywhere. I shut off the TV. Between the coffee, spicy sandwich, and scotch at Bibi's, my stomach roiled.

I was blotto. I needed fresh air. I filled a glass with water and went out on the deck.

Something bothered me, even through the alcoholic haze. Something. ... That's what it was. While talking with Kathleen, I'd realized I couldn't remember my parents' funeral. What had she said? I drank some water. What was it? Oh, she'd said my Mom's parents hadn't come. I set the glass down on the floor and rubbed my face. Glancing up at Paugus Bay, I pictured standing at the water's edge some-where, holding my sister with Kathleen's arm around my shoulder. I know my parents were cremated. But where were their ashes? I fumbled in my pocket for my phone and called her.

"Hon, we scattered their ashes out over the lake near where you lived. Are you OK? You sound a little … tipsy."

"Why can't I remember, Kathleen? Why can't I remember any of that?"

Silence.

"Please tell me."

"Angeline, you were … very drunk that day."

Just like now. I leaned on the railing. "Did I talk? Did I say anything? Did I. …"

"You blamed yourself for their death. You cried so much, you almost choked. I took you and Sophie back to my place and stayed with you. You kept saying if you'd stayed in touch more, if you'd come back once in a while, if you'd … well, words to that effect. You were inconsolable."

I wiped my eyes with the hem of my shirt. "I don't even remember any of that. It was like it didn't happen. I don't even remember not remembering."

"Hon, I think you should rest. You sound—"

"Drunk."

"Yes."

"Angeline, you are not to blame for the deaths. They were two very dysfunctional people, damaged somehow. You were a wonderful daughter and sister to Sophie. Please, let this be the beginning of some healing and—"

"Thank you, Kathleen."

But I'm not sure she heard me because I stumbled to the

door to get inside, dropped my phone, and almost fell. But someone took my arm, startling me, making me cry out.

"It's OK, Ang. It's me, Gerard. Let me help you."

I turned. "What the hell?"

"Let's get you into bed before you fall and break something."

"Stop stalking me!" I choked and felt my head spin. I tripped on the threshold. I schlorshed water down my front. I somehow had grabbed the water glass.

Gerard gripped and maneuvered me toward the bedroom. I remember putting the glass down very carefully on the counter as we passed the kitchen. Somehow the only thing I could think of as I collapsed on the bed was how pathetic I was. So drunk I couldn't remember my own parents' funeral. The last thing I saw was Gerard's face leaning over mine.

In the morning, when I woke, the sun shone brightly through the blind slats. The bedroom door was closed. I sat up too fast and felt the stab of a migraine. Next to me on the nightstand was a glass of water and two aspirins. I took them. Then I noticed I was out of my day clothes and in my nightclothes. Suddenly, I was fully awake. Had he undressed and dressed me?

I recalled calling Kathleen. I needed to call her back to tell her I was fine other than a massive headache. And somehow, I remembered everything she told me. Maybe I'd become adept at drinking and remembering. I'd had enough practice.

I needed coffee. When I opened the bedroom door, light filled the room. I squinted. Two windows were open for air, and I smelled something I couldn't describe until I realized it was the lake. I checked the door. It was locked.

I shuffled to the coffee maker. It was ready to go. I pushed the button.

On the high cafe table, I found a note.

"Call me when you're awake. G."

"Sure thing," I said aloud, hearing the words bang in my head. I found my phones, one on the table, one in my hand-bag. Both were low on juice. I plugged them in. It was ten-forty-five. I'd slept all that time? Crap.

After I drank a cup of coffee, I poured a second one, trying to get my brain engaged. I ran my hands over my breasts and stomach. So what if Gerard saw me naked? Big deal. But seeing me so drunk embarrassed me. I remembered his face looking down at me. Drunks are not pretty things. So what? What did I care?

Part of me cared. My pelvis area thrummed. Traitor.

I had to admit it. I sipped my coffee. I was a little turned on.

After my second cup of coffee, I picked up Gerard's note and laughed off what could have happened last night. If he got a good look at me naked, that should turn off any kind of sexual attraction. After Sophie, I'd look like an old mare.

I needed to see Bibi. I worried about Bibi. I was sure she was confused and upset. Screw Gerard. If he had news, he would have said so. I'd call him on the road.

After getting dressed, eating a protein bar, taking more aspirin, and locking the cottage, I headed out. When I called Gerard, he picked up on the first ring. "How are you feeling this morning?" he asked.

"Rough."

"I have news. Meet me at Restaurant 99. I'll buy you a lobster roll."

"News? What news? I'm headed to Bibi's."

"Ang, you're going to want to know this. See you in twenty." And he hung up.

Did all FBI agents have such bad manners? I wanted to

call Bibi, but I'd wait. Better to just show up and talk more, face-to-face.

My stomach was in knots from last night, from the booze, and worrying about Bibi. Plus, being undressed when I was unconscious, the legalese being "intent to molest." I would try to act like it was nothing, but really I was pissed. But why be pissed? I was the one who got so drunk I couldn't remember anything. I had to blow it off.

The chain restaurant at the mall outlet on the way to Tilton didn't sound like the kind of place you could get a decent lobster roll.

At the restaurant, Gerard sat in a corner booth with wine in hand, chatting up a waitress. I approached, probably smirking. He saw me and waved. The waitress looked disappointed.

I slid into the booth. "So, what's the news?"

"Ah, you Americans. Always in a hurry."

"Oh, don't play that game, Gerard. Besides, according to you, you're half American."

"Yes, the top half," he said, then laughed.

"Very funny."

"How's your head?"

"Thanks for the aspirin."

"You're welcome."

"Do I have to eat first before I hear the news?"

"That would be nice."

"I'm not looking for nice. I'm looking to move on with my life."

Gerard sipped his wine while watching me closely. I may have blushed. "Ang, not that you asked—or ever would— but you undressed yourself and were sound asleep in bed by the time I wrote the note and prepped the coffee."

I didn't say anything, but I felt my shoulders relax.

"You look nice today."

I rolled my eyes. "I wish you hadn't said that because I know it's a lie."

The waitress was suddenly there, smiling at him and ignoring me. He ordered lobster rolls for both of us and coffee for me. A gallon might get me up to speed. I asked him questions about Bibi, some I already knew the answers to. We managed small talk. When the lobster rolls came, I stared down at them.

I hadn't had one of these—well, not since after my parents' funeral. There were a few things you'd eat when you're in New England that aren't available on the West Coast—full-body clams, flakey onion rings, and lobster rolls. But my stomach was still a mess, and I wasn't sure it could handle the rich seafood.

Time for business. "OK, so you said you have 'a protective watch' on Bibi. Any evidence of her involvement in Betty and Link's enterprise?"

His mouth was full. He shook his head. I took a bite of my lobster roll and realized I was starving. It was delicious. I ate half of it before I stopped to pick up my coffee mug. The heat felt good on my hands.

"OK, out with it. What do you have?"

He swallowed and dabbed his napkin against his mouth. "We have new findings. We arrested two men for killing Steven Hastrick."

I set down my coffee. "But why did *you* arrest them? Why didn't local law enforcement arrest them?"

"It's not a local issue. We suspected the men were hired to kill him, so we worked with the locals. The men talked. Our suspicions were corroborated. The murder became part of our investigation."

"Who hired them?"

He paused for effect before saying, "We think, but have no proof, it's Betty's successors, Ralph and Rena."

I leaned forward and scanned his face, looking for an explanation. Then it clicked. "Of course!" I smacked the table. "If they could get rid of Hastrick, Bibi would inherit."

He leaned back in that slow, sexy, relaxed way he had and tilted his head, looking positively full of himself. "*C'est vrai*. Correct."

I wanted to say *I know what* c'est vrai *means, asshole.* But screw it. I drummed the table with my spoon, processing all this. Bibi was going to be one rich woman by the time the legal shit was straightened out. "Damn. This new crew is really merciless."

"It wasn't just them. Betty first put together the hit. She wanted revenge for Bibi. But she never got to it. She died before she could arrange the hit in Kauai. You distracted her. You were a surprise."

"Killing someone for your goddaughter? That's one scary godmother."

"Yes," he said. "The Godmother, the Movie."

I chuckled. The Frenchman made a joke. "OK, this looks simple on the surface, but why would *she* go to Hawaii? She could have handled it from Boston, had her henchman do it, or hired someone to do it. Why put herself at risk?"

"We don't know—unless she was really after you. Mike followed you, remember? The other explanation is that she didn't have connections there. So she had to be there to find a way to get rid of him without raising flags. No one on the island knew he had a major inheritance. He had a piece of land, but no one knew his real name. Because he was considered homeless, no one cared to look into him. Everyone just considered him—what do you call it?—a weirdo?"

"But how could she possibly cover up murdering him?"

"Betty was clever. Here's what I've pieced together. She did her research and recognized how heated the environmental issue was on Kauai."

The waitress came over and filled our water glasses.

"Betty played up to a local environmental leader and extremist, advocating for a visible and extreme incident that could be blamed on one of the GMO transnational companies. What was the sacrifice of one man when these four companies were poisoning Kauai and killing his people?"

The waitress came back and asked if we needed anything else, directing the question at Gerard. I gave her the stink eye. She moved on. Gerard didn't seem to notice.

"Betty had money. She'd pay for one or two men willing to get rid of someone for a fee. The idea was to plant evidence pointing to one of the companies—Dow, BASF, Syngenta, or DuPont."

I snorted. "As if any of these companies need to get rid of one pesky activist." My heart thumped hard against my ribcage. Sadly, I had an idea whom Betty first contacted. Aisake was the leader of the environmental activist group I had done legal research for. He was Iolana's friend. I wasn't going to mention his name in case it wasn't him. "Who was it?"

"Aisake Thompson. You knew him, correct?"

My head still hurt, and I drank some water. A mosquito bite on my leg itched, and I scratched it. All these Kauai events and tie-in were tough to follow with a hangover.

"OK, that explains possibilities for why Betty was on Kauai. So she organized a hit on The Grim Reaper, and she also took a cabin near me because her henchman Mike had followed me."

"We think so. Or before Link died he let her know you were headed for Kauai."

"No, it was Betty's henchman, Mike. Link didn't know where I was going. Wait." I was remembering the cliff, Betty and her gun, me close to the edge. Yes, that was it. "Betty told me it was Mike. She did have him follow me." I rubbed my temples. The lobster roll wasn't sitting well on my stomach. I closed my eyes, wondering what else I was forgetting. When I looked up, Gerard squinted at me as if concerned or trying to read my mind or both. "OK, so Betty was dead. Then I moved up into the hills of Kauai. Then who was it who tried to kill my dog? Still Betty and Link's gang? The Boston Duo who took over?"

"The same man whom Betty hired and one of the men who killed The Grim Reaper. He's the one we have in custody."

"That's good. You've caught one of them at least."

"He told us who his partner was. He's singing like a canary."

I snorted. Couldn't help it. "Now you sound like a famous forties movie actor."

"I hoped that would make you smile."

"So, what about my dog?"

"Betty somehow found this guy for hire after she arrived in Kauai. He was paid to kill Hastrick, but not until she went home. Of course, she never made it home. Later, the Boston Duo hooked up with him and hired him to kill your dog and to kill Hastrick. I imagine Ralph and Rena knew about the money you held, and killing the dog was supposed to scare you into handing it over to them. After that, they planned to get rid of you, too, according to Betty's wishes. She was not a good loser."

I had to think about that. It all sounded too pat. Something wasn't right.

"What was Gus doing on Kauai? What was his purpose?"

"To protect you."

I stared into my coffee. Damn. That's what I'd told Bibi.

"Are you sure Gus was there to protect me? I thought that was your job."

"Not officially."

I kept my eye on him. He had a good poker face.

"We were investigating the crime group. We knew you were extorting your Ashley Madison dates. Still, with your sister involved in the crime group, we wanted to keep an eye on you for that, not that petty extortion you were doing. Gus was supposed to keep an eye on you and keep you out of our way. But he didn't."

"Well, too fucking bad. It happens to be my life, you know?"

"Angeline, if Gus hadn't been there, you probably would have been killed. Betty had to put Mike on Gus, so that left her to take care of you."

I sighed and picked at the remainder of my lobster. "I liked Gus."

"Everyone did. He was a different breed."

I was glad to hear that and smiled, remembering his bad Liverpool accent and the crazy 60s outfit he wore for our Ashley Madison rendezvous at the Hotel Vintage.

I swallowed hard. "Now what? Betty is dead. With the arrest of this guy and his info about Ralph and Rena shouldn't that close the case?"

"We need some kind of financial records to prove their criminal activities. I don't think we'll find out anything more from this guy. He's just a thug hired out for cash."

We ate in silence, or I should say he ate in silence. I asked for a box to go.

Finally, he said, "What do you plan to do with Bibi?"

"What do you mean?"

"Take her back to Oregon, or you move here? I hope you're not asking her questions about Betty. I hope you haven't given her any info."

"What would I give her? She's already scared that you're going to arrest her for being a member of the crime group. She just wants to do her art and grieve over her losses."

"So you told her about Sophie."

"Had to. She was Bibi's twin."

Gerard nodded. "Was she pleased that you're her sister?"

"No. When I told Bibi about Sophie, she fell apart." I swallowed hard. "It was awful. Bibi's hands flew to her neck as if she were in pain, as if she could feel a rope tighten around *her* neck."

Gerard lost his cheery veneer. His face went gray, and he hid his hands under the table. Then his phone buzzed. He picked it up, looked at caller ID, and said, "Excuse me." He left, heading toward the men's room.

I finished my coffee. A little while later, I called the waitress over.

"May I have the check please?"

"Your dining companion paid it. Is there anything else I can bring you?"

When Gerard didn't return, I figured he'd received an important call or done a runner. Too much to picture Sophie hanging in that blue dress. I wondered how much guilt he felt, how much he'd grieved over her, how that grief manifested with him.

I left the restaurant and headed to Bibi's, forgetting to take my leftovers.

Bibi's house was shuttered and locked. Her car was gone. I walked around the house twice, looking for life. No dog barking. No car. Blinds pulled.

Had she fled? Had someone kidnapped her? Or had the FBI arrested her?

The only place that didn't have blinds was the dining room. I peered in. The dining room table was empty, as was the cabinet behind the table. No photos, no art pieces. Shut up like a summer home.

If she'd been kidnapped or the FBI had arrested her, her laptop would be gone, but her personal photos, art, printer, and paper would still be there. The place would also be a mess after they'd rifled through everything.

I kicked the side of the house.

"God damn it!"

Bibi must have packed up and split on her own. But why?

I needed to think. At the end of the pier, I dropped down, lit a cigarette, hugged my knees, and stared out over the cold lake.

B ack at my cottage, I opened my empty suitcase on the bed and stared at it. I had no idea what to do. I called Gerard every fifteen minutes with no luck. I grew more suspicious with each call. What was he up to? Why did he do a runner at the restaurant? Was it due to guilt about Sophie when I talked about her suicide? Maybe.

Or was *he* in trouble? Who had called him?

I imagined Gerard dead. I plopped down on the bed and cried. Like a broken water main, the tears wouldn't stop. It wasn't just Gerard. I was exhausted, the fight drained away. All I'd wanted was a connection with my one remaining sister.

Sure we were worlds apart. But couldn't Bibi and I learn to love each other, find some common ground?

I wiped my face dry in the bathroom. A chill shook my body, and on the verge of being sick, I leaned over the sink. Five gallons of coffee and rich lobster on a hangover stomach? What was I thinking?

I looked in the mirror. I didn't look like either of my

sisters. Maybe Mom had had several partners while in Boston. Perhaps none of us were Dad's.

What if that were true? I felt a ping in my chest. I needed to get a DNA test.

After guzzling a glass of water and brushing my hair, I packed. I'd visit Kathleen first before taking a flight out tomorrow. Maybe she'd remembered more. Maybe she'd remembered more details about Mom's escape to Boston. But Kathleen had said Mom didn't talk to her about that.

A knock on the door swung me around and set my nerves clanging.

Oh, my god. Gerard.

I was so afraid for him while full of anger for him leaving without a word, I opened the door and swung a fist at him, connecting with his chin. He jumped back.

"Ang, easy. Desolé. I'm sorry. I—"

"What the hell happened to you? Don't you care about anyone else? You left me in the restaurant, and I had no idea what happened. And where the hell is Bibi? What have you done with her?"

He looked puzzled. "What? What do you mean?"

"Where are your two goons who were supposed to be protecting her?"

"What are you talking about?"

"Bibi! Who the hell do you think I'm talking about? Bibi's gone."

"Are you sure she's not there and not just at the store?"

"Of course I am. The dog's gone, so is Bibi's computer and all her personal things."

He pushed past me into the cottage, pulled out his cell, held up a finger, and made a call.

I couldn't hear much but a "Yes," and *"Tres bien,* good."

Then "OK," and "Let me know." He hung up and turned to me.

"Bibi is fine. She's back in Boston. She's decided to cooperate with us and tell us everything she knows."

"So she's safe?"

"Yes."

"What about the Boston Duo?"

"They left town. We held them for forty-eight hours but had to let them go."

His cell rang again. He answered. "OK," and "Yes," and "Good." He smiled. "A female and male operative are there protecting her. Plus, she's answering questions right now."

I swallowed hard. I hated to think of Bibi in the middle of this if she was innocent.

"Can I see her? I'd like to speak to her again."

"I suggest you use FaceTime or Skype, but *after* she's done answering our questions."

"She's going to feel alone. And scared."

"She called a friend who is with her. The friend will spend the night until she's no longer in danger."

I felt a twinge of envy. Of course she had friends. I looked outside at another storm brewing.

"Where's your phone?" he asked.

I took it from my shoulder bag and handed it to him. He touched a few spots on both his and my phone then gave it back. "That's Bibi's cell and contact info."

I tucked my hair behind my ear. "Merci."

He smiled. "Look, I'll go get us some clams and onion rings, and maybe salad?"

I didn't want all that fried food. "Pick up some clam chowder for me."

After he was gone, I changed my clothes. My hands

shook. I needed to get my mental shit together. I crossed the street to the deck that hung over Paugus Bay. In an Adirondack chair, my head back and eyes closed, I let the breeze muss my hair and cool not only my face but my temper. I was pissed at Gerard, at his constant messing with me.

The breeze brushed over me, and I concentrated on Mom, here at one of the lakes, the many times we were with her. The smell of the lake reminded me of her. She was a water baby, would swim whenever she could no matter the temperature of the water. I don't remember dad being with us at the lake. Where had he been? At work? But I did have one memory of my dad in relation to the lake, a good memory, one of a few, but a major one.

I was fifteen and lakeside with my girlfriend, Diane. We stretched out on a blanket. The sun warmed our bodies. The breeze brushed over us. When Diane's boyfriend showed up, he said I looked good in a two-piece. I blushed. She slugged him on the arm, and they took off. I expected her to come back as she was my ride home. After an hour, I began to worry. I had to get back, or my dad would ground me.

Then two seniors from my school showed up. One dropped onto the blanket next to me and told me I was cute. He reeked of alcohol. Then he pulled his Depeche Mode t-shirt up, grabbed my hand, and tried to shove my hand under his swim trunks. I yanked away, jumped to my feet, and rolled him off my blanket. He was so drunk, he just laughed. Shaking, I picked up my things, walked a mile to a restaurant, and called my dad to come get me.

In the car, instead of getting angry, Dad patted my knee and said, "Good girl. You were right to call your old dad." He put on some Jefferson Airplane, and we sang all the way home.

I was still smiling when I heard Gerard yell my name from across the road. "Angeline! Dinner!"

I looked toward the cottage, the sun lighting him up, and for a moment saw my father. I felt the pull of home from the past, something I hadn't for a long time. I dashed across the street.

41

Gerard and I ate in silence as ominous dark clouds across the bay hung in the air forecasting more thunder and lightning. Gerard practically wolfed down the clams and onion rings, belying my belief that the French had pristine manners. I ate small bites of clam chowder and was glad I'd ordered it as it comforted my upset stomach. As my brain cleared, I thought of Tempest.

"I'm tired, Gerard. I want to go home and start again. I want my dog. I miss her." No way would I admit that I had nothing and no one else. "Are you really going to get my dog back?"

When he didn't answer, my heart sank. So Tempest was gone too. A promise made in haste. A promise he couldn't or wouldn't keep.

I stood and went to the picture window. Lightning razored across the sky and reflected in the bay. A second later, thunder boomed. The wind came up, fierce and frightening. Within minutes, branches fell from trees. Leaves blew across the driveway.

I balled up my fists so tight my nails broke the skin. I

wanted to break Gerard's skin. He needed to be punished for everything he'd caused.

When I felt him behind me, I whipped around and smacked him hard. He jumped back. His cheek flamed pink.

"*You* killed my sister. You may have forgotten, but I haven't. You thought you were so smart. Did you *really* think she'd understand that you were faking the break up with her? Why would she doubt you? She wasn't in your world of duplicity. She took you at your word."

I stepped forward and smacked him again. He stood there, taking it. Small specks of blood from where my nails cut my palms streaked his face.

I practically growled. "Why didn't you call Sophie? Why didn't you tell her the truth? Or maybe that wasn't the truth. Maybe you didn't love her. Maybe it was all part of your job. Maybe you didn't even think about her."

Gerard held up his hands as if to ward off the blows of my words. He backed into the counter and turned away, covering his face. The sobs were almost silent. After a minute, he blinked hard, pushed past me, and headed outside. Somehow, under the awning, even with the wind, he managed to light a cigarette. His hands shook. I wanted to hate him. Instead, I felt sorry for him.

After he finished his smoke, he stayed there for the longest time. I tossed the food remains, crumpled up the napkins, and threw them in the trash. Then I kicked the trash can.

When I looked back through the sliders, he was still standing there. Had he ever felt the full force of Sophie's loss until now? Had either of us? All I'd done is walk around being angry at the injustice and trying to stay alive.

I searched for my cigarettes, found them, lit one, and joined him. The wind whipped my hair over my face, so I held my hair back with one hand and took a long drag. I exhaled and looked over at Gerard.

He didn't look at me when he said, shouting over the wind, "I was wrong. I just thought our love was stronger than that. I should have known she was fragile." He paused. "Yes, I was and am still too 'wrapped up in my job.' In the past, I would have considered Sophie's suicide collateral damage. This job turns you cold."

I waited, this time feeling the truth of the confession.

He looked at me. "I could *not* tell your sister. She was not good at keeping secrets."

That was so true. I smoked. The wind flicked burning ash from my cigarette.

"Ang, I'd do anything to bring her back. But she's gone. Maybe I am guilty. Maybe that's why I keep you in the loop. Maybe being close to you is my mea culpa or my punishment because you remind me of her."

"Remind you of *her*? Oh, come on." My foot tapped.

He grabbed my arms.

I shook him off. "Don't."

"Angeline, listen to me. I keep you in the loop because I need you, and I think you need me. I want you here. You know what's happened. You and I are the only people who can get justice for what this crime family has done."

I looked away and finished my cigarette. I might not be an attorney anymore, but I hadn't forgotten how complicated it was to dole out justice, how gray the area between right and wrong, the rule of law, and rule of outlaw. Plus, we were all human. And humans made mistakes. Like he did. Like I did.

He leaned on the railing. "Can I sleep on the couch tonight?"

We were now in semi-darkness. The wind had died down, and large droplets of rain smacked all around us.

"The FBI can't afford a hotel room?"

I didn't wait for him to answer and went back inside, where I stared at the scotch bottle before putting it away.

Gerard came in and stood at the counter. "Angeline, I consider us a team. I thought we wanted the same thing—justice for your sister."

"Yeah, right. As if that will ever happen. Betty and Link are dead. That's my justice. Who else do we have to kill to make this right?"

I surprised myself with that admission.

When he didn't say anything, I said, "Screw that, Gerard."

I tried pushing past him, but he pulled me back, turned me around, and pressed me against the counter. We were inches away from a kiss. Again. Our eyes locked. I could feel myself about to give way as my body flooded with a sexual rush. I wanted to maul and bite him, to touch him—

He smiled and said, "Thank you for killing that piece of *merde* Link. Betty deserved to die too."

I slipped away, my hands now fists. My heart constricted. I felt ill. Did he think calling me a murderer was sexy?

I was so tired of being used and explaining myself. I'd killed both Sam and Betty in self-defense. *Self-defense.* Gerard didn't have feelings for me. He was using me to keep my sister alive.

"Angeline?"

I said nothing.

"You know what I mean. You know that I'd never turn you in."

I opened the hope chest in front of the couch, pulled out a blanket and pillow, and threw them on the couch. I sent a cold, hard look at Gerard and headed for the bedroom, then closed the door and locked it. I was done with him. I would keep Bibi from his FBI clutches.

Once in bed, I made my plan, a mental list, then fell asleep.

42

The next morning, I woke to the sound of a dog barking, a high-pitched noise, almost a yowl. I stumbled to the kitchen and looked outside. Gerard's vehicle was gone.

On the couch, he'd left the blanket neatly folded with the pillow on top. That pissed me off. He could have put it back in the hope chest. But maybe he wanted to remind me that he'd been there or he was a good house guest, tidy, non-intrusive.

Then I discovered he'd also set up the coffee maker. I flipped on the switch. As I waited for the coffee to brew, I opened all the blinds. Leaves and small branches flew by. The dog was still at it, yapping, the kind of noise that got under your skin and made you want to throttle the animal. Tempest had a wolf's howl. A lusty bay-at-the-moon wail. I remembered last night, Gerard not answering me about his promise.

Forget him. I'd get Tempest home ... when I got home. I didn't need him.

After drinking a mug of strong coffee, I remembered the

mental list I'd made before falling asleep. I wouldn't go to Boston. Bibi didn't need me. She had money, a decent lawyer, I'm sure, and friends. She knew about the FBI and how to keep herself safe. She was tough.

If she wanted a relationship with me, she'd make the next move.

In the meantime, I'd prove to her I didn't want anything from her. I just wanted to be sisters. After I dressed, I called my lawyer and got him started on a will. Bibi would inherit everything of mine. He advised against it. "Not so fast," he said. But I wanted the will done and sent to her. Where was the jeopardy? She already stood to inherit Betty's fortune as well as her adoptive parents' estate.

I did cover myself. I had my lawyer add a clause that would nullify the inheritance: 1) if Bibi were found to be complicit in any of the crime group's activity, 2) if she was found guilty of any criminal behavior, or 3) if anything suspicious happened to me that could be traced back to her. If she didn't inherit for any of those reasons, my wealth would go to the local humane society. People just weren't worthy.

As I drank my second cup of coffee, I looked through the tourist brochures about New Hampshire—the White Mountains, the Lakes Region, the historical sites. I didn't find one about Benson's Wild Animal Farm. Did it exist anymore? The Loudon Motorcycle Races? I'm sure *that* was still a big deal. All the places from the past, not that I ever went to them, brought back a sensory overload. A young girl's dream of going to these places with her classmates. Instead, that young girl spent lonely weekends wondering what her classmates were doing, then overhearing about it later in the cafeteria amidst laughter and the joy of having fun. Sometimes I knew the classmates. Sometimes they were strangers because I was in a new school.

One time Mom and Dad took us to see the Old Man of the Mountain, a rock face in the White Mountains. But in 2003, giving way to weather, gravity and time, it collapsed, a memory now, seen only on license plates, route markers, and the state quarter. New Hampshire no longer existed for me. Even the state motto left me cold. "Live Free or Die." How did a John Birch motto become the state's?

I needed to get out of here. The wind had died down, and I opened the slider for fresh air. Outside, the traffic along Paugus Bay drove out the calm of the water, the bird-song, the tinkling of wind chimes. I didn't recognize this place anymore. As hard as I searched for myself here—and for the family I did and didn't have—the more I missed Oregon.

I wrapped the blanket from the couch around me, the blanket Gerard had used. It was comforting, but I couldn't sit still. I paced the living room. His scent, a coppery smell mixed with aftershave, wafted up from the blanket. I rubbed my chest, that hollow ribcage of nothingness.

Time felt unreal here, neither past nor present. A feeling flooded me so fast my body sagged. My legs went weak, and I dropped onto the couch. Hard. Never had I felt so rootless and unmoored, so totally orphaned. Not even after my parents died. Maybe after Sophie was buried. But then I was filled with vengeance. Not this.

Sophie used to say, "Let the universe handle it, Ang. The universe will give you an answer, a direction. Quit trying to control everything." I used to laugh at that. This time—even though I trusted my brain more than Sophie's words—they pulled me together.

As I washed and dried the few dishes I had dirtied and

packed my carry-on, I tried not to think about any of this. The bay water shone brilliant and cold in the foreground, dark opaque blue in the distance. Mom used to joke about how we'd go swimming as soon as the ice melted and, when our lips turned blue, would have to call us out of the water. We couldn't stop shivering. On hot, muggy days, she and Kathleen would sit in their lounge chairs, smoking Winstons, and sipping iced tea, beer, or gin and tonics. They'd take ice from the ice bucket and melt it on their face, then drop it down their bathing suits. They took every chance to go topless. When it was time to go home, Mom would wrap a towel around Sophie. Kathleen, smelling of baby oil and cigarettes, would wrap a towel around me, hug me, and call me *sweetie*.

Kathleen.

I was glad I had decided to see her before I flew back to Oregon. Maybe, just maybe, she had thought of something else to tell me about my parents. Or maybe I just needed to be wrapped in her warmth.

43

After calling Kathleen, I locked up, took one last look at Paugus Bay, and headed to Tilton.

Inside Kathleen's building, a crew of painters and carpenters were downstairs, giving the space a new colorful interior. Kathleen gave me a hug, and I hugged her back, holding on like I had when I was a kid. After I let go, we went upstairs, and I followed her into the kitchen. After running water into her electric kettle, she laid out the teacups and saucers, along with a teapot. Her hair was in a French braid, and she wore gold palazzo pants and a black blouse. Kathleen was stunning, and it wasn't even noon yet.

"Am I interrupting something? Are you expecting someone or going somewhere?"

"I have some people coming to talk about renting downstairs, but that's not for a few hours."

Kathleen had a hard time looking at me. What was up? As she ladled two scoops of loose tea into the pot, she asked, "How have your days gone?"

I filled her in as she set a timer for the tea to brew, then took down a container of biscuits and arranged them on a plate. I wanted to say don't bother with the cookies, but it seemed she was taking her time. I wasn't being paranoid. Something *was* bothering her.

After I'd finished telling her about Bibi and the last few days, leaving out the Gerard sections, of course, Kathleen said, "Bibi will come around. Family ties are strong, even if she doubts you are sisters. After she's been run through the mill, she'll reach out."

Run through the mill. Mom used to say that too.

When the tea was ready, she poured it into two cups set on saucers and handed one to me. We sipped in silence as if waiting for the other to begin. In the background, hammers hammered, and electric tools drilled.

I didn't know where to start. "Go ahead, Angeline. Is there something else you want to know?"

This startled me.

Her expression turned kind, empathetic. The Aunt Kathleen I used to know. I wasn't sure what I wanted, and somehow I needed to let whatever was stuck dislodge.

I swallowed hard as I watched her face. Without thinking, I blurted out, "Is my father my father?" Sweat puddled under my arms and along my upper lip.

She didn't answer right away. Her expression didn't change. She was considering her answer, or she knew the answer and was afraid to tell me. Finally, she said, "No, hon, he isn't. He isn't your biological father, but he *was* your father."

I set down the teacup, no longer thirsty. "How do you know?" I said, my voice sharp, accusatory. The Old Man of the Mountain crashed down, and my family finally fell apart, completely.

She sighed. Tears welled in her eyes. "Let's take our tea to the living room."

That did it. "No. Tell me about it right now."

She leaned back against the counter, her palazzo pants fluttering around her ankles.

I leaned on the kitchen table. The noise from downstairs stopped, creating a heavy silence. I waited.

"Angeline, I thought you'd never find out, and sometimes ignorance *is* bliss. Then when you found out about the twins, I knew I had to tell you the truth."

"The truth?" My voice squeaked. "Kathleen, you should have told me at my parents' funeral."

She shook her head. "I was in shock. I felt guilty for not getting your mom out of there in time. I wasn't thinking of you and your sister. I was too busy blaming myself for your mom's death."

"Yes, it seems *everyone* was busy thinking about Mom." I stood up and crossed my arms. "Did you ever think to find us later and let us know? That would have been the decent thing—"

A teacup sailed across the room and smashed against the wall four feet to my left. Wide-eyed, I looked down at the broken fragments, then up at Kathleen. "Damn, Kathleen."

She stomped her foot. "As if your parents did the decent thing?" Her face flushed red. "Do you know how *hard* it was to be your mom's best friend? It was always about her. There I was, concerned about her well-being while my daughter was hooked on heroin, and I couldn't do anything for either one." Her arms flew up from her sides like wings battling the wind. "Was your mom there to help me, though? No. Yet every time your father got emotionally abusive, and I also suspect physically abusive, she'd call me. Kathleen to the rescue." She blew out a long exhale and swiped at her eyes. "One time, I insisted that she leave him. She shouted at me, 'You don't understand!'" Tears coursed down her face. She was trembling. "She was right. I didn't. Your father killed my best friend." She made a groaning noise. "That's the same year I lost my daughter to a drug overdose. If it hadn't been for my husband, I wouldn't have survived all that."

I was speechless and felt battered. I hadn't moved, couldn't. I wanted to leap across the table and strangle her. I also wanted to run to her and wrap her in my arms. But I was too busy seeing the reality of my past blown apart, too busy wanting to strangle the real culprits, my parents.

She wiped the tears from her face and blew her nose on a paper towel. Her mascara had run. "I'm sorry, Angeline." She gulped back more tears. "I felt I had to keep my promise to Annie and not tell you girls."

"A promise to my mother?" I struggled to keep my shit together. The tears balled up in my chest. I stepped forward. "My mother? Do you know what I've thought all these years? 'Oh, poor Mom. She was so badly treated.' Yet, she was having affairs? Did he even know? I knew they weren't monogamous, but us kids? She didn't protect us. I was always covering for her, making excuses so Dad wouldn't get mad. I even took responsibility for an old phone of his that she broke and was grounded for two weeks. Even then, she didn't tell him the truth. What the hell, Kathleen?"

I glared at her. My father wasn't my father. Just great. "Well, is that it? What about my real dad? What else haven't you told me?"

Kathleen put her hands together as she had at our first meeting like she was praying. "Your father was sterile. Remember me telling you about the Weirs incident when your dad and mom went on a date with my husband and me? He'd just found out that day. If I'd known, I would never have announced my pregnancy to them that night. That was why he was in such a bad mood."

By this time, my brain, like a hyperactive child's, couldn't settle on what to ask next. Oh, how I wanted to beat the pulp out of someone. Unfortunately, those who deserved it were dead. But not their damned secrets.

Kathleen swept her tears away. "One day, your mom stopped by my place on the way to Boston. She asked me to watch you while she looked for a place to live. I was so happy she was leaving Ron." She rolled her eyes. "She was gone ten days, and when she came back to get you, I asked how she did. She was going back to your dad. I could tell she never intended to leave your dad. She went off to have a good time. She was all flushed and excited. I was so angry. I yelled at her and said I couldn't take it anymore, that our friendship was finished."

Now she had my attention. "What did she do?"

"She didn't understand why. I said you lied to me, told me you were leaving Ron."

"Did she admit that?"

"No. She told me she went to Boston to get pregnant."

"What?"

She nodded. "I was stunned. I called her crazy, and she looked like I had punched her. Then all the excitement drained out of her." Kathleen let out a long sigh and rubbed her forehead. "That's when she told me that your father, when in Vietnam, had worked with toxic chemicals, and that had made him sterile. That's how they lived most of the time, on his VA disability."

The noise downstairs resumed and was almost a relief from the strained conversation. I held up my hands. "Mom used to say I had my father's hands. What a joke." Maybe she meant my real father's hands.

This was insane. I rubbed my cheeks and walked back and forth, kicking the broken china cup aside. Kathleen waited. I finally said, "That means Dad knew all along that us kids weren't his."

"According to your mom, they made a pact. The first time, he was willing to let her have sex with another man so she could get pregnant, but no affair, just sex. When and if she did get pregnant, everyone had to believe the baby was his. She was sworn to silence. And no one knew about his sterility except the VA."

"But Mom told you."

"Yes."

"So the Boston trip resulted in the twins. She must have had sex with a lot of men. Was that also part of their arrangement?"

Kathleen, looking every bit her age, said, "Your mom had no trouble getting pregnant. She had two abortions before meeting your dad. Just between her and me, I used to call her Fertile Myrtle." She watched my face, the lines on her forehead deepening. "I'm so sorry about all of this, hon. I'm sorry I kept all this from you. I'm sorry I threw the cup. There's no excuse for that."

"So, Mom went to Boston. Was Dad in the loop on that one? Or did he think she was leaving him?"

"I don't know. Honestly, I don't. I was getting pretty tired of how they lived their lives."

She took another cup from the cupboard, poured herself some tea, and sipped it with a slurping sound. She now looked fragile, beaten down, grief worn. I wondered what Mom looked like before she died. She had no courage at all, none. Yet, now I was so pissed, I whispered, "Those two deserved each other."

Kathleen said nothing. When she moved to a chair, she sat like she was in pain. I sat down too. She placed both hands in her lap and looked over at me with the kindest eyes I'd ever seen. "Should I go on?" she asked. I nodded. "I still don't know if your parents were taking a break, or if it was an attempt at getting pregnant again. I was terrified for Annie. But she called me months later to tell me she was pregnant again and that they were both so happy, and you were going to have a little sibling."

I thought about this for a bit. "So maybe dad needed her to go further away this time to get pregnant? Did he know who my father was?"

"Your mom said no. But the man was in a neighboring town. It was more than once. In fact, I remember your mom saying something like "if I didn't love Ron." I got the impression it was more than just a tryst to get pregnant."

"I can't imagine how my ... father felt." I was having trouble referring to him as *Dad* or even *my father*.

"When your mom said she was still seeing this man after you were born, I was so angry, I yelled at her to grow up. She was like a child when someone gave her attention. I told her if she continued to see this man, it would end badly. She told me she couldn't stop seeing him, so I said, 'Well, move away!' and they did."

"I don't understand how my father dealt with this."

"They were both, you know, very centered on themselves and each other. Not in a healthy way. Even after the twins were born, they seemed happy, at least for a while. You seemed fine."

"Fine? Dad was obsessed with Sophie. I felt pretty left out. He kept saying how much she looked like Mom." I was dizzy and leaned my head in my hands. "Damn. This is so ... so freaking bizarre. This is my family! I'm in my forties, and I'm just finding out all this?"

Kathleen seemed to snap to attention. "Angeline, I know this seems bizarre, but think about it. Your parents loved each other so much that they were willing to have a family in a way they both agreed upon. You knew they were different, that they did things their way. As frustrating as that is to you, they loved you girls."

I smacked the counter. "Oh, right! They loved us so much they waited to kill themselves until *after* we were out of the house."

Kathleen stood. "Let's go sit in the living room, get more comfortable."

We went to the living room. Kathleen lowered herself into a chair. I paced.

"Angeline, your mom meant so much to me. But I was overwhelmed with the problems I had with my daughter." She sniffed and this time pulled a hankie from a pocket in her palazzo pants. "Do you know that Annie and I talked about traveling together? We both wanted to go to Paris. It was a dream for both of us."

"Paris? Really?" I sure wasn't going to tell her I'd been there—or why.

"Yes, Paris. Why does that surprise you?"

"I don't know. I guess I never thought of Mom traveling. She seemed like a nester."

"Your Mom had a thing for Paris. She was a romantic, you know. Always hopeful, thinking things would get better, living in a dream world."

A knock sounded on her door. While she answered and spoke to one of the workmen, I thought about Paris—and Gerard. I felt sick. For the first time, reality sunk in. I'd tried to kill him.

I kneaded the muscles in my neck. My shoulders were bunched up around my ears. Now I had to face the reality that my father hadn't been my father. Was my real father out there somewhere? How did Mom meet him? Did he love her? Was he married? Dorothy Parker said it right: "What fresh hell is this?"

Kathleen returned to the couch. She cleared her throat as if preparing to tell me something else.

"What?" I said. "I don't care what it is, just tell me. Get it over with." I plunked down on the couch. "Sorry. I'm just ... you know?"

"I know, hon. I know, believe me."

Now I felt terrible. I'd tried not to think about my parents over the years. If I did, it was mainly about my mom, how much she'd put up with by marrying my father. But now that he wasn't blood, he was all I could think of. What had it taken to be that much in love with a woman and to let her have *their* children by other men? That just killed me. They had a good motive for what they did. It really wasn't any different from what people did now with artificial insemination from a sperm bank. Only my parents got the sperm the old fashioned way. And the sperm donors knew nothing about it.

"Are you sure you're all right?" Kathleen asked.

"Yes, just wondering about my biological father. What else was it you wanted to tell me?"

She cleared her throat. "Those FBI agents? They showed up here yesterday. They wanted to know why you'd come to talk with me, what we talked about. They wanted to know what I knew about you and that FBI agent Gerard Duvernet."

I jumped up. "What?"

Kathleen quietly said, "What's going on, Angeline? Are you in trouble?"

I threw up my arms. "That's what I'd like to know!" I walked to the window. The SUV was there across the street. "Those sons-of-bitches."

Kathleen joined me.

"What exactly did they ask?"

Kathleen was shoulder to shoulder with me. "They asked about you and this Gerard, if you had a relationship with him."

"That we might be screwing suddenly tops Bibi's safety?"

I pulled my cell from my pocket. "Excuse me, Kathleen." I made the call.

44

G erard answered.

"Gerard? Why are those two goons asking questions about you and me? What in hell gives them the right to—"

"*Arrêté*, Angeline, stop, wait. Let me explain."

"Where are you?"

"Boston."

"Why?"

"I'm finishing up here."

"Finishing what?"

"Not over the phone. I'll meet you at the Manchester airport. Your plane leaves this afternoon. I'll meet you at the moose near the baggage claim area in an hour."

The moose. Yeah, right. I knew what he meant, but I was done being ordered around. "I'm not meeting you. I want to stay—"

"You don't have a choice. Don't approach the 'goons' as you call them. Just get in your car and drive." Then he hung up.

"Damn, damn, damn!"

Before I left Kathleen's, I asked, "Are you sure they were FBI agents?"

"Hon, I wouldn't know a real FBI badge from a fake. So the answer is no. I should have been more careful."

"If they show up again, check their badges and take down the info. If they let you do this, they probably are FBI. If they leave, nada. To verify, call the FBI and ask them about the badge numbers and names."

"I can do that?"

"Of course. You should."

"OK, I will. Thank you. I wish I'd known that." She reached out, held me by the arms, and looked into my eyes. "Are *you* going to be all right?"

"Yes, no worries." Of course, that was a lie, but I didn't want her to worry.

My lip quivered. "Thank you, Kathleen, for telling me about my parents. And I'm so sorry about your daughter. And my mom. I wish—"

"I know, hon, I know." She gave me a long hug and kissed my forehead like my mom used to do. "Call me whenever you want or need to talk. I have Skype."

"I will."

"Do you know where you're going?"

I nodded. "Yes," I said, my voice breaking. "I'm going home."

45

From the very start of this dangerous cat and mouse game, who to trust remained the major challenge. I watched for the SUV as I drove away from Tilton. It didn't follow me. If they were FBI, maybe Gerard had called them off. I was meeting with him, after all. If they weren't, why weren't they following me?

While driving to the airport, I thought more about my biological father. Who was he? Would I be able to find him? If I did, would he see me, believe me? I had to try. One of those DNA sites could track him down or at least find relatives who might know him. What if I had a big family out there somewhere? I'd lost a sister and a husband and now possibly Bibi. I wanted a family. But would I want *that* family, if it existed?

After I parked, I found the moose statue in the baggage area. Gerard wasn't there. It had been over an hour. My anger grew. Whatever Gerard wanted or was going to try to force me to do, well, he could eat *merde*. I was done. I'd said that before to myself, but this time, I had nothing to give. He had nothing I wanted.

I waited and checked my phone for messages. My jaw ached from my teeth grinding, and my clothes felt itchy against my skin. I paced. I desperately wanted a cigarette. I needed a life, but not this one.

After fifteen minutes, I decided to give him fifteen more and set the timer on my phone to alert me. Maybe Boston traffic had been worse than usual. If so, that was saying something.

When the fifteen minutes were up, I grabbed the handle of my carry on and headed toward the escalator. I was about to take my first step up when Gerard shouted my name. I reluctantly turned around and had to use every ounce of restraint not to knee him in the gonads.

"Ang, shall we sit over there on the bench?"

I couldn't say, *Do I have a choice?* My jaw felt frozen shut. Good thing he didn't take my arm. Once again, his time was more important than mine.

At the bench, we sat. I left a foot of space between us.

"Damn, Gerard, get on with it."

He scooted over next to me, so close I could feel the gun he was packing.

I glanced up at him. He had bags under his eyes and hadn't shaved. Plus, he was in the same clothes he'd worn at the cabin.

"Those men who questioned Kathleen Glanville? They weren't FBI."

Under my breath, I said, "Oh, just freaking great. She better not be in danger, Gerard. She better be protected, if that's even po—"

"The Bureau assigned someone to watch Kathleen. They are nearby. They've been keeping an eye on the SUV. If those same two go to her door, the agents will be on them right away. I can vouch for that."

He was hoarse, and he smelled. I glanced at his face. His eyes were bloodshot. "God, Gerard, what's happened?"

"Do you have any mints?"

I gave him a couple.

"Something went wrong with the job. Someone reported me to a higher-up as going rogue. They've been monitoring all my movements, calls, and communications."

"Wouldn't you have known they were monitoring you?"

"Not necessarily."

"How does an FBI agent go rogue? What does that even look like, Gerard? And why? Why suspect you?"

"I've done some things outside the Bureau's parameters. For one thing, when I was with you the other night, I turned off my communications with them, my wire."

"You were *wired* when you were with me?" If we'd been alone, not in a public place, I'd have yelled it. Instead, it came out like a hiss.

"At first, we didn't know whether to trust you or not. We didn't know if you were involved with the Boston crime group."

I shifted to look at him square on. He squirmed. Yeah, he'd better squirm. "Tell me, Gerard, how could they believe that? After all I've been through."

"I didn't believe it, Ang, but I had to keep monitoring you in order not to raise suspicion."

"Suspicion?"

"I suspect someone in the Bureau is dirty, someone in the field, maybe higher up. I don't know. I can't tell you any details. I've already said too much."

Suddenly, I wanted to lie down and take a nap or a long night's sleep with no dreams. "What are you going to do now?"

"I don't know. All I know is this stops me from protecting

you. This means I have to go to DC and answer questions. The agency may contact you."

"And just how will I know it's really the agency, not someone pretending to be or someone who's dirty?"

"Demand to meet at any nearby FBI office or call in their credentials. You know that. The problem here is I don't know if they'll be legit or agents under the control of a dirty Bureau member."

I checked the time. Almost time to head to security. "Gerard?" He looked up. "Are you rogue?"

"*Non*. This is my life, and I believe in the work." Now his accent was thick, plus he was glancing up and down the baggage area. "In Boston, I was questioned about my personal feelings for you. They accused me of working more to protect you, maybe even working with you, instead of going after the operatives of the crime group. They think I might jeopardize the case they've built by doing something foolish."

"Like what?"

"Like killing one of the crime group's members."

"Is that true? Would you do that?"

"I shouldn't have stayed over at your cottage. That was unacceptable. I can't show any bias or be involved with a suspect."

I knew from my lawyer days that everyone was a suspect until they weren't.

"What do they suspect me of specifically?"

"The murder of Sam and Betty."

I wanted to say, *So what? They were criminals who wanted to kill me, so I plead self-defense.*

But I didn't. Instead, I asked, "Are you? Involved with me?" When he didn't answer, I asked, "Does the Bureau know about you and Sophie?"

"Yes, but that was part of my undercover operation. Plus, they knew you were an asset and could draw out the crime group when they went after you for Sophie's Maryland stash."

So, I was just an asset.

He stood. "Angeline, someone wants my badge. Someone wants me out."

"What are you going to do now?"

"I don't know. Find out who's after me in the Bureau."

I rechecked my phone. I had to leave. "I have to go. I'm going to miss my flight."

"Yes, go, Ang. Go home. This is my problem. Just trust no one."

He didn't have to tell me that.

As I whirled my carry-on to my side, he said, "Ang, Bibi told us everything she knows. She was free to go, and no charges will be filed against her."

"Thank you for telling me that. But now she's vulnerable to the crime group, right? Or is that too obvious to mention?"

He shrugged. Then he took my hand and pressed it to his lips. "I won't see you again. I wish you every joy in life."

Confused, I said, "What?"

"Go, before you miss your flight, Angeline." He let go of my hand, smiled, and once again looked like the Gerard I'd known in Paris.

When I didn't go right away, he stepped back and said, "Bon voyage. Have a good flight."

I shook my head, exasperated.

At the top of the escalator, I turned to wave good-bye, but he was gone.

46

I don't remember going through security or showing my ID and ticket. I don't remember finding my gate. I vaguely remember turning my phone on airplane mode.

When we landed at Dulles, I woke with a start, and while getting out of my seat, I almost tripped and fell. Two men caught me. One took down my suitcase, and I thanked him. I was exhausted.

Somehow, I managed to make my way through the Dulles airport to my San Francisco gate, plus nabbed a coffee. Along the way, I sipped my coffee, and my body came online again.

On the flight to San Francisco, I pictured Gerard taking me to the Palace Hotel, my surprise as we entered, our short time there. It was absurd, but now that I'd never see him again, I missed him. Plus, I feared this wasn't the end of the FBI and the crime group. Without him, I *did* feel vulnerable. But I had to believe once I was home, I'd get my strength back and take charge of my life again.

My thoughts turned to finding a comfortable house to

buy—how many rooms, what style, where, how much. Maybe someday Bibi would call me and ask to spend time together. I would build a new life, something fulfilling, something that would use my skills and knowledge of the law. Or maybe not.

With my notepad and pen, I made a list of all the things I would do after I rented a car and had a hotel room.

- Check with Iolana on Tempest
- Find a rental house or furnished apartment until I can buy
- Call my lawyer
- Check finances
- Determine which neighborhood I want to live in
- Determine what I want and need in a home
- Check in with Hank's old business partner to see about his health
- GET TEMPEST BACK note: house needs to have a kennel
- Get DNA report on me, find a genealogist to help, and try to find my father
- Call Snoop. Any more info on Bibi?

I hated to "snoop" on Bibi, but my old lawyer habits were hard-wired, and I needed to be prepared, do my background checks, make sure Bibi wasn't part of the crime group despite what Gerard had told me. I wondered if my biological father was like me? My parents sure weren't. They, as some people expressed, flew by the seat of their pants.

At the San Francisco airport, I had time to eat at a restaurant and relax. I was on the West Coast. I was close to home. Eugene would look so good.

In the bathroom, I freshened up before heading to my

gate. The East Coast ennui had lifted, and when we boarded, I was excited. I took my seat in first class, happy to be next to the window for this short flight. Hopefully, the plane would take off before the fog rolled in.

As we taxied, I thought of something else for my list, took it out, and started to write.

The man sitting next to me had boarded at the last minute. He said, "You make lists too? I like the old-fashioned way of doing that. It somehow gives me comfort."

I looked over at him. Thankfully, I have a poker face. He was a looker. Thick silver hair, bright hazel eyes with a twinkle, perfect white teeth, and a gold earring in his right ear. He was tan, too, and not the fake kind. But he wasn't my type. A little too slick.

I wasn't sure I wanted to chit-chat, so I just nodded.

He said, "I can't make lists on my phone." He took out a pair of silver-framed glasses and slipped them on. "I use a small notebook like you. I remember the list better if I write long-hand. Do you?"

I tried to dismiss my suspiciousness. Had I grown so guarded I couldn't enjoy a friendly little conversation with a man?

He took his notebook from his jacket pocket and showed me the cover. "Something I picked up in Morocco," he said. The cover looked like papyrus and was imprinted with simple block gold letters. NOTEBOOK.

I nodded because it was classy.

"I buy small, beautiful notebooks whenever I travel."

I gave in to a conversation. He seemed intelligent, a little too talkative, but sincere. Obviously, he traveled often. "What type of notes do you make?" I asked, noticing his hands—long fingers, no rings, square at the tips, no manicure or fuss. In fact, he had somewhat ragged nails. I liked that. It made him more human, not so perfect.

He turned slightly toward me. "Oh, my notes can be everything from don't forget your vitamins to call my research assistant for an update. I mix personal and business."

I'd forgotten what I was going to write on my list. "And what would that business be?"

The flight attendant interrupted us to ask if we'd like champagne. I think she thought we were together. I was about to say, "Not for me, thank you," but my seatmate said, "Yes. Lovely." She smiled at him and gave us each a flute of champagne.

I looked out the window and thrummed my fingers on the tray.

"I'm sorry," he said. "I should have told her we weren't together."

I took a sip. "Not your fault. It was her presumption that irritates me."

"I understand." He turned the notepad over and over. "Are you interested in my notes?"

"No. Actually, I'm interested in your hands. They're the hands of a white-collar worker, but the nails are somewhat ragged." I waited for him to react and expected him to take that as somewhat of an insult.

"I'm afraid I don't go in for manicures." He laughed self-consciously. "Not in my line of work. You asked what business I'm in? I'm a chemical engineer."

My mouth must have dropped open because he pulled his head back and grinned. "Did I say something funny?"

"No, not at all. It's just ... it's funny that. ..." I squirmed and shook my head in disbelief. "It's just that my late husband was a chemical engineer."

"Oh! Well, that *is* funny. I mean, it's such a coincidence. What was his name, if you don't mind telling me?"

"Hank. Hank Porter."

"Hank Porter! You mean the Hank, who was working with the Chinese on the polyols?"

Now I was gobsmacked. "Yes! Did you know him?"

"I didn't know him. I knew of him. I had met him. I was working on a similar project for a team of investors. Hank was way ahead of us." He paused. "I'm sorry to hear of his death. That must have been terrible for you."

"I can't believe this." Now I wondered who this guy really was. "Out of curiosity, how did you hear about his death?"

"Through the professional grapevine. Was he ill for very long? Oh, so sorry, I'm sure you don't want to talk about this with a stranger."

"No, I really don't want to talk about it at all." I looked away and choked back the lump in my throat.

"I'm terribly sorry," he said again.

After I composed myself, I said, "Please. No worries." I needed to change the subject. "Where's your office?"

He brightened, relieved. "Seattle, Singapore, and San Francisco. But I'm going to Eugene to meet with one of the new tech companies. I personally invest in startups. Do you live in Eugene?"

This guy had a knack for answering a question, then asking one. That could be excellent professional training in interpersonal skills, a characteristic of a curious mind, or someone who had been trained in undercover work. Men rarely conversed this way with a woman. Usually they talked about themselves *ad nauseum* as if the woman were dying to know all about them, showing little interest in the woman, as if we were all the same.

This guy waited for my answer without jumping ahead. I decided to find out more about him and held out my hand. "I'm Ang. And yes, I'm going home to Eugene."

"I'm Patrick, and I live in Naples, Florida."

We chuckled, shook hands, then the safety regulations interrupted our conversation, and the plane taxied down the runway.

When we were in the air, we shared the *Wall Street Journal* and the *New York Times*. We found plenty to talk about. He liked theater. He had worked for the government at one time in R&D, but he didn't say what department. He'd been married for twenty-two years but was divorced, no kids. The similarities accumulated. I wanted to make a list of them, but couldn't, not with him sitting there. At one point, Patrick wrote in his notebook after reading something in the *New York Times*. Or I think that's what he was noting. I couldn't see what it was. I wanted to know.

"May I ask? What did you just add to your notebook?" This would let me see how forthcoming he was when asked questions. Plus, I was curious.

"Have you ever kept a list of observations? I track all the unusual things I see, read, or hear."

"*That's* what you're doing? Seems you'd be writing all day."

"I'm a bit of a voyeur. Or as the French call it *flaneur*."

That startled me. "Are you French?"

"Heavens, no. I'm Scottish."

"And you keep these little notebooks because. ..?"

"Because I find humans fascinating. When someone does something unusual, I write it down." He leaned in close to me and said, "For example, to our left—don't look. That gentleman just dipped his finger in his champagne and licked it. Why would someone in first class do that?"

I told him that as a lawyer, I'd seen enough unusual human tics across the board to last a lifetime. He laughed and wanted to know more about that. I told him what I could. I didn't tell him I was disbarred. We wouldn't see each other again—unless he was FBI. God knows I was now suspicious of everyone being FBI. I told him just enough about me to make myself interesting and to make him feel relaxed. The more people talked, the more they tripped themselves up if they were lying or were after something. He was also on his third refill of champagne. I was still on my first.

But I was conflicted about how suspicious I was. I did want to talk with him. He was different and had nothing to do with my former life. When was the last time I had anyone interested in me or my life? I'd been living in an alternative universe, not of my making. Even now, I was still a prisoner in that alternative universe. I *couldn't* talk truthfully about what I was doing, what I had been doing. Would I ever be able to have another relationship where I was one-hundred percent honest with a man without scaring him away or being suspicious? I needed to be careful. With Patrick, it was easy as we had many things that allowed me to stay away from the personal. I looked over at him, writing away in his notebook. He glanced up, winked, and continued writing. I felt a ping, something close to caring about him, almost attraction. Maybe I was just starved for a healthy relationship with a man.

The plane descended. Cloud cover hung over hills of dense grays and dark greens with house lights widely scattered in the distance. The outskirts of Eugene at dusk. That jolt of the familiar, that word *home*. I leaned my head on the window, feeling the pull of a place that had once been mine and would be again. I was a cynic at heart, but this place had a different hold, something close to yearning.

"Can I take you to dinner?"

Patrick snapped me out of my homecoming.

"I really enjoy your company," he said.

When we landed, we exchanged numbers, made a plan, and after we disembarked, we said goodbye at the car rental desk. While I waited outside for my hotel shuttle, I thought of all the questions I'd ask him two nights from now at the restaurant. In the back of the shuttle, I watched the industrial area change to city. Interesting that Patrick had heard about Hank. But in that field, many of the engineers knew about each other, or followed each other, especially the hotshots. Maybe I shouldn't have made a dinner date with him, but no big deal. I had more important things on my mind.

At the Inn at the 5th, the bellhop greeted me and took my bag. I looked around and took in the city where I'd have my new beginning. Once settled and in my own place, my dog by my side, I'd let the universe open up to me.

I laughed. Yeah, right.

47

In my hotel room, I opened my suitcase on the bed. In it, my gun was in a locked hard case. After unlocking it, I loaded it, made sure the safety was on, and slipped the gun into my purse. The rest of the suitcase's contents, a few miserable pieces of clothing and two pairs of shoes, would force me to go shopping, which I hated. I had as yet to learn to shop online. How did anyone buy clothes without trying them on?

My cell needed recharging. I would do that after talking to Iolana. Stretched out on the bed, I called, but she didn't answer. I didn't want to leave a message. I wanted to hear her voice. An hour later, she still didn't answer. Hopefully, she was all right.

At a nearby boutique, where I knew the owner, I bought two new outfits and gave in to buying a dress that the owner said would show off all my good parts. I'm glad *she* knew which ones were good. It looked sexy and sleek, but did I really want to wear it on a date with this guy? With no sister to talk to about him, I did something I'd never done before. I told the boutique owner, Andrea, about Patrick and asked for her opinion. Her first words were, "He sounds too good to be true."

Boom.

After I left with my bag of new duds, I wondered why Andrea hadn't asked where I'd been or said anything about my absence. Maybe it was only a big deal to me.

That night I couldn't sleep. Why had I agreed to this dinner? I didn't need the stress or the cramping stomach. The night was starless with no moon. I walked around the stores and restaurants on Fifth Street, smoking a cigarette under street lights. It was strangely quiet for a city until a train rumbled by, vibrating the ground beneath me, blowing its ear-splitting whistle. I breathed the crisp, moist air, taking big gulps, trying to calm my nerves. I thought about going to Le Bar and having a few drinks, but I needed to cut down. Mentally, I went through everything that was causing my anxiety and gave myself permission to feel scared. I was starting over, but there were too many leftovers. Plus, I wasn't out of danger yet. I knew that.

Someone stepped out from under an awning. Startled, I stepped away. The man headed in the opposite direction, his hood up, his smell wafting after him, that of unclean clothes and unwashed body. "You could be homeless, so be thankful." That was another thing I had to stop—talking out loud. I looked around, finished my cigarette, and headed back to my room, where I watched movies for a few hours until I fell asleep.

The next morning, while drinking coffee in the cafe, I called a pet relocation service. Tempest wouldn't need to be quarantined. I wrote down their info and called Iolana again. This time she answered.

"Iolana, it's me, Ang ... I mean River."

Silence.

"Iolana?"

Shit! I'd forgotten to call her with my new number. I was slipping.

"Oh, River, where have you been? I tried your old number, but it was disconnected."

"What's happened?"

"It's Tempest. I let her out two days ago, and she hasn't come back."

I stood up and banged my knee on the table. "Not again."

Iolana spoke with someone in the background.

Had the crime group taken her?

"Who's there with you?" I asked as I headed back to my room.

"Friends. Some from the activist group, some you know. We've been out searching for her."

I tried to think. "Could she have gone to my old house or the Plantation?"

"We searched both places. I don't understand. Tempest has been fine. She sits on the stoop sometimes as if waiting for you to come back, but nothing else. I'm so sorry, River. This is upsetting."

My heart pounded so hard it was painful. If the Boston gang—and they were a gang as far as I was concerned —*had* taken her, wouldn't I have heard from them by now? Then my mind went into overdrive. She could have been hit by a car and thrown in a dumpster. Or shot by a local who hated strays, although I'd chipped her and she had a collar.

"Iolana, what about the vet?"

"We checked there first and the Humane Society. We also called the chip company to see if anyone had found her, but no one has."

I reached my room but couldn't get my key card to work.

I slid down the wall, sat on the floor, and covered my face with my hands.

"River? River, you there?"

I rubbed my face and wiped my eyes on my sleeve. "Yes, I'm here."

I looked up. A man stood over me.

"What are you doing?" he asked.

I struggled to stand. "I can't get my key card to work."

"I'm sorry, but you have the wrong room." He pulled out his card, swiped it, and opened the door.

"Who's that?" Iolana asked. "What's happening?"

I explained, then stood and brushed myself off. "Iolana, is there anything I can do?"

"We'll keep searching. I'm so sorry. It's all my fault. I should have—"

"Stop, please. It's not your fault. I appreciate everything you're doing and have done. Are *you* OK? Has anyone bothered you?"

"What do you mean?"

"Has anyone asked about me? Come to your house as FBI agents? Have you seen any suspicious vehicles outside your house for long periods?"

"No. Nothing unusual. Until now, with Tempest. But she could have gone off chasing something. She'll be back, River. Really. She'll be all right."

Iolana didn't sound convincing. I asked a few more questions until I reached my room on the next floor, unlocked the door, and flopped down on the bed.

"Where are you?" she asked.

"I'm back in Eugene. To stay." Then I told her briefly what had happened since Kauai and what my real name was.

"Oh, my," she said. That was Iolana. Never too surprised

at anything she heard. "A sister? Does that make you happy?"

"It would if this Boston gang wasn't mucking it up."

"Can't your FBI friend help?"

"No. He's out of the picture."

"Look, we'll keep looking for Tempest. Please, don't worry. We'll find her."

I wasn't so sure of that, but I said, "Thank you, Iolana."

Then I gave her my new contact info and said aloha, and we hung up.

The cell felt heavy in my hand. I rolled my bottom lip between my teeth. Doing nothing was not an option. I could not lose that dog. If the Boston gang had taken Tempest to put the screws on me again, I had no choice. I called someone I thought I'd never talk to again.

48

Gerard's number was disconnected. I pounded the bed, swore, and went over to the liquor cabinet. Asshole.

As I grabbed a single size bottle of whiskey, I caught my reflection in the mirror. "Get a life!" I said. "Suck it up. Do what you need to do." I put the bottle back.

To mellow out, I made a to-do list, including items I'd need to do in case the Boston gang was still after me.

- Call Iolana for the name of a PI
- Call the dog chip company to give them my current info
- Get another place to stay asap
- Call my lawyer, tell him my situation in case something happens to me
- Call Bibi and ask her if she's ok and if she's noticed anything suspicious

I called Iolana first and told her what I wanted.

"Yes, I know a good PI, but he's cantankerous."

When I called, the connection was noisy and crackled like an old landline. His voice was gruff. I told him why I wanted to hire him.

"You want me to find a dog?"

"Yes, a dog. Got a problem with that?"

He snorted. "No, not if your money is good."

I told him this was no ordinary dog abduction, just report to me where Tempest was. Don't try to get the dog away from whoever had her. Once I filled him in, he said, "Now I'm interested—in getting paid *and* in the case."

Yeah, and I was sure his rate went up with my explanation.

My lawyer, after hearing my story, called a friend who had a B&B. A room was available. I could move that afternoon.

As I was packing my few things, Patrick rang to ask if we were still on for the following night at 7:30 at the nearby French restaurant. I hesitated. He waited. Now that I'd heard his voice, I figured what the hell. It would be a distraction.

"Can we meet someplace different? And do it tonight?" I asked.

"Of course. What do you have in mind?"

He was way too flexible and eager. I told him about a little place in a different neighborhood. It was another of those places that no one would suspect I'd frequent. But I went there when I'd wanted to slip out of my lawyer persona, drink, and play solitaire on my phone. I gave him the address and bumped the time to eight-thirty. Again, he was all too amenable.

I moved to the B&B, but was restless and had hours before I had to get ready for dinner. Maybe walking would take my mind off everything. I headed downtown at a fast clip. The young and the homeless had taken over Broadway from Oak Street to Charnelton. Kesey Square was filled with pot smoke. A young woman danced to the drum of a young man. I stopped to pat a few of the dogs and surrendered a few dollar bills here and there.

But I kept feeling a presence as if I were being shadowed. Maybe the Boston gang? But why would they keep after me? I was small potatoes, a few million. Even trying to talk sense to myself didn't work. I headed back to the B&B, this time at a faster pace, almost a jog. When I got to my room, I was sucking air and holding my sides like a marathon runner.

I think I had a case of PTSD. It was the only explanation for my instant anxiety and paranoia. How I longed for the days of being a lawyer.

In my room, I stripped off my clothes and took a long shower. After blow-drying my hair, I pulled on a white sweater and black slacks and knotted a geometrically designed scarf around my neck. My mood was still lousy. So much for a date.

At the restaurant, Patrick waited for me. I was glad he wasn't one of those people who thought being late was fashionable. He didn't try to hug me or shake my hand. We had a table in the back and quickly fell into talking. Or I should say he did. There were more questions, but I stopped them.

"That's enough about me." I flashed him a smile. "How did it go with the startup?"

"I'm going to back them. An impressive young team. Brilliant business plan and product. This is when I love having money."

"In this political climate, it's good to know that people like you are using their money to help the next generation."

He ordered a martini. I ordered a scotch.

"So, tell me what you do as a chemical engineer?" I knew enough about it to catch anything that might be bogus.

But everything he told me seemed genuine. He could "talk the talk," a language Hank had patiently explained over the years just as I had patiently explained my legalese.

Patrick was on his second drink when I asked him where he was from and had lived. He told me about Illinois, Boston, and even Paris, where he had lived for a year before he married. But as soon as he told me that, he asked if I had any sisters or brothers, if my parents were alive, much more personal questions than I wanted to answer. I answered his questions with quick responses. "My parents are dead, and so is my sister. You know Hank is too. It's been a rough couple of years. I went home to New Hampshire for some closure, and now I'm back to start over."

He seemed genuinely sympathetic, even empathetic. I wanted to believe him. I tried to imagine that I had a future, and it included someone bright and engaging like him. Maybe not like him, but close. He felt more like what I thought a brother would feel. Easy, nonthreatening.

But I felt he was too much in my business with the questions, and, after feeling someone following me this afternoon, my guard was up.

We ordered and ate, all the while I tried to get more specific info out of him. Early on, he'd decided not to have kids, didn't want to add to the population. When I asked him about his ex, he said they were still friends and that it just hadn't worked out. He gave me general answers with no specifics. But at the same time, I didn't trust people who spilled their guts. That must have come from my New England genes. I'd never been comfortable with the way the West Coast people tended to tell all.

Patrick's cell rang. He wiped his mouth and said to me, "Excuse me. I'll be back in a moment."

He took the call outside. I swallowed my drink then spied his jacket on the back of his seat. I stood and, while watching the door, pulled out his notebook and opened it.

I leaned into the light from the candle on the table. All the notes, page after page, were about me—everything we talked about on the plane, his impression of me, some details I hadn't given him, like my birthdate, place of birth. But he could have gotten those online, I suppose. His last comment was, "She seems friendly and open, but she's definitely afraid of something. She pauses often, she considers everything she says before saying it, and her eyes are troubled. She will not trust me for a long time."

Trust him?

Any trust I had for Patrick right then flew out the window.

I shoved it back in his jacket and took my seat, my hands shaking, my eye twitching. I ordered another drink. I had no idea how I'd deal with him now. Was he connected to the Boston gang? The FBI? Something or someone else?

When he came back, I asked him if everything was all right. "Just a business call," he said. I wouldn't question him tonight about his notebook. I needed to get my thoughts together and figure out an approach. Like a trial, I needed to ask everything in the right order and with a strategy. One strategy included calling Snoop. Right now, I tried a method I'd used with clients who were holding back, lying, or nervous.

I was amazed at how quickly I dropped into the fake easy-going, somewhat anxious, but charming criminal defense lawyer. Most people will talk when they think you *like* them. A male criminal defense lawyer acts like a superhero, lots of quiet bravado and no-nonsense. But if a female criminal defense lawyer acts that way, men are suspicious. Charm works much better. Hardened criminals don't fall for it. They know the game. But it's always worth a try.

After dinner and more casual conversation, he asked, "Is everything all right?"

This surprised me. I thought I was carrying on quite well. So I said, "Yes, but I think jet lag caught up with me."

He seemed to accept that.

We passed on dessert. Patrick insisted on paying, and while he was paying, I ordered an Uber.

As he helped me on with my coat, his hand brushed the back of my neck. I yanked away. He asked if he could drop me off at the hotel.

"Thank you for offering, but I have an Uber coming."

Outside the restaurant, the sound of jazz surfaced from a nearby music hall. My car arrived. Patrick kissed me on the cheek. We said goodnight.

"Is it all right if I call you?" he asked.

He *is* too good to be true. And he filled his notebook with every move I'd made.

I nodded, but I wouldn't be answering that call. The Uber pulled out. I couldn't get back to my room fast enough.

49

There was one person who had my back—Snoop. When I returned to my room in the B&B, I called her.

She answered right away.

"Yes, Angeline, River, Angeline."

"Haha, Snoop, you must be feeling better. Over your crud?"

I waited for her to say something. She waited. She won. "OK, look, I need you to do a few things. This time, I'm going to pay you."

"I can use the change."

"Here's the info." I gave her what I knew about Patrick. "I need a complete profile on this guy."

"No worries."

"Is it safe to be doing this, Snoop? I mean, the—"

"You know me. No worries. Feds are slow. I'm fast."

"So? What about Bibi?

"Nothing yet. Still catching up from being sick."

"Hey, have you ever had any luck with finding a dog?"

"What, you think I'm God? Get real."

"OK, that's a no. Have you ever been able to get a transcript from an FBI interview?"

"Yeah. But it's tough."

I gave her what I knew, the date that the FBI supposedly interviewed Bibi and where. "Let me know how much and where to send the money."

"Send what you think I'm worth."

"Hon, I'd go broke."

I heard her titter, kind of a sweet little giggle. She was so damn cute.

Around ten o'clock, Patrick called. I let it go to voicemail.

In the morning, I woke to the steady beat of Oregon rain. My phone vibrated. It was the real estate broker. She'd found "a lovely little house that fits all your requirements." Cottage style, lots of light. We met an hour later. By mid-afternoon, I'd bought a house. It was spendy, way more than Hank and I had paid for our old house and not even as much square footage, but the market had changed since then. I thought about driving by my old house, but I just couldn't.

When I stopped at the market for a few deli dinners, I could hear Hank say, "Whose turn is it to pick out the ice cream?" My chest filled, the memories overwhelming.

Then Patrick called again, jerking me out of my sorrow. He left a voicemail about calling him and hoped I'd enjoyed our evening. I put the deli items back and was leaving the market when I saw my old boss with his arm around a young—very young, too young—beautiful woman. When he looked up and recognized me, he was going to say something, but instead turned back to his companion. My stomach turned. I felt nauseous. I wanted to yell and warn her, but they were gone. This piece of shit was probably still acting out his fantasies, and I couldn't touch him, not like his pal, the politician, who finally went to jail for rape. I'd made sure of that. I'd lost my law license over that, but it was one decision I'd never regretted.

I drove to a nearby bar where I ordered a martini. After staring at the olive, I ate it. I swallowed the martini in three gulps and ordered another. Why had I come back here? What did I have here but memories of the dead and a few friends?

I was sipping my second drink when my cell rang.

"Hey, Ang."

A long pause. I was almost giddy.

"Bibi! I'm so glad to hear from you."

"I hope so after I tell you this." She was breathless and wasted no time. "I told the FBI everything I knew, and they let me go. This is depressing what with losing Betty and everyone gone." The noise on her end sounded like an airport. "Even my friend who helped me doesn't want anything to do with me now after hearing I went to the Feds. She won't even return my calls."

"Do you need me to come to Boston?"

"No. When the estate is settled, everything will be sold. I'm at the airport and moving to Hollywood, Florida."

"Florida? Will that be a good change?"

"They have an artists' community there. I bought a condo, but I can't move in yet, so I rented an apartment for now. I need to get out of here. It's been a bitch."

"And it has bad memories now."

She didn't say anything. I thought I heard a sniffle. I felt bad for her.

"Do you know anyone in Hollywood?"

"A friend from art school. He said it's cool and would be good for me. The sunshine will be too."

"I'm happy for you, Bibi. It seems like we're both starting

over." I was a little tipsy from the martinis. This was like a lifeline.

"There's something else." She sounded like she didn't want to tell me.

"Go ahead. I'm a big girl." I hoped the bit of humor would lighten her fear even though I was scared of what was coming.

"The Feds asked me a lot of questions about you ... and that Gerard guy? They seemed almost more interested in that than the crime group."

Fuck.

I tried to remain unconcerned. "I heard that too. I'm sure they still want me to be bait for the Boston Beanies."

She curled her lip. "We don't call Boston Beantown. Only outsiders do that. How'd you know Boston was called Beantown?"

"Growing up in New Hampshire. You know how we feel about Massachusetts. Taxachusetts. Massholes. You get the drift. No offense."

"Not new. You don't want to hear what we call people from New Hampshire."

"Glad I moved years ago." I wanted her to stay on the line. "Hey, I just bought a house."

"Cool. Look, I have to go. They're calling my flight. Sorry I can't talk more."

"Sure, OK. Is this number good to call you?"

She said yes, and we hung up. I headed back to my room, happier than I'd been in a long time. I made another list.

- Check in with PI in Kauai.
- Have money transferred to my account.

- Get the room sizes of the house, floor plan, from realtor.
- Buy minimum of furniture for now.
- Buy car.
- Get post office box.
- Buy new laptop.
- Try to stay strong.

I hadn't listened to Patrick's voicemail yet, so I decided to suck it up, and I did.

"Angeline, this is Patrick. I'd love it if you called me back. I'd like to be friends. I enjoyed our time together."

I wanted to call back and say, "Oh, really? Is that why you made such detailed notes about me?" I was done with him. He'd leave, and that would be that. What I didn't understand was why, when we were on the plane, would he draw my attention to his notebook if it weren't innocent?

I sighed, sick of trying to figure out everything. I just wanted to be in my house with my laptop, maybe doing research for an environmental group as I had on Kauai or something else worthwhile like working to stop human trafficking.

Or, hell, what about reading a good book or making fudge?

I laughed at that one. Me, make fudge? Hank was the cook. I was better at takeout.

When the cell rang in my hand, I almost dropped it. I hoped it was Bibi calling back. I really wanted to have long conversations with my new sister.

The caller was the Kauai PI. He couldn't find Tempest or any sign of her. What, he only spent hours on it and gave up? I thanked him anyway and paid his measly amount via PayPal.

So much for that. Still, I couldn't let it go. There had to be a way to find her and get her back.

The next morning, I was headed to a coffee shop when my burner rang. A call on the SIGNAL app, so I knew it was her.

"Hey, Snoop, do you ever sleep?"

"Not lately. You've got another one."

"What do you mean?"

"Remember when I couldn't find anything on the Frenchman? I can't find anything on your Patrick Toth."

"Crap."

"Yeah, you really attract these Bozos."

"Haha. Thanks. But that's not good news. He's probably a Fed."

Silence.

"All right. How about Bibi?"

"Lots on her. She's legit. She's your sister? Wow. A black woman? Different fathers or mothers?"

I'd never heard her talk this much.

"Long story, Snoop. Whatcha find?"

Everything Snoop told me, I already knew. Until she got to the end, to the financial info. "She's going to be one filthy rich bitch. With Betty's inheritance, her parents' estate, and the portion of the partners' business—"

"Wait. What do you mean a 'portion of the partners' business?'"

"Betty's partners, the ones who took over the business."

"That's Ralph and Rena, Sam's brother and Betty's cousin."

"Right. And they're still in business. I suspect someone is protecting them since they haven't been busted."

Maybe the Bureau's mole was involved with the crime group. Corruption was everywhere.

"Interesting, Snoop. I didn't know Bibi had a piece of the operation."

"Yes. Since turning twenty-one."

I wondered why Bibi hadn't mentioned this. She must know about it.

"There's something else. There's another partner, a silent partner."

"Who? When?"

"I'll find out for you. Recent."

"Yes, please do." Who the hell could that be? "Let me know as soon as you can. Thanks, Snoop."

After hanging up, I called Patrick. I couldn't let this go. I needed to know what he was up to.

"Hey!" he said, sounding excited. "I thought maybe I'd chased you away."

"How about meeting here at the Market in half an hour? I need coffee."

"Sounds good."

I spent the half-hour considering a strategy and how to trap the prick in his lies.

50

The rain fell hard and cold. I ran from my car to the market's French cafe, kicking myself for not dressing warmly. I bought a house coffee and picked a table away from the crowd and the entrance.

When Patrick showed, he seemed nervous and unsure of himself. Whether that was put on or not, I'd find out. He didn't start in yapping. All he said was, "I'll be right back. I need some tea."

When he came back, he had a to-go cup. I knew that scent. "Peppermint tea?" I asked.

He nodded. Suddenly the talker had become mute.

"Let's get down to the real reason you have an interest in me. I didn't buy your whole act. You asked too many personal questions and answered very few of mine."

He opened his mouth to say something but didn't.

If he were FBI, I'd bet he'd been strategizing, too. I waited him out, knowing he couldn't keep silent for long.

Finally, he said, "I'm sorry you don't believe me. I guess I came on too fast." He did look remorseful. "I guess I do ask too many questions. Really, I just wanted to get to know you."

I smiled and locked eyes with him. "I don't believe that, either."

His mouth twitched. Oh, he wasn't liking this one bit.

"Tell me, Patrick, or whatever your name is, what do you want?"

"What do you mean, 'Whatever your name is?'"

I snorted.

"Why are you being so unkind? All I've done is show an interest in you as a possible friend. Maybe more. But I don't deserve this."

I sat back and wondered how long he could keep up this fake front.

"OK, Patrick, I apologize. But I need you to explain something to me."

"What is it?"

"Why is your notebook full of details about me, not lists like you said?"

He struggled to keep still but had to pick up his tea to hold in front of his mouth. He blew on it as if to cool it, but his face turned hard-jawed, thin-lipped, and squinty-eyed. Every bit of the Patrick he'd shown before disappeared.

"You looked at my notebook. When?"

"When you were taking a call outside."

"Are you paranoid or mentally ill?"

"Are you FBI?"

Now he looked amused. "Why would you think I was FBI?"

"Because you have no info on the net, nada. Your company doesn't exist. You don't exist. Or at least Patrick Toth, the chemical engineer from Naples, Florida who knew Hank, doesn't exist. So what's the deal?" My voice was loud enough to make two women at a nearby table stop talking and look over at us.

He leaned forward and folded his hands together, probably so they wouldn't strangle me. "You should do your homework better. My company isn't public. I don't grant interviews. I'm not on social media. I do all my work anonymously. I don't want anyone to know about me. My patents are under my corporation's name. Everything I do, I do as secretly as possible because someone is always trying to steal this kind of work. Hank should have explained that to you. And I did meet Hank. If he were alive, he could attest to that."

"So you understand my paranoia. At least you should."

"Why would you think I was FBI?"

"You really don't know much about me. Even though I told you very little about me, I shouldn't have told you anything."

"You haven't answered my question. Why would you think I was FBI?"

"I'm not answering that question. What I will say is I'm sorry that I had to snoop in your notebook, which you still haven't explained."

"Tell me about the FBI, and I'll tell you about the notebook."

"No. I think I'll pass."

Now he looked crushed, like a little boy who was told he wouldn't get an iPhone for Christmas.

It was a stalemate. We held each other's gaze until he stood, held out his hand to shake, and said, "I'm sorry it turned out this way, Angeline." We shook. Then he picked up his tea and walked off.

I rubbed my forehead. I'd overreached, hoping to force information from him. I knew I came off as a bitch, so that would end any interest he had in me. Snoop could double-check everything he told me. Obviously, he was using a false name, and he sure seemed paranoid about his business. I wish Hank were alive. So many things I should have paid attention to about his business, asked questions about. Still, I'd been so busy trying to put criminals behind bars. I wondered if Patrick *did* live in Naples. It didn't matter now. He was gone. Something else I didn't have to worry about. Unless he *was* FBI, which now I doubted. He had no poker face. I popped an aspirin.

After drinking my coffee, I called Iolana again, but no answer. I rang Gerard. The number was still disconnected. I deleted the number. I thought about calling Kathleen, but I was too tired. A friendly voice was much needed right now.

Back at the B&B, a large bouquet of tropical flowers had been delivered while I was gone and set on the credenza.

The note with them said, "I hope coffee together leads us to a closer understanding. Patrick."

"Closer understanding?" I said. "What the hell does that mean?" I didn't have time for this bullshit.

I crumpled up the note and threw it away.

51

The rain continued over the next few days. I worked on my list.

When I called Snoop and told her what Patrick had told me, she said she'd keep looking.

My new BMW was delivered. I was smoking again, not just one a day. But not in the BMW.

I got an internet provider for my new super-fast, memory-loaded MacBook.

I bought furniture to be delivered when the house closed. Luckily, no one was in the house, so I didn't have to wait to move.

An acquaintance, an interior design consultant, audibly gasped when I called her and told her who I was. She was so professional she didn't bring up the rumors that had circulated after I disappeared and was classified as a missing person. I didn't hesitate to tell her that after everything I'd been through, I spent a year in Kauai working through my grief. That was my tag line with everyone. It stopped any further questions, and usually, if I were talking to them in person, they hugged me. This became a ritual of sorts, and it surprised me that so many people knew about my disappearance and took this at face value.

I hired the interior decorator. I just couldn't do it myself. It had always been Angeline-and-Sophie. Mom used to call us Sisters-Times-Two. I had the list-making-get-things-done management skills. Sophie had the artistic touch—and so did Bibi. Suddenly it felt like they were the sisters-times-two, and I was "the other one." How had Mom ever dealt with giving up Bibi? Too many questions, questions that would never be answered.

I threw myself into creating a type of sanctuary with my house, a home where I could forget the past and work toward a future, whatever that might be. The realtor got it right about the house. I loved the little gazebo behind it. I also loved the kitchen. Hell, maybe I'd even make fudge. Someday. Doubtful. I was never that bored.

I hired someone to put a kennel in the backyard. I would remain optimistic about Tempest. I had to. But not knowing was killing me. How hard had the PI tried? To him, Tempest was "just a dog." Well, not to me.

I moved in two weeks later. My footsteps echoed when crossing the wood floor. I loved the intimate living room and fireplace. Outside, the rain continued. No one called except my lawyer and the interior decorator. After I moved in, I set up a small work area with my new laptop. I needed a printer.

In a new document, I wrote down everything I remembered about Patrick. Then I started writing down everything about my parents that I'd learned. I found Linda, a genealogist, who told me what to do to first start researching my father. I joined ancestry.com and sent off my DNA in the form of spit, then paid for the monthly services so I would hear from others who connected with me.

I wasn't sleeping well. Iolana and her crew had stopped searching for Tempest. I hadn't heard from Gerard, and I had to finally let that go. I cried. I wasn't getting Tempest back.

I downloaded "Tainted Love," and kept it on repeat. I burned candles. I was going to say goodbye to them all, the whole lot of them—Sophie, Hank, Mom and Dad, Tempest, even Gerard. I wasn't, however, willing to say goodbye to Bibi. I needed to keep her, even if it was for an occasional call. Maybe we could get together for Christmas.

I would change. I needed something, I just didn't know what.

The weeks passed. I'd hoped to feel normal again, at least somewhat. So much had happened, and I wasn't sure if I was OK, really OK. I kept dropping things. A few times, I ran for my gun when I heard voices outside. Most of the time, what I'd heard were normal street noises—kids, one of our elderly neighbors swearing at something invisible, the garbage truck. I wanted to believe I was no longer in danger and my past was past. I let the tears run, the sobs sob, the aches run their course.

One night, I curled up in my chair with a blanket and a fire in the fireplace. I'd bought a book. I didn't go in for all the Eastern religions or religion at all for that matter. I didn't know what else there was. But while browsing in J. Michael's Books, I found a copy of *The Encyclopedia of Women's Myths and Secrets*. That matched my lawyer's brain, something new to learn. Plus, I'd been dealing with so many secrets lately I figured it might give me some insight—to what I didn't know. At least this knowledge was something that had a different spin from what usually attracted me. I looked up Sophie's name.

"Canonical adaptation for The Gnostic Great Mother. ...

Sophia once represented God's female soul, source of his power. ..."

It went on for about fourteen paragraphs. Whoa. Where and when had all this history been lost? Or probably destroyed? Well, what else was new?

The fir sap spit and popped as it burned, making me edgy. I tried to focus.

So, Mom had given Sophie that name. Had she known? Maybe had a sense that Sophie would have made a great mother? But why had she called me Angeline? That was so off base. Mom had never considered me an angel.

Curious, I looked up the root of my name and found what other cultures had called angels: apsaras, Valkyries, Horae, Houris, Peris, fairies. And then this:

"A guardian angel was a personal Shakti who watched over a man and took him into her ecstatic embrace at the moment of death."

Well, hell's bells. That was a beaut.

Mom once told me that she'd had dreams about how to name us, so I wasn't surprised. Then I thought of Bibi. Didn't Kathleen say that Mom had named her that, and when Dad left her at a Boston fire station, he'd pinned a note with her name written on it? Or had Bibi told me that?

I Googled *Bibi*. It could, of course, be short for Elizabeth, but I didn't think so.

Then up popped Ebíbí, a Yoruba Nigerian name for the month of May.

Sophie had been born in May.

I took a big leap. Mom had named her Bibi as a clue that her father was Nigerian. I wondered if Bibi had ever thought of where the name came from. I would call her in the morning to tell her. Right now, it was too late to call with the three-hour time difference.

The light rain suddenly turned to a downpour and the wind battered the windows. I stood and closed the curtains.

In the kitchen, I poured a few almonds into a clay bowl, but knocked over the bowl. The nuts went flying. I scooped them up and was headed back to my chair when a truck with a loud motor pulled into the driveway. I set down the bowl and picked up my phone. A door opened, and a gruff man's voice said something I couldn't hear. I turned off my reading light and headed to the credenza in the hall where I kept my gun in my shoulder bag. I made sure it was loaded.

A man's voice said, "Shh. Quiet, for fuck sake." The screech of metal on metal made my heart race and my breath quicken. The front door was locked, but there were plenty of ways to get in, including breaking a window. I tried not to move. More metal on metal screeches. The man spoke again in a hushed command. "That's it. Let's get out of here."

I waited until the truck pulled out of the driveway and headed down the road, the muffler backfiring and adding to my fired-up nerves. I sniffed the air, hoping not to smell gasoline or something burning. I shook myself, trying to regain focus. I had no idea why a truck would pull in here without making their presence known or what the noises meant. Maybe they were dumping off some metal garbage bins because they didn't want to pay for garbage service. I needed to chill.

But I couldn't. I waited. When I was certain they were gone, I took a flashlight in hand and the gun in the other. I unlocked the door and peeked out. The metal sound came from a rusty cage that sat at the bottom of the porch stairs. My brain flashed Kauai and the men who had almost killed Tempest. I raced down the steps. There was an animal in the cage.

Rain dripped down my face as I flung open the unlocked cage door. I shined the light on the inside. I gagged and fell back. It was a dog. Oh, God, no. I scrambled to my feet. Then I squatted to look closer. It was some kind of roadkill, but it wasn't Tempest. I covered my mouth and backed away. Bile rose to my throat.

In the house, I splashed water on my face. I was about to call the police when my cell rang. A male voice.

"You stashed a couple million of ours. We want it. We'll send you instructions on how to transfer it. Do it tomorrow, or it won't be an animal in that cage next time." He hung up. He hadn't even tried to disguise his voice. But I couldn't tell who it was. No one I knew.

I sank onto the floor and rocked back and forth.

52

I stood, shaky and chilled. Far from calm but resolute. Any lawyer knows those two things don't always ignite together. But once they mingle, they can make shit happen—and fast. I would end this. I would wire them the money. This had to end.

So in the morning I did.

I followed the instructions, wired the money, and closed the Maryland account. Then I called the police to say someone had played a terrible prank and told them what was in my front yard. They sent an officer from animal control to take care of the cage and roadkill. He asked if I was all right followed by a few questions that I answered. My eyes were swollen. I looked like hell. The officer apologized and said how sorry he was. I nodded. If only he knew.

After he left, I called Bibi, needing a connection, if not friendly, at least family. She didn't answer, so I left a message, telling her about her name and asking her if she'd ever tried to find out about her lineage. I explained I was looking into our genealogy and wanted her to know how much our connection meant to me. I hung up. Actually, Bibi was the only person who meant anything to me now.

My nerves fired on high again. This nightmare seemed to go on and on. But I'd done what they'd asked. That better be the fucking end of it.

The memory of that dead animal in the cage brought on a major crying jag. They had their money, but would I get Tempest? I doubted it. Those bloodsuckers didn't care. I had no doubt the Boston gang would go after what Hank left me from the business. I needed to subvert them somehow. Maybe by sending them the money I'd bought a little more time.

I dabbed at my eyes with a paper towel. I remembered the dog we had when I was little, right after Sophie was born. Dad brought it home, some kind of hound. I can't even remember its name, but I loved that mutt. When we moved, we couldn't get a place to live that would let us have animals, so dad gave it away. I didn't know it at the time. All I knew is that one day we had a dog, the next we didn't. It was weird that I just now remembered that.

I zapped a frozen meal in the microwave, but couldn't eat. I could always get another dog, but the thought made me nauseous. I shoved the meal into the fridge. Somehow, Tempest and I had a connection. I hoped Bibi and Otto were safe. If Bibi weren't part of the Boston gang, what would keep Ralph and Rena from going after her part of the business, even her inheritance? They could blackmail her as they did me and if they didn't get the money, kill her. But from what Gerard had told me, it didn't sound as if these two were the "heavies" of the outfit. Gerard thought there was someone else heading the gang. But we had nothing, nada, not a clue as to who it could be. Unless Gerard was holding something back.

After making an appointment with a security company, I almost called Bibi again. If she knew where her money came from and how, what then? From Snoop's new info, it sounded like she'd benefited well from the "business."

The next night I pulled all the curtains and kept my gun handy. This time, after pouring a healthy two fingers of scotch, I curled up in my chair and watched shows on my laptop. Buying a TV was still on my list.

On the second night after the roadkill delivery, while searching for a movie, I heard a vehicle pull into the driveway. What? No!

I yanked on my boots, grabbed my gun, turned on the porch light, and opened the door. This time the truck was more of a small U-Haul. I couldn't see through the driving rain. Holding the gun at my side, I waited for a figure to emerge. The figure in raingear bounced up the stairs, took one look at me, and staggered backwards.

"Whoa-don't-shoot-don't-shoot-I'm-just-a-delivery-guy." A white-knuckled grip on the rail, he walked backwards down the stairs.

"Quick. Tell me. What do you want?"

"I ... I ... Are you ... Angeline ... Porter?" He stuttered. "I have a ... delivery for you."

The guy raced to the back of the truck. He looked like a kid.

I stuck the gun in my back waistband, zipped up my raincoat, and pulled the hood over my head. The automatic porch lights were on, and I looked around outside. The vehicle had no signage.

I had to shout above the rain's din. "What's in the truck?"

The guy shouted back, "It's a dog."

I stopped like I'd hit a wall. "It better be alive."

"It is, it is, honest!" He nodded so hard I thought he'd snap his neck.

I raced to the back of the truck. I yelled, "Tempest?"

The guy struggled to open the back. I took deep breaths as the door rolled up. I couldn't see inside. He took a leash from a hook. My chest hurt. My eyes adjusted to the lack of light. There was one cage in the truck.

"Tempest!"

There was a familiar woof, then a whine. I moved closer. "Hurry," I said. "Please."

The young man opened the cage, leashed Tempest, and walked her to the end of the truck. Tears rolled down my cheeks mingling with rain as I hugged her. She whined and licked my face. She was home. I hadn't lost her. "Oh, thank heavens."

I was a mess. Laughing, I said her name over and over, and in a giddy voice I said to the young man, "Thank you. Thank you so much. I'm sorry about the gun."

The delivery guy lifted her down to the ground, handed me the leash, and asked me to sign his bill of lading to say he'd delivered the dog. His hands were still shaking. I signed. I was so happy, I went to hug him, but he jumped back. I apologized. He hurried to the driver's seat, jumped in, and locked the door, duty done. Crazy lady's signature on the delivery notice.

The delivery notice. The bill of lading. I needed a copy. I hadn't even looked at it. I knocked on the window. "Wait!" I yelled. "I need a copy of the delivery notice."

The guy jumped, started the engine, and rolled down the window an inch. "I can't, lady. I was told not to."

I pretended to go for my gun. He grabbed the clipboard, ripped a yellow copy off the bottom of the papers, and slid it through the window opening. "Is that it?"

It got wet as I shoved it in my pocket. I nodded. He backed out fast and was gone.

When I looked down, Tempest jumped on me. I rubbed her head and ears, and we went into the house. She was wet, and so was I, but I didn't care. I needed this. One single win and it meant the world. How had I become so attached to a dog?

After wiping down Tempest with a towel, I pulled my uneaten meal from the fridge and fed it to her. I put out a bowl of water then poured some scotch, sat on one of the bar stools, and watched her, wiping away tears. She checked out the house, sniffing every corner in every room. "That's a good girl. This is your new home." Her tailed wagged. Her eyes were bright, but she smelled and needed a bath. Then she flopped on the floor at my feet and fell asleep. Just like that.

As Tempest's chest rose and fell, I thought of Gerard. If I had his number, I'd call and thank him. I knew the thugs wouldn't return Tempest if they'd had her. Why bother? So it had to be Gerard. He deserved an apology too. I hadn't kept my end of the bargain in helping him put the Boston Beanies away. I'd cut and run. I'd gone to see Bibi. The FBI could bring this group down, but I thought Gerard wanted me in it with him to finish the job, more like bringing closure to losing Sophie. But our connection was more than that. What it was I couldn't say. Something primal, like experiencing a dangerous situation together. And we were still in it.

Now it seemed I was in deeper than ever with having Bibi as a sister. If she had a cut in the organization, did that mean she was receiving stolen money, or was the inheritance from Betty's legitimate wealth? The FBI had found nothing on the home and business computers, so that meant the criminal end of the business was kept separate and on other computers that probably belonged to Ralph and Rena. I wondered what was said between Bibi and the FBI, what they asked her when they interviewed her. What did they now know? What had she told them? Had she given them info on where to find all the files?

I ruffled Tempest's ears. She woke and licked my hand.

I sat down again, sipped the scotch, and with a pen and the notebook I kept in my purse, I scribbled a list of possibilities.

- Does Bibi have part of the illegal business side and does she know it?
- Ralph and Rena could want her in the gang to make them look legitimate.
- What exactly does their criminal enterprise look like on paper?
- Is Bibi a foil of some kind?
- Could Bibi have taken over for Betty? (Not likely. Nothing in her demeanor, language, or our conversations pointed to that. Even her mannerism showed she hadn't lied.)
- Unless she's an excellent actress.

An excellent actress. Maybe. I chewed the end of my pen. I wasn't a great judge of character in this case. I *wanted* to believe Bibi was innocent. My gut said she was. But my brain was wired to believe evidence, not a hunch.

Lawyers also needed to be aware and careful of their biases and prejudices. If Betty had mentored her, Bibi could easily be playing all of us for fools. I needed a transcript of her interview with the FBI to see if what she told them matched what she told me. A case against an organization like this was always difficult, especially if the group was involved with crooked politicians and law enforcement. Sometimes, however, it only took one discrepancy to lead to incriminating evidence.

Tired, I curled up on the couch with Tempest and watched an episode of "Women Who Kill," the show that used "Tainted Love" as a song for the 1980s part of the story.

Sometime in the future, I'd find out the truth. But for now, this moment, I was content with paying off those thugs and having Tempest next to me, licking my fingers. She loved salt and vinegar chips.

When my cell rang, Tempest growled. The ID read NO ID. Then the caller hung up. When it rang again with NO ID, I answered.

53

"Hey, Snoop."

I heard a muffled voice in the background.

"Hello?"

I was about to hang up when Gerard said, "It's not Snoop. It's me. I thought I told you to stop communicating with her."

"Gerard?" I sat up. "Where are you? Are you all right?"

"Angeline, you must stop communicating with this hacker. Do you understand?"

"No, I don't. If you won't give me a reason, I'll continue to use her. Can you tell me if she's putting me in danger? Is she dangerous? Part of the Boston gang?"

"You need to trust me."

I laughed. "As if I can trust anyone." I paused. "Tempest was delivered yesterday."

"Did she arrive safely? Was she in good shape?"

"Yes. She's right here next to me on the couch."

"Good." He sounded tired.

"Thank you for getting her back to me and keeping your

promise." I waited for him to say something. "Where did you find her?"

"I can't stay on, Ang. I just wanted to check on Tempest and hear your voice."

Hear my voice? "I'm happy to hear your voice, too. Can you give me your number in case I need to call you?"

"No, Angeline. That's not possible. I just wanted to say ... hello."

I bit down on my lip and said under my breath, "Oh, for fuck's sake, Gerard. What the hell is going on? You looked terrible at the airport. Are you back on the Boston case? Do you need my help?"

"I can't talk, Angeline. Please do me a favor and keep a low profile. I want you to know that I'm trying to keep you safe."

"Safe? I paid off the Boston gang. Hopefully, they won't come after the rest of my money. But I'm scared for Bibi. Please tell me you're keeping her safe too."

He didn't say anything.

"Gerard, did you hear me?"

"*Oui.* Yes."

"Is there something you need to tell me? Is Bibi all right?"

"I must go, Ang. I miss you. I'm glad you have Tempest."

What? "It's not fair to call like this then—"

He hung up.

Damn him! And screw that. It didn't sound like he was going to keep Bibi safe. Why was he being so secretive? Some big FBI operation to take down the Boston group?

A sudden chill shot up my back. Maybe it was coincidence, maybe not, but why did I get Tempest back right after I paid the money? Tempest had been gone a while. I'd been back for weeks. Gerard had had time to find her, or

have one of his flunkies find her, and return her to me. I
didn't like the timing, and I hated coincidences.

"What an idiot," I said out loud. Tempest looked at me
as if saying *You're not talking to me, right?*

Now the questions piled up. How had he found
Tempest? Who had taken her in the first place? How did he
get her away from whomever had her on Kauai? Or had he
known where she was all this time? Why would he do that?
How was it he sent her two days after I paid the money? He
didn't sound surprised when I told him I'd paid off the gang.
Maybe he was still undercover. He could have been the one
to force me to pay the gang to prove he was one of them. He
knew how much that dog meant to me. Those thugs
wouldn't know to use Tempest as a bargaining chip.

My monkey mind would not shut up. I hugged Tempest
and pulled the bowl of chips away from her stare. My heart
raced. My cell rang. I checked the ID. Patrick. I let it go, but
of course, he left a voicemail. I deleted it.

The bill of lading. I jumped off the couch, scaring
Tempest and berating myself for not thinking of it earlier.
Stupid! I raced to the bedroom and took the bill of lading
from my pants pocket, flattening it on the bed. I couldn't
read it in the dim light and went back to the living room and
my reading lamp.

Under the lamp, I read the sender's name and address. It
was a pet relocation service. The owner: Angeline Porter.
The sender: G. Duvernet. Where were the forms? There had
to be forms. Nothing traveled without forms, especially a
pet. They'd have to show vaccinations at the very least.
Perhaps that was handled by the service. Maybe being FBI,
Gerard had special dispensations. I'd call the pet relocation
service in the morning, but I didn't expect to learn anything
new.

I plopped onto the couch. Tempest jumped up and laid her chin on my thigh. The rain beat a steady curtain around us. The night would be a long one. One thing I knew from his call: I wasn't out of this mess yet. He hadn't called just to find out about Tempest. He'd called to tell me he was trying to keep me safe which meant I wasn't safe.

And he hadn't answered my question about Bibi.

54

In the morning, I woke early, my hackles up. I wondered if the mob would come after the money I had in trust and would Gerard be working with them. Since he hadn't answered my question about Bibi being safe, I assumed they would also go after her inheritance when it became available. They could play Bibi and me against each other, saying they'd kill the other sister if we didn't turn over what we had. But they could only do that one time. So which one of us had the most money coming to us?

I had Hank's business buy out. Bibi not only had the inheritance from Betty, but her brother's estate too. I'd bet on her. That meant they'd want her money and would threaten to kill me if she didn't turn it over to them. But I didn't mean that much to Bibi, not yet anyhow. And if she were already in the gang, they'd come after me anyway and pick me clean.

But I wasn't going to let any of that happen. I'd been moved around like a piece in a dangerous chess game for too long. I could clean up this mess with a strategy. That's what I did as a lawyer—usually clean up other people's messes. I'd won most of my cases. An excellent strategy could fire me up. Time to get back into the fight for justice—or at least something resembling it.

I jumped out of bed and tromped to the kitchen, Tempest right behind me. I let her out back to do her business. Then I slammed together some coffee, ate a blueberry muffin, and checked both my phones. Nothing on the burner phone.

When Tempest came in, she lay on the tile floor, asleep again. She'd been through so much. I didn't like thinking about what that was. The early morning traffic whizzed by, and children noisily walked to their schools. Cars headed out of driveways. Everyone moving.

On my phone, I Googled the name of the pet relocation company on the bill of lading and called the one I found closest to Kauai in Honolulu. As I waited for the call to go through, I pictured Gerard the last time I saw him at the New Hampshire airport, haggard, wrinkled clothing, bloodshot eyes. What had happened to him? How could he have arranged for Tempest to be delivered to me?

"Hello. Honolulu Pet Relocation. This is David."

"Hi, David." I told him I had my dog sent to me by his company. The animal was in terrific shape, no problems there, but I'd received no papers, such as vaccinations or a health certificate. I gave him the info from the bill of lading.

I could hear the keys of his computer tap. Then he said, "Would you excuse me? I have to put you on hold."

That usually wasn't a good sign. I waited.

"I'm sorry, Mrs. Porter, but we have no record of that transport. The bill of lading invoice number doesn't match our records either. We don't even use that form."

I asked him if there were any other companies by that name, as it seemed pretty generic to me. He said not that he knew of. I asked if there was any other way he could help me. He said maybe check some of the other pet relocation companies. Then he said, "Your pet had to have flown. Maybe an airline could give you some info? Also, the number in the red box isn't ours. Have you called it? It's not a Hawaii number. I tried calling it, but it's been disconnected." I hadn't called that number as I could barely read it as a phone number. I thanked him and hung up. Then I blew up a photo of the bill of lading and wrote down the number. Even then it was difficult to read.

What could I do now? I could have Snoop check out the bill of lading and see if she could find out anything else. I could also put her onto finding out what airline Tempest flew on, and if there was a way to check private flights. The only other way to find out was to force Gerard to tell me, but I didn't have his number.

He was in no position to do anything if he was undercover. He sure couldn't keep me safe. Hell, I couldn't even keep me safe. None of us could. That was a fallacy, an illusion even. There was no safety in the world.

Time for me to take charge of my life. There was no way I could return to a normal life. I needed to be part of bringing down this criminal gang. Where was that badass lawyer I used to be? Time to drag her out of hiding.

I sat down at my computer with my mug of coffee and opened a new document. I would start with the usual: make a list of unknowns and try to answer them or create the steps to find the answers.

- The main question: is Bibi involved with the gang? Ask Bibi for everything she told the FBI.

- Can I get a transcript? Ask Snoop if she could get a copy of the interview.
- Have Snoop get info on Ralph and Rena, the bill of lading, and who has the financial files for the gang's operation, if that's possible.
- What is Gerard's main operational goal—to bring down the Boston gang or find out who is the rogue FBI agent? Is the rogue FBI agent possibly the head of the mob or just getting paid off to leave them alone? Can't find out anything until G contacts me again. If he contacts me again.
- Tell Snoop that Gerard told me not to contact her. See what Snoop says about this. Trust Snoop? Yes. Why? All her info so far had been good. Then why does Gerard want me to cut off communicating with her other than what she's doing is probably illegal? Go with gut. Trust her.
- Patrick: who is he? Check with Hank's engineering buddies who worked with him in China. Call the florist shop to see how he paid for my flowers. He could be FBI. OR what if he *is* the rogue FBI agent? Could that be possible? And what would he want with me?
- Kathleen: keep her informed? No, not yet.
- The Gang: time to bring them down. I don't want them out there doing this to other people, especially women. So much hangs on Bibi not being part of the crime group.
- Hope that G. contacts me.

I went to work. First, I made a call to Snoop.

After I gave her the little info I had on Ralph and Rena, I told her that Gerard told me not to contact her.

"Do you have any idea why?"

"The Feds are salty with me. I've been a target."

"Why? There are plenty of hackers out there to chase."

"I've been trying to out a couple dirty FBI agents. These agents are like doctors and lawyers, always sticking up for their own even when their own are breaking the law. Let me deal. What else?"

"Wow, bring down Feds? Power hacker."

"No cap. I mean, seriously. So what else do you need?"

"I have a bill of lading for the delivery of my dog." I told her about my conversation with the pet transport company. "Can you find out where it came from and any other info about it? And if possible track down what airline transported Tempest."

"That it?" Snoop asked. "Send me a photo. Here's a guerilla email address for me. It's untraceable, will last twenty-four hours then disappear."

I wrote down the address. We hung up. I sent the photo.

Now to find out about Patrick. I called the florist Patrick had used to send me flowers. They said he paid cash. Shit. So that was out. I asked the woman to describe him. She did. He'd made an impression. It was Patrick. But he left no information or contact, not even his phone number. Now I was confident he was either FBI—or maybe someone associated with the Boston gang.

After another cup of coffee, while staring at my screen, an idea popped into my head. How about Googling Betty Snayer's name, Bibi's so-called godmother and dead gang leader? Damn. I was slipping. I should have thought of that right away.

I found several Boston papers with articles on her life and death. The press had little to say about her estate, only that law enforcement had frozen her assets until their investigation on her death and business enterprise was complete. No mention of the partners. Someone was keeping it pretty hush-hush.

I ticked off my list's completed actions and added, "Buy printer."

Time to call a few of Hank's engineering pals who were with him in China and ask about Patrick.

55

A fter leaving messages on two of Hank's engineering associates' phones, I took my coffee and Tempest to the backyard, where I sucked down the moist air and raised my face to the sky. Under the gazebo, the weak sun streaked through the slats. For a moment, a blanket of melancholy covered me, making me heavy, loaded down both in body and soul.

"Pull it together. This is you. You're on it. Buck up."

Revisiting my graveyard of loss was not an option. I was alive and would rebuild my life here. Just to double check, I entered the number on the bill of lading into my phone and called it, expecting to hear a disconnected message. Instead, Gerard answered. I almost accidentally hung up.

"Gerard, it's me. It's important."

"Then hurry, Wendy. What's up?"

Ah. OK, someone was with him. "Answer yes or no." I told him about Patrick as quickly and thoroughly as I could.

"Is he FBI?" I asked.

"I don't know. What's his name again?"

I gave it to him.

He halfway covered the phone as he said, "Yes, it's an old girlfriend. She's having trouble."

"Two more things. First, I need the transcripts of the FBI interview with Bibi. I want to know if what she told me lines up with what she told your lot."

"OK, I get it, Wendy, but I don't have time for this right now. Sorry. If he's bothering you, call the cops. Look, I'm meeting someone. I have a date. I have to go."

I almost shouted, "Second, were you responsible for sending Tempest to me or was it someone else? Did you do it through FBI channels?"

He hung up on me. Again. I wanted to belt him.

But he *had* given me some info. He was with someone who couldn't know I was on the other end. He said he had a date. That would imply he was back in the gang hustling rich women as he had done at the beginning with Link.

I set the phone on the bench and rubbed Tempest's ears. She groaned and put her head on my knee. But when my foot tapped, she pulled away. I rubbed my chest. My face burned. That did it. Take a stand, one way or the other. Make a decision. My gut said I needed to keep Bibi safe, therefore I would work on the assumption that she was not part of the gang. As soon as I decided that, my heart's rapid beating slowed. A good sign.

Then my cell rang. It was Bibi. Synchronicity.

"I was thinking about you," I said.

"Ang." Her voice was hard-edged and angry. "Someone was in my apartment when I got back from walking Otto."

"What? Is anything gone?"

"No. That's not the problem."

I waited.

"It was Shawn, Betty's old girlfriend."

"What?"

Her voice grew deep and ragged. "She was sitting in my computer chair. The bitch said, 'Hi, Bibi,' as if we were old friends. Scared the fuck out of me!"

"How did she get in?"

"No clue. I've rented an apartment at the CIRC on Holly-wood Circle because I was told they have great security. My apartment is on the eighth floor. Somebody let her in."

"What did she want?" I went back in the house for my smokes.

"Shit, Ang, she was dressed in haute couture, I mean like expensive. She'd never dressed like that with Betty. Full-on makeup, clear-eyed. I don't think she was coked out either. Her hair was professionally streaked and blown out gorgeous. It used to look like fright night. I almost didn't recognize her."

Outside, I lit a cigarette, thinking fast. "How did Otto respond?"

She snickered. "He growled at her at first. Then Shawn called him over. She pulled something from her pocket and gave it to him before I could stop her. I grabbed Otto and tried to take it from his mouth, but he'd already swallowed it."

"Is he all right?"

"Yes. She told me to relax, it was just a doggy treat." Bibi hissed. "She knew about him. She was prepared. That's so fucked up."

"I don't like where this is headed."

"Right? Well, the bitch has joined the business with Rena and Ralph. She's a partner. She said she bought in. I don't believe that."

"Did you get Shawn's full or real name?"

"She said her name is Talia Shawn Diamandis."

"Greek. From Boston?"

"I don't know! I didn't ask for a resume." She was almost shouting.

"Sorry. OK, tell me what she wanted."

"She said she wanted to let me know about her becoming a partner in the business, to get reacquainted, to give me her condolences in person, and to say that she hopes I'd consider becoming active in the business since I was a partner." Bibi took a deep breath. "I said I'm no partner. I was given an inheritance."

Bibi yelled at Otto to go lie down.

"She said something like, 'Sweetheart, you are a partner and you should start acting like one.' This bitch is younger than me!"

Amazingly, my mind stayed clear. "What was her end game, I mean, what did she ask of you?"

"She said there would be a meeting of the four of us soon, and I needed to attend. It was like she ignored me completely, the shysty."

"Then what?" I took a deep drag off my cigarette.

"I said, 'What about Betty? You took off right after she went missing, never contacted me, and now you're here, not a pixel of remorse or loss. What about that?'"

"Good for you. What did she say?"

"She said, 'I miss Betty every day.' I called, 'Bullshit.' But she just kept smiling, like I was amusing."

"A psychopath."

"That's what I thought, the frickin' *slampig*."

I didn't need to ask what *slampig* meant. Plus, Bibi's Boston accent was slipping through the more she talked.

"Did you ask her what your role would be in the business?"

"Nah, but I did ask what *her* role was in the business.

Guess what she said? Straight out, no jive, she said, 'I launder the money.'"

"Holy shit. She said that?" I almost choked as I inhaled. "Did she say anything else about the business?"

"No. She stood up, all hoity-toity, and said, 'Everything will be perfect, Bibi. You'll see. We won't dump you in right away. We'll walk you through everything.' I told her I didn't want to be walked through. She just laughed and said, 'It's so nice to see you again.'"

Whoa. This was not good.

"Then she tried to kiss me on the cheek. She patted Otto and left. Cool as could be. I didn't even get to ask how she got into my apartment."

"Are you in the apartment now? If you are, call and get secure locks on that door so no one at the CIRC who has a key can get in. Or move someplace else."

"She'd find me wherever I went. I won't hide. I'm not playing this bitch's game. Besides, now I have some dirt on her."

"True. But she's obviously been planning this move for a long time. Do you have a photo of her?"

"No. She hated having her picture taken. Even Betty couldn't get one. She always turned away."

"Look, I'm going to have my contacts find her, or at least try. She might be a ghost, you know, using some dead person's ID. Let me look into it. In the meantime, what are you going to do?"

"Maybe if I go along, I'll find out what she's up to. Maybe I can get a photo of her."

I loved this new tough sister.

"When I get some dirt on her, I'll throw her under the bus. Even if it brings down the business. I've lived without money before and I can do it again."

"You haven't received anything from Hastrick's estate yet?"

"No. It takes months, maybe even years until the lawyers straighten it out."

"I'm taking the next flight out."

"No, don't. I'm glad you're there though."

"I've been through this before with this group, Bibi." I wasn't ready to tell her how Betty was involved. The meeting she was going to with Rena, Ralph and Shawn would probably reveal that. Let someone else give her the shitty news.

After we hung up, I called Gerard and got a disconnected message. I doubted it was disconnected. Just a ploy to keep unwanted callers away. But he could have destroyed that burner right after my last call. I'm sure the FBI supplies of burners would need more than one landfill.

Again, I opened my suitcase on the bed. Tempest trotted into the bedroom and sat at my feet, looking up with that dog-wise understanding that I might be leaving again.

56

I n case I needed to make a quick trip to Bibi's, I found two lovely women with great references who cared for dogs. Tempest took to them right away, nuzzling their hands, leaning against them, taking a biscuit. I gave them a gentle warning not to give any info to anyone who asked about Tempest or me.

After meeting them and on my way to Office Depot to pick up a printer, my cell rang. I answered without looking at the ID.

"It's Patrick. Don't hang up, Ang. I need to apologize. But I have something important to tell you first."

I was in no mood for cat and mouse conversations.

"Spit it out, Patrick. I'm busy." I gunned my car past a semi-truck.

"My name isn't Patrick Toth. My name is Ian McKnight. I'm your brother."

A pale-blue vintage Thunderbird passed me. The license plate read *THDRBRD*. "No shit, idiot. Talk about redundant."

"What did you say? Angeline? Are you OK?"

"Give me a second, will you?"

I had to force myself to slow down and get in the right hand lane. "This is not a good time. So, you're claiming to be my brother? How would you know that?" I heard him swallow and exhale.

"I'm your half-brother. My dad is your biological father."

I kept my eyes on the traffic. My hands sweated on the wheel. My brother. My brain would not process this. Patrick. The guy I thought might be either FBI or part of the Boston mob.

"Ang?"

"I'm here. " I struggled to say something. "How do you know this?"

"I told my dad I was going to do one of those DNA tests. He said not to, not until he and I talked."

"And?"

"I'm sorry. I had to get to know you before I told you. I was trying to be careful for both of us."

"Look, I'm driving right now and this has me shook. Can I call you back in a few minutes."

"Of course."

I hung up and slowed to take the exit onto Coburg Road. My body felt like it had been injected with speed. I didn't know what to think. It made sense, though. All three of us girls had different fathers. I knew that from Kathleen. But all of this was too much on top of everything else. My nerves were so fried they crackled.

I pulled into the parking lot at Office Depot, took a few deep breaths. A half-sister. A half-brother. My biological father. Finally, I felt chill enough to call Patrick back. "No," I reminded myself. "Ian. His name is Ian."

When he answered, I said, "So, Ian, your father is my biological father?"

"Yes."

"Does he know about me?"

"Yes."

"Any proof of this?"

"He saved photos of your mom and the letters she wrote to him. Her name was Annie, right?"

"Yes." I was shaking. "He has letters? From my mom?" My voice croaked.

"Yes. He said he was willing to share them with you, if it will help."

I had no idea how it would help other than to prove they wrote to each other.

"You do realize that the whole thing you did on the plane and in Eugene freaked me out. I thought you were FBI. Or a ..." I didn't want to say mobster, so I said, "stalker."

"I'm so sorry. I've never had to deal with anything like this, and I wasn't sure about you. I did some research and read about you in the paper and online, how your sister committed suicide, your husband died, then you disappeared, leaving behind an inheritance. I was trying to see what kind of person you were. I didn't want my dad disappointed or hurt." He paused. "Why would you think I was FBI?"

I rubbed my eyes. What could I say that wouldn't take an hour or two to explain?

"It's a long story, and I don't have the energy to tell you right now. Plus, I'd like to see those letters from my mom. But right now I have a major family issue." Yeah, issue is right. "I might be heading to Hollywood, Florida to help my half-sister."

"Half-sister? OK. I happen to live in Naples, Florida. I didn't lie about that. Naples is only a few hours away from Hollywood. If I can help in any way, please, I'd be happy to."

"Ian, when can I see the letters Mom wrote to your dad? It would really help. Along with anything else he can send to me to prove he's my father. You said he has photos? Can you text them to me?"

"Since you were a lawyer, I understand you need evidence. I'll have him email the photos and anything else he thinks is appropriate."

I smiled at this. "Thank you."

"I'm with you, Angeline. Whatever you need, just call me."

That caught me off guard. "You don't know what you'd be getting into. It's actually dangerous."

"You don't know what I can bring to the table, either."

"Look, let's talk later. And thank you for offering to help. I think it's a little crazy under the circumstances, especially with you not knowing the situation."

He laughed. "No worries, Sis. I can always say no if it's that crazy."

I laughed again, this time a little hysterically. "OK, Ian, I need to go into Office Depot and buy a printer. We'll talk later."

I hung up. So did my mind. It went completely blank from the overload.

I don't remember picking out a printer or paying for it. Outside, the rain came down hard and cold, dissolving my fogginess. I dodged standing water, raced to the car, and put the printer into the trunk.

I was soaked and shaking much worse when I pulled on my seatbelt. Tempest licked the water from my hand. As I headed home on 205, a convoy of Army vehicles drove by. The men looked so young. How did soldiers do it, go into battle? I'd never thought of it before. Never thought of what it took to know what to do, how to do it, even when trained.

What kept them from being paralyzed when they first entered combat? What did the brain do? How could anyone be prepared for the unexpected? A soldier had to have a mission they believed in. At trial, you had a mission. You prepared as thoroughly as possible and knew that the unexpected could happen, that you'd done your very best. From there on out, it was a matter for the opposition, judge, and jury.

But in these times of uncertainty and in my new situation, I had a second chance to get justice for a sister, and I needed to stay focused on that. I would keep this sister alive.

When I was a lawyer, I was never at risk. That is, if I kept to the law. Now I'd put myself in jeopardy again. And it wasn't just to fight for Bibi. Now the stakes were greater. I was done with this gang, this mob, how they were using us, how they thought they had power. We'd see about that. I had to bring them to justice before they did anymore harm. Now I was feeling like my old self, the Angeline Porter who had fought for those who needed me. I was back in the game.

57

After I fed Tempest, I opened my laptop on the kitchen's island counter. Ian had sent a text saying he'd emailed a few letters and two photos. He had more, but he thought that was enough to prove our connection. I was still a little shaky and wasn't sure how I'd react to what I was about to read and see. I pulled up the email, downloaded the zip file, and opened it.

Mom's letters to Ian's dad were over-the-moon love struck—and emotionally hard to read. I recognized her handwriting but was shocked by what she told him about Dad, such personal confessions, her fear, her insistence that she had to stay with him. I scrolled through the letters, thinking I couldn't be more shocked until I came to the photos. Mom looked radiant. The one with the two of them made me cry.

"Damn, Mom! What were you thinking?" She had piled up lies like rocks in a quarry. She'd obviously loved this man with all her heart. Yet, she kept telling him she couldn't leave Ron "because he would kill himself."

"Oh, Mom. He killed himself and you. That wouldn't have happened if you'd left him."

But maybe it would have. I didn't put it past my dad that he would have gone after both mom and Ian's father, maybe killed them both. But I would never know, would I?

I enlarged the photo of them again and slapped a hand over my mouth. I had my father's eyes and mouth, his brown hair. I choked up and let out a cry. This was my father. I had a father, a living father, and we looked alike.

I shut my laptop.

When I pulled myself together, I guzzled a glass of water and paced the kitchen. Being a cynic, I couldn't help thinking that this might not be a good thing. Why did I need a father after all this time? Besides, I had no idea what he was like or if we'd get along.

Plus, this was distracting me from something more important right now. All I could hear was Bibi's brave but scared voice on the phone. They weren't going to do to her what they'd done to Sophie and me.

The phone rang.

"Angeline, I can only talk for a minute."

"Gerard? Good. Listen, Bibi's in trouble, and I'm going to Florida. But first, can you send me the transcript of her interview? I need to know if what she told the agency aligns with what she told me. And I have to tell you about—"

"Angeline, no. Stay away."

"What? You asked me to be bait for this gang. I'm ready. I want to bring them down before they get to Bibi."

"*Non.* Don't."

"Why? You need to tell me. Give me something, damn it. I'm going to Florida no matter what you say, so let's talk."

"You won't change your mind?"

"No."

There was a long exasperated sigh before he said, "Then I will meet you there."

And he hung up—again! *Bâtard*.

OK, maybe he had an operation in place that he wanted me clear of and *was* trying to keep me safe. But the time for that was long gone.

58

As I made preparations to go to Florida, I called Snoop on our Signal connection. I needed info on Ian McKnight and Shawn Talia Diamandis.

"Congratulations. You have testosterone in your family," Snoop announced like an ultrasound tech announcing the sex of a baby.

I laughed. I loved this gal. "So Ian McKnight checks out?"

"Yup. Everything he told you about himself is true. He lives in Naples, he's an engineer and doesn't put anything online, I'm guessing because of research and patent stealing, etc. He has no social media or website."

"Anything personal? What about photos?"

"Some public records like his driver's license photo. That matches your description. His father is listed as living in Naples too. Swanky place on the coast, but not so bougie that he ranks with the wealthy. Legitimate as far as I can tell."

I was sweating. "What about this Shawn Talia Diamandis?"

"But before I tell you about the woman, you should know that Ian—" There was a loud click, a buzz, then silence.

"Snoop? Snoop, you there?"

The connection went dead. I held the phone out and stared at it. Shit.

I waited. Snoop didn't call back. I tried calling twenty minutes later. Nothing but a loud buzzing noise. I tried using Signal to text. It wouldn't go through. Fuck.

I hung up, took the phone out to the garage, and smashed it with the blunt end of my ax. Then I threw the pieces in the bag I kept for dead burners. Later, I would throw the parts in different trashcans. My heart pounded, this time fearing for Snoop. I had to call Gerard back. He'd better not have messed with Snoop.

My iPhone rang. Bibi.

"I talked to the manager of my apartment," Bibi blurted out, no preamble. "He's apologetic, but he doesn't think anyone on his staff would let her in."

"The evidence says otherwise. It would be hard for anyone living on service wages to turn down a big wad of cash. Someone let her in." I took a deep breath. "I'm taking the next flight out, Bibi. We need to figure out what to do about Shawn. I'll send you my info. Don't worry about picking me up. I'll rent a car."

This time she didn't try to stop me.

"I'll call my brother when I get there. He lives in Naples and has offered to help. I'll have to bring him up to speed. He might bail though when he hears what this is all about. We need to close ranks on this woman. I think this is going to get messier and more dangerous before we put the gang behind bars." I wasn't going to mention Gerard. Or what just happened to Snoop, my hacker.

Silence. I don't think what I told her registered.

"Are you all right? Can you go someplace safe until I get there?"

"I'm fine. I lived on the streets of Boston. I think I can handle it."

She'd said this before, probably to bolster her courage. Playing tough. Probably all right for now.

After I hung up, I traipsed into my bedroom and while packing what summer clothes I had, I thought about Bibi and me killing Betty. Maybe if I proved how much I wanted us to be sisters, to be close, *and* gave her proof that Betty tried to kill me first, she would forgive me for Betty's death. But it would be tough. I'd killed her godmother, the woman who saved Bibi from a life on the streets. But my gut said that no matter what evidence I had to establish Betty's guilt, she'd probably hate me for killing her godmother. I had to try, however. I had to show her that I would always be there for her and truly wanted us to have a relationship. But first, I needed to bring down the mob.

After dropping off Tempest, her bed, food and bones at the ladies' house, it was all I could do not to cry. By midnight, I was in an Uber on my way to Portland to catch an early non-stop flight to Fort Lauderdale.

I called Ian. He didn't pick up, so I left him a message to call me.

I passed towns and farms, and cars and trucks traveling south. The car seemed to hit every rough patch of highway as I tried to write out my thoughts and make a list. I felt sick leaving Tempest again, but she seemed excited to see the two women. A brief thought had hit me as I pulled away from their home, and they waved—what if I didn't come back? What if something happened to me?

I shook this off and checked my phones to see ... what? I

had no texts, no messages. I texted Bibi and reminded her to write down everything that had happened, to make sure she'd kept a log of exactly what Shawn had done and said. I also said that we should exchange passwords to our devices and laptops, just in case something happened to either one of us. I didn't want to freak her out, but I also wanted to make sure our bases were covered.

I called Gerard with my new burner number, but he didn't reply. I had three extra burners in my shoulder bag. I looked out at the hills and mountains in the distance, the cell towers visible, connecting everyone. I had to concentrate, think about what I'd do when I was with Bibi and Ian. Was this even necessary?

I wrote:

- Bibi needs backing. She's alone.
- *G and I need to work together.* He also has to fill me in on what he's doing.
- Ian seems to have a level head, but I won't involve him unless it's absolutely necessary. Then again, can I trust him? I don't really know him.
- What did Snoop start to tell me before we were cut off?
- What *happened* to Snoop? Was she busted? Or was it something else? G. needs to find out and tell me.
- Big question: why is Shawn not in Mass.? Did she follow Bibi to Florida?
- Could this be a trap for me? For us?
- And why did Shawn admit to laundering money? Why show her cards? Probably to implicate Bibi as a gang member? She could have recorded

their conversation. Did I tell any of this to G?
Can't remember.

- I should be keeping a log of everything. What the hell's the matter with me? I can't even follow my own advice.

Screw that. I had a long flight, and I could make my notes on the plane. That would get me in the right head space for when I landed. I could do a few more things. I could use my own investigative chops to research Ian and Shawn. While online, I'd look up a few pointers on how to defend myself, just in case. It might just come down to me and Bibi. Ian was an unknown at this point. He might hear what I had to tell him and run for the Gulf of Mexico and a boat. Anyone with any sense would.

It didn't matter whether he was in or not. This time I'd find a way to destroy Shawn and that mob. This time was a fight to the bitter end. I was done hiding. Done playing the victim. If I was going to end up a victim, I was going to go down saving this sister. No more running. Like in the wild, when you ran, the bear would run after you because you acted like prey and you were done for. Sometimes, though, if you stood your ground, put your arms in the air and looked frightening, growled and hissed and yelled, the bear retreated. This time, I was ready to stand my ground. Even if the bear took me down.

Thank you for reading Tainted Times 2*!*

If you loved *Tainted Times 2*, please leave a review on Amazon and Goodreads.

Readers and fans keep the energy and words flowing. It's the lifeblood of an author to be read, enjoyed, and appreciated.

I love my fans. If you want to know more about me and my life, my work, my interests, sign up for my newsletter on my website www.valeriejbrooks.com.

Again, thank you! And welcome aboard.

AFTERWORD

In this second of the three thrillers, Angeline Porter found her way back to who she was at the beginning—a tough, active legal mind and warrior for justice. She now has a sister she can help and won't be anyone's pawn again.

As she heads into the next chapters of her life, she'll land in Hollywood, Florida and BOOM, she'll fight for her and her sister's life. But all is not as it seems, as usual.

Yes, Gerard will be back. He's between a rock and a hard place being undercover while trying to keep Ang safe, which he isn't very good at. The poor guy. He knows there's a rogue FBI agent who is messing up the works, but where to put his focus?

Ang doesn't care what he does. She'll have her hands full and have to cover her own derriere. Seriously. But now she's ready.

I hope you're ready for Angeline pitting herself against the mob—and trying to find out who is really out to get her.

Sign up for my newsletter for all the info you'll need to follow this and the last of her spine-tingling story.

ACKNOWLEDGMENTS

Love, gratitude, and thanks go to:

Best pal and co-conspirator, Jan Eliot, creator of the internationally syndicated cartoon strip "Stone Soup."

My stellar LitChix writing group: Chris Scofield, author of *The Shark Curtain*, and Patsy Hand author of *Lost Dogs of Rome*.

For support in so many ways: Lois Jean Bousquet, Tom Titus, Susan Glassow, Judith Watt, Kirsten Steen, Grace Elting Castle, Quinton Hallett, Terry Brix, Sofia Dimitru, Mary Jo Comins, Karla Droste, Kassy Daggart, Johnnie Mazzocco, Nicky Connors, Marlene Howard, Tracy Miller, Samantha Ducloux Waltz, Jessica Maxwell, Linda K. Smith, Becci Crane, Kent and Debby Brooks, and Wendy Brooks.

Wendy Kendall, my co-host, on our new Crowdcast THE INVESTIGATORS BOOK GROUP

To my support group in New Hampshire: the fabulous Michelle Saia at the Book Warehouse, Tilton; my life-long friends Kevin Walsh, Jane Lamanuzzi, Nancy Rand, Bob Read, Gus O'Connor, Linda Walsh, and Vicky Chase.

Thanks to fellow bloggers Heather Weidner and Ana Gigoriu-Voicu for interviewing me and helping get the word out.

Ludwig's Book Reviews for reviewing *Revenge in 3 Parts* on his blog of extensive thriller reviews.

Howard Robertson & Margaret Robertson for the opportunity to read at the Lane Community Readers Series.

Scott Landfield and Tsunami Books and Jeremy at J. Michaels Books for keeping the faith and continuing to give writers and authors a home base.

Cindy Casey & the fabulous crew at Vero Espresso House.

Oregon Writers Colony for providing a second home and writing retreat at Colonyhouse in Rockaway Beach, Oregon; Wordcrafters; Willamette Writers; Pacific Northwest Writers Association; and Sisters in Crime.

Elizabeth George Foundation for a grant that led me to writing noir.

The residencies that gave me time and immersion to explore my writing: Hedgebrook for Women, Playa, Villa Montalvo for the Arts, Soapstone, and Vermont Studio Center.

My family. You lift me up and carry me along, always.

My pooch, Stevie Nicks, who took over one of my writing desks but has been a lousy editor. Plus, she can't sing.

My one and only, my heart and soulmate, Dan Connors, the best traveling companion and scout ever.

ABOUT THE AUTHOR

VALERIE J BROOKS' first in the Angeline Porter trilogy *Revenge in 3 Parts* was a finalist for the Nancy Pearl Book Award.

Her short stories were published in *Scent of Cedars: Thirty-two Promising Writers from the Pacific Northwest* and *France, a Love Story: Women Write About the French Experience.*

She received an Elizabeth George Foundation grant and the Monticello Award for Creative Writing. As a literary activist, she served as Associate Fiction Editor at *Northwest Review* for four years, was a Board of Directors member of Oregon Writers Colony and Eugene Ballet, was an advisor for Artists in Schools program, and co-founded Willamette Writers Speakers Series. She's a proud member of Sisters in Crime.

Valerie enjoys life in Oregon with a nearby large family and lives in the McKenzie River Valley with her husband Daniel Connors and their spirited Havanese pooch Stevie Nicks.

SIGN UP ON VALERIE'S WEBSITE TO RECEIVE HER NEWSLETTER PLUS JOIN HER ON FACEBOOK for give-aways, noir news, interesting noir fiction & film facts, and freebies.

FOLLOW HER AT

www.valeriejbrooks.com

facebook.com/noirtravelstories

FOR REVIEWS OF MYSTERIES, SUSPENSE & THRILLERS

https://valinparis.wordpress.com/

FOR SOCIAL MEDIA

pinterest.com/valinparis/

twitter.com/ValinParis

instagram.com/ValinParis/

Made in the USA
Monee, IL
07 March 2021